THE EPIGRAM BOOKS COLLECTION OF

BEST NEW SINGAPOREAN SHORT STORIES

VOLUME ONE

THE EPIGRAM BOOKS COLLECTION OF

BEST NEW SINGAPOREAN SHORT STORIES

VOLUME ONE

JASON ERIK LUNDBERG

SERIES EDITOR

E
EPIGRAM BOOKS / SINGAPORE

All short stories copyright © 2013 by their respective authors
Introduction copyright © 2013 by Jason Erik Lundberg
Cover photograph © 2013 by Darren Soh

All rights reserved
Published in Singapore by Epigram Books
www.epigrambooks.sg

Edited and curated by Jason Erik Lundberg
Cover design and layout by Lydia Wong

Published with the support of

NATIONAL ARTS COUNCIL
SINGAPORE

National Library Board, Singapore
Cataloguing-in-Publication Data

The Epigram books collection of best new
Singaporean short stories. Volume one /
edited by Jason Erik Lundberg. – Singapore :
Epigram Books, 2013.

pages cm

ISBN : 978-981-07-6234-6 (paperback)
ISBN: 978-9810762353 (ebook)

1. Short stories, Singaporean (English) I. Lundberg, Jason Erik, 1975-

PR9570.S52

S823 -- dc23   OCN855522655

This is a work of fiction. Names, characters, places, and
incidents either are the product of the authors' imaginations
or are used fictitiously. Any resemblance to actual persons,
living or dead, events, or locales is entirely coincidental.

First Edition: October 2013
10 9 8 7 6 5 4 3 2

CONTENTS

vii	Introduction • *Jason Erik Lundberg*
01	The Tiger of 142B • *Dave Chua*
26	The Hearing Aid • *Vinita Ramani Mohan*
33	The Illoi of Kantimeral • *Alvin Pang*
41	Lighthouse • *Yu-Mei Balasingamchow*
60	Seascrapers • *Stephanie Ye*
72	Because I Tell • *Felix Cheong*
79	Sleeping • *O Thiam Chin*
94	Agnes Joaquim, Bioterrorist • *Ng Yi-Sheng*
107	The Dispossessed • *Karen Kwek*
120	Harmonious Residences • *Jeremy Tiang*
137	Randy's Rotisserie • *Amanda Lee Koe*
145	The Protocol Wars of Laundry and Coexistence • *Koh Choon Hwee*
160	Zero Hour • *Cyril Wong*
171	Walls • *Verena Tay*
190	Copies • *Eleanor Neo*
200	Welcome to the Pond • *Wei Fen Lee*
212	Scared For What • *Ann Ang*
225	Joo Chiat and Other Lost Things • *Justin Ker*
235	Anniversary • *Phan Ming Yen*
239	The Borrowed Boy • *Alfian Sa'at*
260	Contributors
269	Honourable Mentions

Introduction

Jason Erik Lundberg

SINCE THE MID-1990S, Singaporean literature has largely been dominated by two genres: poetry and stage plays. These two literary forms were so prevalent in 2003, the year that I visited Singapore for the first time, that a trip to independent store Select Books (then located at Tanglin Shopping Centre) became an eye-opening revelation about the local literary culture. Other than Catherine Lim's short stories and novels, not much else besides self-published titles with poor production values was frankly on offer in terms of local prose fiction. Coming from the USA, where poetry and plays have only a sliver of the prominence and readership of prose, I was pleasantly astounded to see these two forms supported by Singaporean readers. Novels and short stories by Singaporean authors had of course been written and published for decades before my arrival here, but at that point in time, were either out of print or existed in such small print runs as to be similarly unavailable.

However, in recent years, short fiction in particular has

begun experiencing a renaissance. Thanks to a plethora of anthologies and single-author collections from Singaporean publishers Ethos Books, Monsoon Books and Math Paper Press, the establishment of literary journal *Ceriph*, and the continuing presence of online journal *Quarterly Literary Review Singapore*, more Singaporean writers are expressing themselves through prose than ever before.

The interest in and pursuit of short prose writing has been additionally helped by the attention that has come with local authors making the longlist of the prestigious Frank O'Connor International Short Story Award: Wena Poon in 2008 (*Lions in Winter*) and 2010 (*The Proper Care of Foxes*), O Thiam Chin in 2010 (*Never Been Better*), Dave Chua in 2012 (*The Beating and Other Stories*), Felix Cheong in 2013 (*Vanishing Point*), and Alfian Sa'at in 2013 (*Malay Sketches*). For the prose enthusiast, it is a very exciting time.

In the past, reprint anthologies in Singapore have mainly been designed as a form of literary canonisation, such as *One: The Anthology* (2012) edited by Robert Yeo and *Telltale: 11 Stories* (2010) edited by Gwee Li Sui, just to give two recent examples. But to date, there has not yet been an attempt to curate the best **new** short fiction being produced by Singaporean writers, as a way to capture this representative moment in time of local literary culture. *The Epigram Books Collection of Best New Singaporean Short Stories*, designed as a biennial anthology series, of which this book is the first volume, is the answer to this lack.

Over a period of around five months, I read through hundreds of short stories in anthologies, collections, magazines and literary journals, both in print and online, published between January 2011 and December 2012, by authors who were either Singaporean citizens or permanent residents. The wonderful National Library system was an incredibly beneficial resource in finding texts that I did not already have access to. In addition, I was allowed to pick from the top prize-winning stories of the 2011 Golden Point Award and Goh Sin Tub NUS Creative Writing Competition, and opened up nominations for consideration via a Submittable portal. At the end of this book, you'll find publication information for all of the stories chosen (which includes the venue in which each piece was originally published), as well as a list of more than seventy Honourable Mentions, in the hopes that you will seek out these texts for further reading.

The keen reader will notice that three of the stories included here were first published in the 2012 anthology *Fish Eats Lion*, which I also edited; lest your temper flare at thoughts of impartiality and unfair favouritism, please be assured that the final decision to include these pieces was left to publisher Edmund Wee. In addition, because of the restriction of the time period, there were some authors whom I would have love to have included, but simply couldn't because their most recent short fiction had seen print before 2011. Also, because of the mammoth task of searching out and whittling down the stories for curation here, I am sure that I inevitably missed some pieces that might have fit the criteria, as would be the case for any editor of a similar publication.

As to the chosen stories themselves, the authors are evenly split between men and women, and range from established award-winners to emerging writers just starting their careers. I did not read the stories blind (i.e. I obviously knew who the authors were), but I put aside consideration of bodies of work and literary accomplishments and focused solely on the merits of each piece I came across. All of the stories I selected for this book had to fulfil the following criteria, regardless of genre or subject matter: exceptional writing, strong narrative voice, compelling plot, memorable characters, and the overall effect of moving me in some way as a reader.

• • •

When I was a teenager and living in North Carolina, one of my most anticipated books each year was *The Year's Best Fantasy and Horror*, edited by Terri Windling and Ellen Datlow, and published by St. Martin's Press. At that time, I only had limited access to short fiction of the fantastic being published in the USA; my parents had gotten me subscriptions to *Isaac Asimov's Science Fiction Magazine* and *The Magazine of Fantasy and Science Fiction*, but there was a wealth of short science fiction and fantasy being published in other venues, and I didn't quite know where to start in order to keep up with it all. However, the Windling/Datlow anthology series, each volume thick enough to kill a dozen spiders in one blow, was indispensible in keeping me current with the truly phenomenal written work being produced; and to my everlasting gratitude, it was consistently stocked by my local public library.

The series ran for twenty-one volumes, from 1987 to 2007 (with Kelly Link and Gavin Grant taking over Windling's role for the final four), and I quickly learned to trust the editors' judgement, even if I did not always agree with some of their choices. Deciding on the "best" of anything is always an exercise in subjective opinion, and one could be driven crazy by questioning why one mediocre story was picked whilst an outstanding work was overlooked, but taken as an aggregate whole, my literary preferences very often lined up with theirs.

As I got older, my reading tastes branched out to encompass mainstream realism, mysteries, suspense novels, and even a bit of romance, but every year I came back to *YBF&H* to encounter the stories that I'd inevitably missed the first time round, to re-read pieces that had already touched me, and to discover new voices of whom I'd previously been unaware. When my writer friends started seeing regular publication, it was also a delight to turn to the Honourable Mentions in the back of the book to find out who'd made it; a highlight of my career was being included twice in this list.

When it came time to assemble the anthology in your hands, I kept *YBF&H* very much in the back of my mind in terms of organisation, standards of quality, and openness to lots of different kinds of writing. Although this book leans more heavily toward realism than the fantastic, it still owes a great debt to Datlow, Windling, Link and Grant, and I can only hope that it lives up to their example.

• • •

It may be an indication of the current cultural zeitgeist that the stories in this volume all deal with loss in one form or another, as though processing the rapid changes that

INTRODUCTION

Singapore insists upon in order to stay globally competitive, and converting these impressions into deep meditations on life itself. Whether it is the loss of matrimonial intimacy in Dave Chua's "The Tiger of 142B", one's hearing in Vinita Ramani Mohan's "The Hearing Aid", youthful innocence in Alvin Pang's "The Illoi of Kantimeral", trust in parents in Yu-Mei Balasingamchow's "Lighthouse", memory and identity in Stephanie Ye's "Seascrapers", childish naïveté in Felix Cheong's "Because I Tell", a loving spouse in O Thiam Chin's "Sleeping", control over the natural world in Ng Yi-Sheng's "Agnes Joaquim, Bioterrorist", neighbourhoods in Karen Kwek's "The Dispossessed", moral assumptions in Jeremy Tiang's "Harmonious Residences", marital harmony in Amanda Lee Koe's "Randy's Rotisserie", familial accord in Koh Choon Hwee's "The Protocol Wars of Laundry and Coexistence", the entirety of humanity in Cyril Wong's "Zero Hour", filial respect in Verena Tay's "Walls", romanticism for dreams in Eleanor Neo's "Copies", social justice in Wei Fen Lee's "Welcome to the Pond", paternal authority in Ann Ang's "Scared For What", personal history and bodily appendages in Justin Ker's "Joo Chiat and Other Lost Things", precious family members in Phan Ming Yen's "Anniversary", or idealistic determination in Alfian Sa'at's "The Borrowed Boy".

Although, at the same time, that is not all these stories are about, by any means. Each examines various facets of the human condition and the truths that we tell ourselves in order to exist in the everyday. Some do this through domestic realism, and others through fantastical fabulation. The styles are as varied as the authors, and no two stories are alike. I am proud to present you, the reader, with twenty separate and unique literary insights into the Singaporean psyche, which examine what it means to live in this particular part of the world in this particular time.

The Tiger of 142B

Dave Chua

THEY FOUND THE mangled body in the evening when the sun painted the skies orange-red. It was an old Chinese man who lived in #17-803. When they printed his picture in the papers the next day, I tried to remember if I had ever seen him. Surely we would have bumped into each another on the elevator? Or I might have seen him hanging around at the void deck, sitting on the stone bench, pretending to play checkers while eyeing the schoolgirls who walked by?

But I could not remember him. He had worked as an accountant at a firm for sixty-one years and was reportedly "an upright, jovial man". His family was in grief over his passing. The paper furnishings for his funeral spilled out onto the island of grass in front of the block.

His body had been found in the corridor, covered in blood and mangled, "as if clawed and partially eaten by an animal," the newspaper said. Had anyone heard anything? Most folks were not in or had their televisions tuned too loud.

The police interviewed the neighbours and took down their statements. The tabloids were full of reports about the killing but had no real clues. The journalists circled the block like vultures in the next few weeks, hoping for a lead. His family padlocked their gates, refusing to answer the doorbell. I passed by the spot where his body was found briefly, but it had been wiped clean. There was not even a smear to indicate his passing or that he had died there.

• • •

"What do you think it was?" I asked her.

"I don't know."

"Do you think it was random?"

"He was an accountant. Those don't tend to have many enemies."

"Maybe he added some figures wrongly."

Her hand brushed my cheek. I loved how soft her fingers were. The radio was still on even though it was late at night, and it was bereft of the DJ's drone and dedications.

"I should play the piano again," she said, moving her fingers in the air.

"You should. It's gathering dust. We don't have that much space to spare for things that do nothing."

"Like your VCR. Throw it out."

"I will, I will. And all those tapes. Don't even dare put them near the player. I'll get the piano tuner," I said, trying to sound useful.

"You know where to look?"

"Yellow Pages. The web. I can do that, you know."

"Your mom called," I said.

"What did she want?"

"Just to talk to you. She had that tone in her voice again when she talks to me. She always preferred your other boyfriends."

"She always prefers someone else," she said.

"She thinks I'm a bum."

"Next time she asks, just tell her that you're doing computers."

"But I'm not."

"Just tell her. She'll stop. She thinks that people in computers make money. If you say finance, she'll have a ton of questions to ask, and she'll figure you out. You just have to dress better and not look like the assistant of a karung guni man."

Chet Baker's *My Funny Valentine* came on, a song that we both liked, and we went into silence and closed our eyes. I was not too sure how we had been together. I was let go from my job about two months back, and I had not been searching hard. I had been avoiding meeting up with friends and not going out. I ate out of cans to save money. Occasionally, I went to the shopping centres when the weather got too warm to soak in the air-conditioning or to the pool where I tried to find an empty lane, which was frequently impossible, but otherwise I stayed home.

• • •

Two weeks later, on the fourteenth floor, an old Indian lady on her way back from the market had seen a tiger about the size of a man striding in the corridor, as though it owned the place. She screamed and dropped her vegetables and started running downstairs. She thought that she heard the tiger following her, and so she ran and ran, afraid that her heart would rip. When she reached the ground floor, she was still running. Then she called the police from a payphone.

The police arrived but found nothing. They escorted the woman to her house, and, after entering, she refused to come out again. She was burning incense and candles and screaming at the top of her voice about what she saw to anyone who would listen. On television, one could see her eyes darting around nervously.

The police had searched every floor and found no trace of the tiger. Not even a hair. There was no evidence except the ravings of a sixty-ish Indian woman.

She put out all sorts of wards, two huge locks, and statues of her Indian gods outside her flat. Some people said she had always been a little unhinged, and her children apologised for her rants, but she said that she knew what she saw.

The story refused to go away, and, though it elicited barely five lines in the main paper, it filled the tabloids. The people from the zoo were tired of answering questions from the press. There had not been a tiger escape, ever, and no tiger cub had been lost or unaccounted for.

"Come down here and count them!" the zoo spokesperson screamed to the journalists. He did say later in the article that there was an increase in the number of visitors.

• • •

When I told her about the news, she seemed bored. She had been having hard days at work and coming back late every night. I massaged her feet clumsily, which made her smile. I told her about what the Indian lady saw.

"If it was a lion, we'd be honoured. They would have parades," she said. "Proof that Sang Nila wasn't deranged claiming he'd seen lions here in the 14th Century."

"Who was that person I saw you with that day? Didn't you see me?"

"He was an old friend."

Her voice was careful. To know more would require navigating around the wall she had put up.

"Have you started playing? I wiped off the dust for you. Even got a piano tuner to come. He made me meet him at the void deck. He was afraid."

"Did he rush through the work?"

"No. Once he was inside the house, he felt safe. He used one of those electronic things. Thought he was going to use a tuning fork.

"Well, I left him to it. I went to the bedroom. People don't like being looked over the shoulder when they work, yah?"

"What did you do?"

"I tried to do some work, but it was sort of distracting. The sounds of him tuning the piano and clucking his tongue in disapproval. Like they were bad children. You feel a bit self-conscious about letting it fall into such a state.

"After a while, he knocked on the door. I must have dozed off."

"So like you," she said.

"Yeah. I went out. He had closed the cover of the piano and put our photographs and other things back, almost exactly as we had it."

"They were not really in the same position. You didn't notice? I did."

"He played a tune. One of Chopin's *Études*. He wasn't bad. His hands still flowed over the keys even though his hands were old. He then asked if I wanted to test it, and I just pressed the C key. I can't remember any of it.

"He asked if we had any tea, and I said yes. Then he stayed and chatted for about an hour. Think he was just killing time between appointments."

"You had enough money to pay him?"

"Yeah, of course I did. So I made him some tea, and we talked. I didn't want to talk about all the silly tiger stuff, so we discussed work.

"I asked him if ours was the worst piano he had to tune, and he said not by far. He said that he was at this mansion a few months ago, one of those colonial black-and-whites, which had a grand piano. It had obviously not been touched for a long time. The whole place was falling into pieces—paint peeling, cats running around chasing cockroaches.

"When he opened the piano, he found that it was infested with termites. Every time he played a key, dust fell out of the piano. He was afraid that, if he played anymore, the whole thing was going to fall apart."

"He must have felt pain. To see something like that."

"Yeah. So he waved goodbye and apologised to the maid. Told her that he couldn't fix it. He never saw the owners of the house.

"There was another time he was tuning this stand-up piano, like ours. He played a few keys, and it was totally off and muffled. He then opened the back and found that there was a plant growing inside. A vine was entangling the strings, choking them."

"You're joking. How could it get light and water?"

"Wow. Someone remembers her biology class. I don't know. Maybe the sides weren't built well? Light could seep in?"

"Hah. I don't know. Doesn't seem very likely," she said.

"Anyway, he finished his story and got up. I paid him, and he left. I followed him downstairs. He was nervous. He clung to the sides of the corridor as we walked. I thought that, if a tiger did appear, he would just jump off."

She smiled a small smile.

"Do you know why I got the piano?" She said. I knew that it was one of those questions she wanted to answer. The opening up of herself took ages, like parting rock.

"Tell me."

"When I was six or seven, I listened to someone playing the *Moonlight Sonata* once, at a shopping centre. Everybody else was rushing around. Nobody heard her play but me.

"I told my mom I wanted to play like that, and then it was a project for her. Boom! The piano, the teacher, the lessons, the scoldings, the practice, the exams. Those things that stripped all the joy of the instrument from you. And you realised the path from A to B was a long, long road."

"And did you ever play the *Moonlight*?"

"I stopped lessons at Grade Five, and, for a month, I just tried playing, but it was so filled with effort and pain that I couldn't manage. I wanted to be like that piano player I saw—so effortless, able to convey the melody without trying. As natural as breathing."

"You can still do it."

"No. Those days are over. I can even barely stand to hear myself play."

"So there was no point tuning it?"

"No, there was. Maybe I'll try playing something. You have to remind me."

"I will."

She folded herself into me and was quiet. I did not move, and we slept with the lights on.

• • •

Nobody reported anything alarming for a week. That was no surprise, considering the number of people hovering around the block. The police hunkered down, but even they could not lend any credibility to the story.

Ten days after the incident with the Indian lady, a mauled body was discovered on the stairwell between the sixth and seventh floor. The ambulances came, and one of the flat-owners on the seventh floor admitted hearing muffled screams in the night.

The next day, the corpse was identified as that of a known loan shark, a man in his mid-thirties named Ah Chan. He was said to be looking for debtors on the seventh floor. He had a parang in the small sports bag he carried, along with black markers. Word got around quickly.

Soon, the papers labelled the tiger as a folk hero, a divine protector placed at our block to defeat evil. The victim's family denied any wrongdoing. Some thought that it wasn't there to kill us but to guard us, though I doubted the Indian woman would agree.

Protector or vermin, the voyeurs were back again, and so were the reporters. There were those waiting for the lottery numbers, but others really wanted more. The beast that haunted our flat became like a god. The stairwell where the body was discovered was covered with incense and flowers. Altars lined the corridors, saddled with shiny apples and mouldy oranges, lit by red lights in the balmy night. The smell from the incense floated up to our apartment, and made our kitchen smell like a temple.

One of the morning shows had a tiger expert who wore a khaki cap to talk about the animal and its behavioural patterns. He described different varieties of tigers. The host then asked him about the kind of tiger that could be roaming around killing loan sharks, and he paused for a while before saying it might be a Sumatran tiger "that had swum over". He wanted to explain more, but they cut to a commercial. After the advertisements he was gone, whisked away.

• • •

"We should feed the tiger," I told her.

"Put out the meat we can't finish?"

"You're eating less. When did you stop eating meat?"

"Recently. There's this new guy at work, and he was telling us about the benefits of being vegetarian. He showed us some documentaries. You'll give up meat too if you know how it's prepared."

"So we should throw out all the meat?"

"You can eat it if you want. I don't care."

"Maybe, maybe."

"What did you do today?" she asked.

"I looked through the papers and sent out some resumes," I lied. "I also found a CD of *Moonlight Sonata*. When I listened to it, I felt so stupid. I've probably heard it thousands of times."

"Yes, they love putting it in movies."

"It doesn't sound that hard to play," I said, trying to encourage her.

"Hah. Maybe when I have more time."

"Why not now?"

"I'm a bit tired. You don't want me to talk about work, do you?"

I shook my head.

She went to shower, and I looked at the ceiling and turned back to the television. I hated the way she smelled after work, an almost acrid odour, though I could never quite tell her

"Do you want me to play the CD?" I asked her when she emerged.

"Play what?"

"*Moonlight Sonata*."

"It's OK. I can remember it," she replied. "They said Beethoven composed it while playing for a blind girl at night. But sounds like bullshit, doesn't it?"

"Probably," I said.

I changed the subject. "So do people ask you about the tiger thing?"

"I had the cleaner lady tell me, and she gave me a charm.

It's in my wallet."

"Hah. Would that protect you?"

"I just think it's silly. It should just go away. When I was coming back, all these people were looking up. They're probably looking into our flat right now. Can you get new curtains and blinds?"

"Sure. Sure," I said.

"What would you do if the tiger came for you? If you were walking, and it was next to you?"

"I don't know. Maybe I would let it eat me."

"Like it would want you. With your lungs . . . give it cancer."

"It's a tiger. I don't think that they're choosy. You think that, when it catches a monkey in the woods, it lets it go? No, it eats. It's not like us."

"Maybe someone kept it for a while, and now it escaped. And it goes back every night."

"We're not next to a nature reserve or even a park. Unless it's hiding beneath the sand of the playground, but it would bake in the sun. There hasn't been a tiger seen in Singapore since what . . . the 1930s?"

"Why do you men think that there's a logical explanation? What if there isn't?"

"Maybe it's hiding in the bushes. Or climbed a tree."

"I'm sure that they checked everywhere," she said. I could hear the boredom in her voice.

"You trust them?"

She nodded. She closed her eyes and went to sleep.

• • •

There was no report for the next two weeks. One of the flats was broken into, and the police uncovered a group of illegal immigrants living there, Chinese workers who protested that they had not been paid and were thrown out by their errant employer. The police did not find any wildlife inside, but the tabloids hinted that they were responsible.

I spent more time walking, trying to stay out of the flat. When she was not there, the emptiness filled it. I had been listening to a lot of piano music, though I would turn it off before she returned.

I stepped up my hunt for work. I did not want her to think that I was not trying. When she came back, I told her about my day.

"I had a meeting today, with this client in town near Tras Street. But there was something not right about the woman."

"Why?"

"After a while, I realised that she had blue eyes. One of those blue contact lenses.

"I was too distracted. I couldn't concentrate on what she was asking. I just couldn't take her sincerely. Eyes window to the soul and all that.

"I couldn't take it. I wanted to tell her to take them off. And what a good impression that would make. She started asking if there was something wrong. And I said no. What else could I say?"

She listened in silence. I tried to justify myself, desperately.

"Then I was leaving, I passed by their main conference room. I could see a group of them in their business suits, the men in their ties, the women in their neat dresses. They had their hands placed together in a pile. They then cheered for themselves. Like a sports team.

"Then one of them came out of the room, and I was almost ready to run off. He was older than the rest, in a long-sleeved shirt. I couldn't escape. He thanked me for coming and he shook my hand. This perfect handshake, with his long-sleeved right hand, with his cufflink which was like a counterweight, looking at me in the face while speaking with perfect sincerity to thank me for coming. I thought about how long he must have trained for that handshake, probably spending hours and weeks, shaking hands with his children or wife. Or maybe there's a handshake club like there are toastmasters, who practise until one day they know they got it. That perfect handshake."

She seemed bored with my words.

"He waved as I left, and I thought how he's found a fit. He's a peg who's found his hole."

"You didn't get the work then."

"No, I didn't."

"There's always something wrong, isn't there?"

"What do you mean?"

"You have to grow up. You can't be this way."

"It's her eyes. How can you work for someone who's lying to herself?"

"Look somewhere else. Behind her. At her chest like other guys do. Anywhere."

"I can't. Why don't you understand?"

She kept quiet and left the room.

• • •

We met our friends, the Lims, at a restaurant in town. As we passed the car park, we noticed their maid standing next to their car. When we were at the table, we saw them already seated, with their two-year-old in a high chair. She cooed at the baby, while I flipped through the menu and made small talk.

They were uncomfortable, but even the tiger was not something they wanted to talk about much. I could sense Simon's boredom. They talked about their children and how much diapers cost, and needing to get a car in Singapore because the buses shook so much they thought that "the baby's brains would turn to jelly".

It was hard for me to fill in the conversation, but I made small talk about soccer and music and bands. But, whenever the talk steered back to work and cars and property, I mostly clamped up again. I went for a smoke and hovered around the car park. Their maid was now conversing with other maids, speaking in Indonesian.

She was still able to keep pace, but I was falling behind. She paid for my share more often than not, and I tried to pay her back. But she always refused. I winded up stuffing it into her purse, never bothering to place it amongst the other bills she kept, but she never brought up how the money got there.

I went for a few more job interviews, and I tried harder. Once, I thought I had landed something, a marketing executive for a company that manufactured light stands, but they never called. I called them back to ask about the position, and a secretary, with the voice of a child, said they would let me know if I got it. But the call never came. I kept it all to myself, and she never asked about how my job search was going. I wondered if she meant it as a kindness.

• • •

She was sitting up in bed, not lying down. She was coming back later. I did not even hear her enter the house.

"Maybe there's more than one. Maybe there's three or four. I mean then it makes sense."

"Why do you want to make sense of it? It just doesn't."

"It's a freaking Singaporean thing."

"It's probably a mad man who's going around dressed in a tiger skin. Wouldn't that make more sense?"

"Maybe. But so unromantic."

"Anyway, maybe a bunch of tigers. What do you call a group of them anyway?"

"Monkeys are bunches. How can tiger be a bunch?"

"I don't know."

"Why are we talking about this? We talk about nonsense all the time," she said.

"Do we? Is it that bad?"

"Why do you think it's here? Whatever is out there?"

"Who knows? Is it eating people?"

"Mangling . . . is it really protecting? Is it all a coincidence?"

"I don't know. Who knows?"

"Are people moving out yet?"

"No," I said. "Prices are too high now. Impossible to find a place."

"Even that Indian woman?"

"She stuck a whole bunch of crosses and sutras on her door.

And she goes downstairs with a pointed stick. I think she has a knife in her bag."

"You should carry one too. In that big bag of yours. Could have a chopper."

"There was a tiger shot underneath a billiard table at Raffles Hotel," I said.

"You're obsessed by it," she replied.

"They used to be common, you know. Tigers were responsible for two hundred deaths in 1884."

"Well it's not 1884 now."

She wanted to say something, and there was held silence before she spoke out.

"I have to work late the next few days. Something major is coming up soon. You may have to eat out yourself."

"That's all right."

"Do you need money?"

"No," I said. I felt insulted but kept it in.

"All right."

She smiled, but I knew her well enough to see that it was something squeezed out of her, as though she had to think hard about it. I wanted to reach out to touch her, but I couldn't. She went to the room and fell asleep.

• • •

There was a suicide at our block. It had been four weeks since the attack on the loan shark. The press no longer had time to send journalists down to scout the place but had offered a reward for any footage. So old folks and others set up camp beneath, watching us, with video cameras borrowed from their children. We called the police to try to get them to stay away, but the area was public property.

When the woman jumped, there were photographs and videos of her as she clambered over the wall. Some of them claimed to have heard screaming, but the agitated voices of the mob drowned out whatever sound she might have been making. She jumped from the nineteenth floor, and some people claimed that she appeared to be running from something.

I watched the footage, and I could not tell. Her face was too much of a blur. A group of folk rushed upstairs to the floor where she jumped but found nothing except her worn shoes tossed to a side.

Then the journalists started wandering the halls again, knocking on doors. I refused to answer any questions and turned off the lights so that they would not think anyone was in. My neighbours were eager to give their views, and so the corridor became lit like a studio.

The woman who jumped lived alone and was retired. She had not kept in touch with her family for a while. The press eviscerated her children for being unfilial and for not taking care of her. The funeral was moved elsewhere as the family wanted to avoid the cameras and the reporters.

A private company wanted to install cameras everywhere, but the residents complained. We were sick of the scrutiny. I opened the windows and saw somebody trying to look in with binoculars. Undoubtedly, I have been marked as one of those who have been acting too mysteriously. The police had not knocked down every door yet, but I was sure that they would be prepared to. They must have files on each of us. We were being examined in every way, and even a minor crime would be enough for them to come in and search our homes.

I emerged from my flat one day wearing a cap, and there was a brief flash from the flat opposite. Someone had taken a photograph of me. I saw a man in his late twenties in a chequered shirt wielding a camera with a lens the size of a tea-plate. Its eye stared at me accusingly. I ran to the staircase and hurried down. I ran so fast that the echoes of my footsteps sounded like I was trying to outrun myself.

• • •

They had been spraying the area around the flat more often. It seemed the pest-killers come here every two weeks and covered the ground in smoky white clouds.

They went to all the corridor and public spaces, in teams of two, and sprayed. Though they wore masks, I could see their nervous eyes. When they came to our door, they clouded the plants continuously.

"You killing the insects or the plant?" I said.

They just bowed their heads to acknowledge my question before moving on.

My neighbour scolded the sprayers. He said his child was having asthma from all the chemicals and fumes.

"Why are they spending so much money spraying? Why don't they catch the tiger?" His fist thumped against the wall, which dropped flakes of paint as he spoke. I could see a large beige dog with dusty patches standing next to him through the grilles of his gate. It smelled of soap, and I could hear it panting.

But the police did not acknowledge the tiger. No one wanted to come out and say that one existed. Who could blame them? There was no physical evidence.

I went back to the flat and fanned away the fumes. The leaky sound the sprayers made continued to fill the morning air. With their masks and hats, they resembled beings from another planet.

• • •

When I returned home, the heat was already seeping through me. I brushed past the tripods on which the digital cameras have been placed. Everything around the block was as it was before. The old folks were still playing checkers or practising tai chi, but the cameras filled the spaces in between. They had sprouted like bamboo. The children played in the garden, never in the corridors, and the neighbours had turned considerate. Nobody played his or her music loud. Nobody hung their clothes past their space. There were no vandals scrawling rude words in the lifts.

I hurriedly opened the door, fumbling with the keys, and slammed it shut. I tossed the tie on top of the piano. It had been another bad day of interviews. In my head, I wanted to shout at them with their own questions. I did not want to look desperate, but I had probably come across as such. On the table were her breakfast and a cold cup of half-drunk tea. She was here. I opened the refrigerator, and all I found was cabbages and fruit. I shoved some grapes into my mouth.

She did not come home one night. I called and called. I received a text message from her that she was working late. I called her phone right after that, ready to plead, but there was no reply.

I was not sure if she was listening. I went out to the living room. There was darkness outside and I wondered if there had been a blackout or that I might be asleep.

I walked out to the corridor towards some flickering lights. I looked down upon the courtyard below where the vacant parking lot was. I did not know what time it was, but it was the deep part of the night. I did not see any lights on in the other flats. Only the street lamps and the corridor lights shone.

There was a light emanating from one of the cars below, and I saw the movement of the couple in the backseat, making love. I wondered about the way they touched, and I longed for hers.

I felt a presence and turned, and it was there. It was larger than a man, and its tail whipped casually around, sweeping the dusty corridor. The fur was messy, sprouting in all directions. It looked old; the eyes, like golden coins, appeared unable to focus. It watched me carefully as it approached. There was a thick, coiled smell around it—freshly cut grass and the sun.

I was stuck there, admiring its beauty. Its tongue curled out around the mouth, and the whiskers were as fine as guitar wire. Its eyes were intelligent and cunning. It knew that it had nothing to fear from me.

It approached, and part of me wanted to run away while the other part wanted to stay and watch, to find out why it was here.

It was only a foot away as it closed the space between us. I could hear everything around me. The slow hum of the car below. The hum of the aquariums. The hiss of the refrigerators.

Everything was magnified. I thought that it could have struck me down with a single stroke. I remembered what she said about fakirs in India offering themselves to tigers, believing that it was a great honour to be eaten by these splendid beasts.

I could see its body coiled, ready to strike and kill. I remained still. Maybe I should curl myself up into a ball and pretend to be dead. I looked into its eyes and saw how old it was. It was a mighty creature that demanded thick jungle and deep skies. It desired the chase and not to skulk around like a thief.

It stopped in front of me and stared. Its fat pink tongue flicked around its mouth, as if considering whether I was worth the trouble. I looked into its eyes and saw my past and myself and her. If I was consumed what would she do? Would I become an anecdote?

I sensed that it wanted me to walk with it. I followed him for a bit. We brushed past my neighbour's pots. The dog started barking. The smell of pesticide came up my nostrils. If I followed it more, I would venture into its magical world. The image of another universe came to me, one where everything here had become overgrown. Snakes hissed from the pots, threads of ants flowed from wall to wall; monkeys would clamber amongst the grilles.

I imagined the piano with the seed growing within our house. The seed would wind between the strings, the roots pressing against the wood, the leaves twisting out amongst the hammers. One day, it would break out from the piano, spreading around the ground, seeking sunlight. It would continue to grow, breaking out and spreading across the flat like a forest. Angry with the life that wanted to deny it, the plant would grow and fill all the empty spaces, invading the surrounding flats, seeking other pianos as though they were lost relatives. It would turn the people out of their homes; they would run screaming onto the streets, clutching their photo albums and their certificates, as the vines and leaves took over. The tiger would be right at home, wandering amongst the now empty halls, listening to the abandoned radios and alarm clocks, pounding for their owners who no longer could silence them.

Toucans would clamber, searching for our pills and tablets, tearing apart old newspapers and stacks of *National Geographic* to make nests. Crocodiles would lay eggs and breed their young in abandoned aquariums. Serpents would dance in and out of our toilet pipes. The jungle would stride boldly on, invading and taking over all the adjoining blocks and eventually the estate.

The tiger seemed to sense my thinking and let out a growl that sounded like a low moan.

There was a time when I would tell her all this, but I could not now. She would dismiss it. Her absence was starting to make me feel how cavernous such a small space could be.

• • •

Then I stopped. I could no longer follow. It turned to give me a look, waiting for me to reconsider. The golden eyes were ancient and cold. It turned towards the staircase and, in a fluid motion, leapt away, leaving me to the dog's frenzied barking.

Eventually I moved and looked at where it had gone. It had fused into the shadows and disappeared.

The mob came about a minute after. I still held my silent phone.

"Did it come here?" the leader said. He held a long parang. He did not look like he knew how to use it. But, with the mob behind him, the tiger would have stood no chance.

"What come?" I said.

"The tiger," he replied. His teeth were brown and stained from cigarette smoking.

"No. You're crazy. What tiger?"

"Crazy? Seventh floor. They found bodies there. The family's Alsatian. Slaughtered. The daughter crying, can't stop."

I shook my head.

"Whatever did it didn't come here," I said.

"Why would it kill them? Maybe they wanted to harm it or capture it," one of the party said. It was a woman with shorter hair than me.

"You think the tiger is some hero? It just wants to kill," the leader shouted back.

The man looked exasperated. "Then join us. Help us hunt it down. The police don't believe us. Nobody else does."

"What can I do?" I said, trying to stall them further.

"Go grab a knife. Chopper, kitchen knife. Anything."

I went back into the flat and the kitchen. I stopped at the bedroom and noticed that she wasn't there.

I took a knife. It was a small one, hardly capable of slicing an apple. When I emerged from the flat, the man almost snorted.

"I don't think you could kill a rat with that but let's go."

I followed them as they methodically went up every floor. Everyone would be awake by now. I glanced at the others. They carried knives, bricks, sticks, even a changkul. I wanted to ask the man, an Indian with red-veined eyes, wielding the changkul why he kept it. Where would he use it? But there was no space for conversation.

Their fear infected them, and they jumped at every shadow. A cockroach crept past, and three of them raced forward to stamp on it. Bits of the vermin stuck to their sandals. The contents of an altar had been kicked and crushed, the red electric bulb still flickering madly.

• • •

We found nothing, and, when the police came, some of them left to hide the weapons they had bought out. I went back to the flat and realised that I had forgotten to lock the gate. I called her name, but there was no sign of her. A great tiredness came over me, but I did not want to sleep.

I called her number, but she did not pick up. The humming in my brain grew louder.

I lifted the cover from the piano and played a key. It hummed. I pressed down on it harder. Then the keys around it. They formed a discordant combination, echoing in the ears and the empty room.

I continued to play the keys, trying to form a chord, a tune. I wished that I had asked her to teach me to play.

I wondered if the neighbours who heard it were cursing me, playing in the middle of the night. After the police left, they would come to my door, with their parangs and bricks and changkuls, ready to smash my bones and cut me into pieces. They would hack the piano into splinters, slicing the wires and keys.

My blood would spill onto the floor and the common corridor, my skin would be dried in the smashing light of the sun, and my bloodied body would be left at the void deck for all to see. I continued to press on the keys and looked to the door, waiting for it to open and the night to rush in.

The Hearing Aid

Vinita Ramani Mohan

RAJU LOST CONTACT with the world of slurs, laments, gossip and praise gradually over a decade. He didn't just wake up one day to discover that every face he encountered moved like a puppet being animated by strings, mouthing words he could barely make out—words that came from far away muffled by white noise and the silence that reigned in his ears. He saw them fade away, the final notes of a song that had begun loud and clear.

He told his relatives that he would never wear a hearing aid because it would only serve as a reminder of something that had been lost. They tried reasoning with him on this point, subtly hinting that it was his pride getting in the way. They showed him the newest models that looked like flesh-coloured lumpy putty. It would look like a harmless tumour growth, no one would even know you had one on, they'd tell him. But it was useless.

Like an ascetic, he kept to his daily routine silently. He awoke at six in the morning and went to the water pump to fill a plastic bucket with water for his bath. He had always been a slender and short man with dark skin and a thick head of hair. His hair had now turned a shocking white. But even at the age of seventy-two, he had the energy to push the pump lever up and down, up and down, working his slim arms, the biceps rhythmically pulsating with the motion of the lever. He would do this for what seemed like an interminable amount of time until the bucket filled. One bucket was for washing clothes, another half bucket for the bath (to be mixed with hot water), another for the dishes, later on.

Then, he'd bend his spindly knees, preparing to bear the load on his thighs and buttocks and haul the bucket to a poorly lit, cement-floored makeshift bathroom in the backyard of the house. His morning bath finished, he would hand-wash his clothes by the now-dry well, lining them up with wooden clothes pegs on a line hung from the tree to the window ledge. Lunch, served by the aged housekeeper who had been working for the family for nearly thirty years, was a simple vegetarian affair—white rice and watery rasam with a vegetable, prepared only with moderate spices and no garlic.

By eleven, his morning errands finished, he'd spread a thin cotton towel on the tiled floor of the living room, crank up the ceiling fan to the maximum level and lie on the ground to sleep. He always slept with his legs and arms akimbo. He seemed as if he was engaged in the yoga meditation posture of Shavasana, or as though he was having an out-of-body experience. It was the only time he truly seemed to be at peace.

The rest of the day was punctuated by one of two things. The first would be a short trip to run errands, an event for which he would iron one of his two white short-sleeve office shirts that he wore with a pair of grey office pants. He would switch to a white sarong if the errand was nearby and more casual. The second was a daily routine. He would watch the news on the television and also listen to cricket and world news updates on a small transistor radio. As he began losing his hearing, he would pull up the living room rattan chair and sit right in front of the television, studying the images closely, as if he was scrutinising a mole on the newscaster's face. He would hold the transistor radio in one hand like a brick and press it against his ear, his eyes wandering and searching his surroundings for the significance in what he heard.

And that was his day. Except, of course, there was his wife, Mala.

They had spent their entire married life in what had now turned into a dilapidated old house in suburban Chennai, built at the end of a pot-filled muddy road. She always seemed formidably strong. It wasn't the way she looked; it was the way she moved and dressed. She always wore her long hair either in a braid (during her younger years) or in a bun (as she aged). She seemed to have a preference for cheap cotton saris rather than the expensive Bengal cotton, or pure silk saris preferred by middle-class suburban Tamil women.

She never wasted time on accentuating the elegance, sensuality or finesse the draping of yards of fabric over a female body could suggest. She tied it high up on her waist, with ill-fitting blouses that always slipped a little to reveal still cheaper white cotton bras. The pleats which hung in front of the sari were supposed to gently sweep the floor and if an Indian woman was to ever spread her legs into a traditional South Indian bharatnatyam dancer's stance, the pleats would unfurl like a fan. But dance poses played no role in her existence. She would tuck the bunched pleats into her waist-band, bearing her legs and cracked heals, so that she looked more like a *dhobi* about to squat on his haunches on a rocky boulder to beat the dirt out of clothes.

Despite the cultural codes of her time, Mala had sought employment as a banker in one of the major national banks of southern India. She went out with her mostly male colleagues regularly and continued to have an active social life after retirement. These were habits that always provided fodder for gossip and moral judgements among the larger network of relatives. Rumours circulated that she had had an extra-marital affair and that this had widened the already yawning chasm in her relationship with her husband. She raised her three daughters like an army general dealing with privates in a platoon: she doled out harsh criticism and shared convivial camaraderie in equal parts. Despite the resentment they felt over the years for the lack of maternal love they received from their mother, all three daughters focused on setting up their own lives, rising against the tide of academic competition. Each did well, two settling on the east coast of the United States and one in India.

Retirement had brought with it a focused interest in religion and ritual. She became an active volunteer with a leading orthodox sect in the Tamil Brahmin Hindu community and spent much of her time away from home on pilgrimage trips. She accumulated divine experiences the way some women accumulated shoes or handbags. If her glaring absence from their home irked Raju, he kept mum about it. Her presence had a way of heightening his anxiety, so he had chosen the lesser of two evils.

Retirement had also brought with it unseen challenges. The critical comments she shot at him on an almost daily basis throughout their marriage had risen in their acridity, and now he was at home to take the blows more often. He never socialised and had no social mores to speak of; he didn't know how to network with the larger community; he had no interests apart from his transistor radio and the stupid news; he didn't desire anything, which meant he didn't have goals or ambition; what kind of a man lacks ambition? Remarkably, he never protested when Mala let out this volley of abuse.

Raju's younger sister felt she could not look on while these embarrassing and hurtful things were being said in the presence of relatives. One day, when his wife had left home early for a pre-pilgrimage logistics meeting, she addressed the issue, filled with emotion and righteous indignation.

He would have none of it. He shouted his responses, forgetting that everyone could hear him perfectly fine. But this habit, which had begun as his hearing worsened, seemed particularly dramatic and charged in the given context.

"That is just how she is!" he let out. "It doesn't matter!"

His face puckered up in an expression that indicated he wanted to dismiss the whole matter. His sister was making a big issue out of nothing. She had to let it go. He emphasized that at least his wife was occupied doing what she wanted to do and that meant she was content.

"I don't need to hear anything. What's being said that's so important for me to hear? I'm okay on my own." His voice had quietened now, as if his own shouting had reverberated somewhere in his head, causing a dull throb.

This defence of his wife made no sense to his siblings and those close to him. In her absence, what was the harm in confiding in his relatives? Would it hurt to concede that the woman was a tyrant, a lioness and a hypocrite who also dabbled in voodoo and therefore had no right to receive the blessings of any saint, god, sacred site of pilgrimage or temple priest? These were the things his sister had wanted to say and that the relatives said to each other afterwards. No one had any qualms about labelling her, hating her ever-so-briefly before returning to niceties, since familial decorum dictated that you must keep your good relatives close and your bad relatives closer.

But Raju never relented. When his sister had tried just once to share a more tepid interpretation of these darker sentiments with him, he had responded angrily. She was his wife and he would not have her name sullied, not even in his defence. That was that.

The routines continued. He would run errands and his wife would make plans for extended journeys across the country to find her god.

There was nothing particularly remarkable about that summer afternoon. In the living room, the relatives, both from abroad and around Chennai, had gathered for tea and conversation. As usual, Mala commanded the floor, drew the energy in the room to herself and steered the conversation, sharing updates, anecdotes and jokes. She had a distinct presence and a wonderful way of entertaining her guests, plying them with stories and delicious meals, homemade desserts and hospitality. On such occasions, Raju would sit mutely in the corner until someone had the courtesy to lean over to his ear and loudly greet him: that was the usual routine.

That afternoon, he seemed indifferent to the lack of attention. His eyes were squarely fixed on Mala. At first, it seemed as though he was looking at her lips to make out the words he could not hear. But it was more than that. He was looking hard and deep, as if hunting for something, or someone else. His eyes seemed to be compensating for his ears, searching for a different tenor from her, a tone that had been familiar before it had shifted to scorn and boredom. In Raju's world of muffled voices and gradual silence, there was the memory of a different voice—one with an affectionate, intimate rhythm; a quiet voice; a loving voice reserved for husbands and wives.

That is how it was, on any occasion that brought the relatives together. He and Mala had to be in the room together, so that they could play-act the roles of a married couple. Even though she did not address him or return his gaze on these occasions, he always kept looking, mutely, waiting without the hearing aid.

The Illoi of Kantimeral

Alvin Pang

HAVING LOST HER vada to the sea, she kept watch every dawn on the beach where she had last caught sight of him, adrift in his skoyak midway between shore and horizon. Every morning at the third ori, before the sun called the world to its labours, she would add a piece of dried kan to her rice phut in an oiled nanal leaf and depart the house without waking chibu, who would more often than not be slumped over her worktable in the smaller inner room of the house, the one with the broken window. The small path which wound around the cliff edge, wide enough only for one to pass, was dewy and treacherous in the dark, but soon opened onto a sandy crescent, bound to the north and south by two ancient breakwaters, and it was to the one further off, which the villagers called davada meral, grandfather of the coast, that she would make her way, clutching her breakfast as she clambered over the slippery rock to the narrow but sturdy plateau.

She would eat with both hands, all the while scanning the

horizon for signs of life, quickly spotting then looking past the lurelights of the sotokan boats and the dim red glow of the jhimcatchers. On occasion a uluabird skimming the surface of the water would take the shape of a distant boat, its one raised wing like a soksail unfurled to catch the shorebound wind. The flipper of a passing bhaphaun would appear for a moment to be a human arm, waving in greeting or distress. It never seemed to rain while she was keeping watch, or of if it did she took no notice, her feet firmly lodged in the crevices of the elder breakwater. Before long the sun would pry the horizon open with golden fingers and the sea would begin to gleam the colour of wet jade. Climbing down from the breakwaters, she would fold her nalal leaf into a little skoyak, leave inside it one last bite of kan and rice, set it afloat where the tug of the waves was gentle but steady, and walk away from the makeshift boat without looking back, as she returned home to her chores.

Have you eaten, chibu would ask as she came through the door.

Yes, she would reply, *and so has vada.*

Then come help me with the prabayong, nurlin, before you go and check the nets.

Yes, chibu.

And she would immerse herself in the day's work until nightfall and sleep.

The villagers were all aware of her morning vigil. *Everybody knows your vada has run away to the mainland,* the nurlins and erlins would tease whenever she came to the village market. *He is the best illukan catcher on the coast, and some big-brana porneu has hooked him for herself.* The village nuebos would give her knowing looks but not once did they offer a word of comfort or advice. Instead, they fussed among themselves to be the first in line at her stall, for she seemed to have her vada's knack of always having the freshest, biggest catch of the day for sale.

Once in a while, one of the erlins her age would come to sit with her on the breakwater before dawn. One of them brought her a stolen container of sweet koomi, which his dabu had fermented, skimmed and filtered under the full moon just the night before. In silence, they had watched the lunar tide swell and foam. The next night, she readied an extra portion of kaniphut for him, but he did not come that dawn or the next, or the one after. Later she found out that his drowned body had been found in a nearby cove, nibbled at by the sea's remorseless denizens, a half-drunk canister of koomi still strapped to his waist. The next dawn, she made sure to set aside an extra morsel in her skoyak offering to the sea.

She was sixteen when the dark-haired erbo came to her, adorned with the seaglass bracelets, earrings and leather skirts of a Mayar's erlin from the neighbouring Johrikanti. Without asking for her leave, he sat down crossed-legged next to her.

You are indeed very pretty, said the princeling, who had come to the island to negotiate passage and trade. *The villagers spoke of a mysterious beauty who appears every dawn on this rock, and now I see they spoke truly.*

She had never thought of herself as beautiful. Big-boned and ample like her vada, her cheeks were flat, her lips thin, her hair a tangled pukk of dirty straw, her arms grown stout from years of pulling at the nets. Still, her eyes were clear and bright, and she cut a comely figure in the pre-dawn gloom. So she remained silent, and watched the sea.

I do not know whether or not you are a sea-fairy, he continued, *but even if you were one of the illoi, so fine and magnificent a treasure should tame you.* He took her left hand in his, placed within it a large pearl, and closed her fingers over it with his own.

Now, he said, as she felt the cool, hard sphere press into her palm, tell me your name.

I have no name, she replied. *My vada disappeared, before he could give me one as is our custom.*

Ah, so have you been waiting all this time for him to come back and name you? Do not trouble yourself. Let me give one to you now.

He kissed her, and pressed her against the sea-moist granite for what seemed a long time. When she came to her senses, he was gone. The sun had risen a handwidth into the sky, the skraws had begun their first hunt, and the grandfather rock was stained with her blood.

The next night, she armed herself with her vada's old kantoo, which over the years she had kept sharp enough to scale and gut a kan without leaving the visible line of a wound. But the Johribo did not come, nor was she certain what she would do if he did. Her vigil, for the first time, felt a lonesome one, and she clutched her vada's blade for assurance. When dawn arrived, she let fall two fresh drops of her blood onto the little skoyak offering and watched the tide carry it out beyond sight, before turning at last towards home.

Her discovery that she was pregnant did not deter her from her daily ritual. Hours after giving birth to her erlin, she made her way to the shore with him at her breast, tucked away from the night chill, and dabbed his dark forelocks with saltwater before taking up her watch. Before long she would prepare two portions of breakfast and craft two nanal skoyaks, as her erlin scratched and tossed about in the nearby sand in the darkness, nameless and unafraid.

Chibu said that the Johribo, who had now become Mayar, had come to their house one afternoon, having heard of her child, assuming it to be his. He would call again to fetch both nibu and erlin home with him, to be formally installed as part of his extended household.

That day she took her finest illukan, which spends its time in the depths and never sees daylight but has the sweetest flesh, and cleaned it fit for a Mayar's table. Into one of its large eye sockets she inserted the pearl he had given her, its lustre matching perfectly the illu's intact deep-seeking eye. Into its gullet she placed her erlin's pacid, carefully preserved in bohoil since his birth. Then she seasoned and wrapped the dish in nanal, and asked for it to be given to the Joharibo when he came, before leaving the house to tend to her nets with her erlin in tow. The gift was received, a small token was left behind in acknowledgement, and the Johri Mayar never again returned to village, sending envoys instead whenever there was business to be conducted.

In time she became dabu, and later tydabu, but she was never too frail to climb the breakwater every dawn; and if the effort required the assistance of a walking cik and a few willing erlins, none thought to speak against it. Kancatchers and meribos, as they headed out to sea or returned from a night's hunt, would try to spot her silhouette for good luck, and the sight of her would steady them, even if the waters happened to be troubled that dawn. After her passing, the villagers placed a driftwood monument on the old breakwater, shaped like a sitting nuebo, her arms outstretched and watching the sea. For years, although no one in the village had agreed or made plans to do so, a kanlam would be kept lit at the monument, from the 3rd ori until dawn, always visible midway between the horizon and the shore.

Did she ever reveal why she kept that vigil every morning? Surely she realised her father would not be coming home?

I suppose it began as a kind of grieving, and then habit. Probably she found her own peace in the routine; time to be quiet and to think. Watching the sea was the one thing she could call her own, that was not hers by right or responsibility. It taught her a way of being in the world that was hers alone.

As a child my vada used to keep her company sometimes, up on that stretch of rock. He said she preferred not to speak a word until it was time to leave, but on the walk home she would tell him stories about the things she had seen while on watch. The flight of bright-winged dhuokan in hunting formation. A forsaken nuebo who had tried to drown herself and her unborn chilin in the darkness but who was startled by a piece of shale tossed in her direction, and changed her mind. Mysterious lights coming from the ruined sky-towers on the far end of the coast, near the great fallen city they say we were once a district of. And her own tale of course: that is how we know to tell it.

So she never did have a name. How did she even manage? And what about her son?

Oh, she had many names. In the stories that have been told of her, she has been called different things, not all of them pleasant. But there was never any doubt what she meant to us. She was the most respected kantookay of the village, and tybo of the marketplace. She was nibu to her erlin, and dabu to his children, and tydabu to us all. And of course she was always nurlin and chilin to her chibu. Did you know that chibu in the Kantiyan tongue means "mother of the heart?" The term for birthmother is "nibu", and it was considered a step less intimate than a woman of no relation who had freely taken up the duty of caring for a child who had been orphaned or cast aside. One had to earn that name, and it was never given without love.

Her erlin, our davada, she named Tilyak, once he came of age. It means "received". Most people think she was referring to the trinket left behind by the Johribo who was our tydavad, because that's what such tokens are called in the language of trade. A kind of receipt. Then again, she always spoke about having received many gifts from the sea in the long years of her watch, so she might also have been thinking of her erlin in that way.

You need to understand, we do not just pick our names out of a dook, with no regard for what we are or may become. When she passed the village had to decide what to inscribe on her grumu. But she had thought of that too. In her hand, on her deathbed, she was clutching this.

It looks like a tiny carved fish.

In the old ikoglyphic language, a fish would be depicted

as facing the other way. In the Kantiyan tongue, the word for island and fish are one and the same, which is why we islanders are also called the Fish People. This is the symbol for an island. There were many such carvings, each indicating a word, and each word linked to a legend. Synga, the lion and the lost city. Nung, the mountain and how it once shed blood tears. Umi, the sea urchin, who showed lovers where to meet on the hidden beach that only appears at nip tide. These ikoglyphs were meant to be strung together and dangled from a belt or worn as a bracelet, like a good luck charm. They were very popular at the time, and were often exchanged as tokens of goodwill.

This was part of the trinket left to her by the Mayar.

Yes, but look at the carving she chose out of the set. The island glyph is the only one that is connected with a song instead of a tale. It is never written down but every nurlin and erlin on the coast knows it by heart before they learn to swim. It is about remembering and forgetting and the tide of time. In the modern script, the refrain would go something like this: **yan kan tibi po meri tanti si.**

We are islands . . .

. . . but the sea is whole.

Lighthouse

Yu-Mei Balasingamchow

THE EVENING YING met Auntie Yoke Lin was also the day she learned that in Singapore, lighthouses did not necessarily resemble the shiny white totems depicted in her storybooks. As her parents' car trundled down the broad lanes of East Coast Parkway, she leaned forward from the back seat, popping her head into the gap between the two front seats. Ahead, the sky was sporadically lit up by a flash of light—not as erratic as lightning, but far too high to be a street light.

"What's that?" She thrust a crooked finger forward, right below the rear view mirror.

From the front passenger seat, her mother batted her hand back, "Don't distract your father." At the same time, her father eased his grip on the steering wheel and said, "It's a lighthouse. To tell the ships that they're near the shore." He tossed his chin to the right, to indicate the beach that lay beyond the expressway, and the ships that lay beyond that.

Ying turned her head to look. In the dusk all she saw were

the broad silhouettes of trees interrupted by flickering, distant lights, a spreading darkness that the red, orange and yellow dots punctured but could not penetrate. Her parents had taken her to the beach at East Coast Park before, but only in the day. She remembered the way the damp, coarse sand had clumped to her legs and hands, and burrowed beneath her nails and into the folds of her clothes, and she had wondered why the British children in her storybooks were always excited about going to the beach—just as now she wondered why the light from the lighthouse seemed to be coming from the landward side of the expressway. "I thought a lighthouse is out at sea."

Her father said, "This lighthouse is in the same place we're going. On top of some flats, high enough the ships can see."

The car gravitated towards the light and passed under it. Ying pressed up against the partially open window on the left side to peer up at the illuminated trail whipping round and round again. "The light is from the orange roof," she declared as her father steered the car off the expressway.

"Yah," her father said as he turned into an enormous car park. "That's how we know it's Auntie Yoke Lin's block." He pulled up beside a tall, chunky apartment building, identical to the others scattered around the car park like so many stern, concrete sentinels against the blackening sky. Ying slid out of the car and looked up. The buildings seemed as tall as the one she and her parents lived in, yet whiter, broader, sturdier and more imposing. Only the light that swept in steady, rhythmic circles overhead distinguished this block from the others. "5000L," she read off the sign as they walked towards the building. "Daddy, are there five thousand houses in Singapore?"

He laughed. "More than five thousand, girl. Come!"

In the lift, her mother punched the round button marked with a plump, bulbous '18'. "Later can we go up to the top to see the lighthouse?" Ying asked.

"Cannot," her father said, "it's not open. It's just a machine, set to switch on the light when it's dark, and switch off in the morning."

Later, while her mother arranged with Auntie Yoke Lin what time Ying would be dropped off every Sunday evening and picked up every Friday night, and what time the school bus would pick her up every weekday morning and drop her off at the car park downstairs after school, and while her father asked Auntie Yoke Lin's son Justin how he liked his school—"I went to the same primary school, you know. You know Mr Wong? Music teacher, very fierce!"—Ying dawdled by the balcony doors and watched for the light that flashed like clockwork across the same path of night sky over and over again. How could that little moving flash be enough to guide the ships far out at sea? she wondered. What was the point of a lighthouse when the shoreline was all the way over there? And why weren't there men working at this lighthouse, or why wasn't the lighthouse a proper tower with men living here, to keep the light working?

"Ying, time to go," her mother called. She was standing by the door with Auntie Yoke Lin. Unlike her mother, Auntie Yoke Lin was tall, had her hair knotted into a bun and wore a loose, flowing, dark brown batik print dress that made her look grandmotherly, even though she was supposed to be the same age as Auntie Lily (her mother's younger sister and hence Ying's actual aunt).

Ying bobbed a dutiful "Goodnight, Auntie Yoke Lin" as she wriggled her feet between the dry, faded red straps of her sandals.

Auntie Yoke Lin brushed a gentle hand against the top of her head. "With her hair like this, she looks a bit like Lily. See you next week, girl."

Back in the lift, her mother murmured something about how much space there was in the flat, while Ying eyed the button for the top floor of the block—marked '24'—and wondered about the mysterious machine on the roof that drove the light relentlessly round and about, always searching the darkness but never lingering in one spot long enough to see anything. Instead of stout, blond men in woolly sweaters and overalls, bearing kerosene lamps and tools, she imagined a mishmash of wires and circuits, wheels and cogs, a metallic Disneyland adventure ride shrunk down into a factory-like room, humming in sync with the beacon that it kept spinning in one place.

• • •

The first night she stayed at Auntie Yoke Lin's, Ying was disappointed that she couldn't see the lighthouse beam from the window. She peered into Justin's room, next to hers. He was sitting on the floor in his pyjamas, meticulously stacking Lego bricks into some kind of structure. "Er . . . Justin?"

"Hah?" He peered up. "Oh, Je Je." He was two years younger than Ying and Auntie Yoke Lin had told him to call her 'elder sister' in Cantonese, a new term to Ying.

"Can you see the lighthouse light from your room?"

"Hah? What light?"

"The lighthouse light." Ying pointed a finger at the ceiling, then towards the window. "You know? The big bright light from your block upstairs. My daddy said it's a lighthouse."

"Here got lighthouse?"

"Got. Upstairs. From your balcony can see little bit."

"My daddy never say." Justin sounded a little deflated.

Ying glanced towards the living room, where Auntie Yoke Lin had the television running while she chatted on the telephone in a mixture of English, Hokkien and Cantonese. "I'm going out to see."

With Justin in tow, Ying padded into the living room and out to the front of the balcony, penned in by metal grilles. After a few seconds, a white light swooped overhead. "See! There, there!" She pointed.

Justin stood next to her, half a head shorter, grasping the dusty vertical metal bars. "Not aeroplane, ah?"

"Aeroplane where got fly so low?" Ying giggled. "Lighthouse, lah. My daddy say one." She started to keep count of the time it took for the beam to come round.

"What are you looking at?" Auntie Yoke Lin emerged suddenly behind. She was wearing a different house dress today, this one dark blue with light blue swirls that reminded Ying of the curtains in the music room at school.

"Mummy, Je Je show me the lighthouse!" Justin kept one hand wrapped around the grilles, the other flapping at the sky. Ying wondered if she was in trouble, if it was time for bed or if they weren't supposed to be out on the balcony.

But Auntie Yoke Lin seemed at ease as she came to stand behind them, her right hand akimbo. "Oh, the lighthouse. That's how I tell people which block I stay. I say, look for the one with the orange roof, or at night, can just follow the light. I think I told your parents also." She turned to Ying. "Everything okay so far?"

Ying nodded.

"Thought you were out here because you were homesick, looking for your house."

"Where's your house?" Justin wanted to know.

Ying could recite her parents' address, but she had only a vague idea of where it was. All she knew for certain was that it was nowhere near a beach or a lighthouse.

Before she could answer, Auntie Yoke Lin said, "Ang Mo Kio, not so near here. Must drive about 30 minutes."

"Is it near where Daddy working?" Justin asked his mother. "You said he went far away."

"I'm not looking for my parents' house," Ying interjected. She didn't want Auntie Yoke Lin to think she was homesick, and her parents had told her not to ask questions about Justin's father. "Last time from my Auntie Jenny's house also cannot see." Auntie Jenny was her mother's youngest sister. She had looked after Ying during the week since Ying had entered primary school, but was now expecting her own child and wasn't confident of caring for Ying and a newborn at the same time. Before that, Ying had been living with her grandmother, her father's mother. But Ah Ma was sick now, sick and forgetful and living with Uncle Chye's family, and Ying didn't think Ah Ma recognised her anymore, even when Ying sang back to her the Hokkien children's rhymes she had taught Ying.

"Your mum say you always drink Milo at night before sleeping. I make for you now?" Auntie Yoke Lin offered.

Ying wasn't tired enough for bed and she wanted to count the timing of the lighthouse beam again. But her parents had also reminded her, right up to the moment they had dropped her off that morning, that she was Auntie Yoke Lin's guest and should behave herself. "Okay," she said.

Justin slipped his hand into hers as they left the balcony. "Tomorrow we see the lighthouse again."

• • •

For a few more nights, Ying watched the light from the balcony. Sometimes Justin joined her, but after the novelty wore off, he went back to his toys. She continued to wander out every few nights until she'd confirmed, with the aid of her wristwatch, that the lighthouse beam took 10 seconds to make a complete revolution.

By then, she had gotten used to being around Auntie Yoke Lin, and asking questions while the three of them plucked bean sprouts for dinner or kneaded dough to make curry puffs. One afternoon, while Auntie Yoke Lin was chopping chillies—the children weren't allowed to help with that particular task—and Justin was playing in his room, Ying asked if there was a way up to the lighthouse from the top floor of the building.

"I donno. Anyway, what for go up?"

"Maybe need to change the bulb," Ying ventured.

Auntie Yoke Lin chuckled. "Maybe," she allowed, "but I donno how they do it, how they go up there." With a practised motion, she used the broad, shiny blade of her chopper knife to sweep the pile of red chilli slices off her cutting board and onto the plate beside it.

"You know how to change bulbs, Auntie Yoke Lin?"

"Yah, I know," Auntie Yoke Lin answered as she grabbed the next bunch of chillies, "but I don't know what kind of bulb the lighthouse has. Must be a very big one. Did you finish your maths homework?"

Before she met Auntie Yoke Lin, Ying had brought back such a dismal mark in mathematics in her mid-year examinations that her mother had worn a grim expression for a week and her father had sat down to read her mathematics textbook from cover to cover. Auntie Yoke Lin had been a primary school teacher before Justin was born, and now at every opportunity she checked Ying's mathematics work.

Ying didn't find mathematics difficult, just uninteresting and tedious. "Finish already. Can Justin and I go to the playground?"

"Bring your book to the table. After I chop this finish, I check your working," Auntie Yoke Lin said—not fiercely, the way her mother would have barked at her, but nonetheless as steady and implacable as her rhythmic chopping.

"Okay," Ying submitted.

Auntie Yoke Lin's dining table was, like almost everything else in the flat, larger than the one her parents had. It could seat six and the three of them usually occupied the end closer to the kitchen, leaving empty the three seats closer to the wall, where several framed photographs and paintings were crookedly positioned: two black and white portraits of families Ying didn't recognise, a picture of the Last Supper reproduced on reflective vinyl, a piece of Chinese calligraphy that Ying couldn't decipher, and a photograph of Auntie Yoke Lin with a man. The photograph of Auntie Yoke Lin reminded Ying of one of her parents, taken before she was born. It too had been taken in a park and Auntie Yoke Lin was wearing her hair in a bob, similar to Ying's mother's hair but more jauntily adorned with a broad red-and-white-striped hairband.

There were other photographs in the apartment, mostly of Justin as a baby or a toddler. He was leaner now, but the squareness of his face persisted. Auntie Yoke Lin was leaner too and slouched more, her head sinking down with her shoulders as if the weight of her bunned hair was pressing down on the back of her head. But she smiled more vividly in person, even after hearing Ying chant her multiplication tables, mistakes and all, for the umpteenth time.

Ying spread out her mathematics books and waited. She had learned the eight times table in school that week and wondered if it would be enough to calculate the size of the bulb in the lighthouse.

• • •

Every night Ying caught a glimpse of the lighthouse beam from the flat, and every afternoon on the lift up after school, she thought about asking Auntie Yoke Lin for permission to go up to the top floor. At her parents' in Ang Mo Kio, she would have wandered upstairs on her own—just as she had wandered into the neighbourhood temple one afternoon, or found a shortcut by following a few older children along a storm drain and through some battered wire fencing.

It was different at Auntie Yoke Lin's. Although she seemed to have no lack of friends to ring up and chat with once she had finished the housework, she rarely left the flat. Several times Ying heard her say on the phone, in English or her native Cantonese, that it had been some time since they played mahjong, yes, she would organise a game soon. But the mahjong table remained folded away, pushed against a wall behind the settee in the living room. The flat remained neat, as if ready at any time for an inspection, but no one ever came.

Except once, just once, when Ying came home after school to find a middle-aged man sitting at the dining table, immaculately dressed in a long-sleeved shirt and dark brown pants. He wore a cord around his neck, bearing a rectangular embroidered cloth medallion. Auntie Yoke Lin introduced him as Father Michael and the adults continued conversing for some time in low tones, too indistinct for Ying to hear from her room. When he was leaving, Ying poked her head out and heard him say at the door, "Next time, when you're ready. But I'll see what we can do." Just before the door closed, "You take care."

One afternoon, coming home from the playground with Justin—where in between dangling from the monkey bars and bouncing on the seesaw, Ying had asked the other children what they knew of the lighthouse, and been met with mostly quizzical indifference and one boy's impatient, "Aiyah, go and see lorh"—she decided she would do just that, go and see. "Justin," she declared as they waited for the lift, "we don't go home yet, okay? We go upstairs and see the lighthouse."

"Can see what?"

"I'm not sure," Ying replied, "that's why we go." The lift arrived and she punched the button for '24' with a tingle of anticipation. She had never been up to such a high floor of any building before, least of all one with the promise of a lighthouse at the top.

When they stepped out on the 24th floor, there were four flats, a parapet between them, and the top of the staircase that ran like a vertical vein along one side of the block—just like on all the other floors. Between two flats sat a door covered with fading, flaking beige paint. Lettered on it in deep red were the words: No Unauthorised Access. Ying walked up to the beige door and tested its silver round doorknob. It was locked.

Justin trailed her. "See what, Je Je?"

Ying jiggled the doorknob, tried twisting it to no avail, and finally placed her hand flat against the door and leaned her ear close, as if checking for a heartbeat. All she felt was the sea breeze coasting across her back; all she heard was the distant grumble of expressway traffic and the closer mumble of television from one of the flats.

"Je Je?" Justin prodded.

Ying shushed him, several times. She wanted to take her time to tap, rap, kick the door, scratch at the keyhole, perhaps even sit cross-legged on the dusty tiled floor till sunset and see if anyone showed up. But with Justin interrupting her every few minutes, she began to feel irritated—with him, with all the adults who didn't know what was going on even though the lighthouse was so important, with whoever was in charge of the lighthouse for keeping it a big secret and not letting her see it, the way children in her storybooks always got to explore and discover interesting things.

"Okay lah, go home, go home," she muttered finally, giving the sullen, stubborn door one last baleful look. She would come back another time.

• • •

At Auntie Yoke Lin's front door, Ying knocked three times as usual. When it opened Auntie Yoke Lin stood there, looking worried although her hair was done up nicely into a ponytail, secured by a shiny gold hairclip. "Aiyoh, there you are. Where did you go? I went to the playground, all the children said you left already." She waved them inside impatiently. A man came up behind her, stern-looking despite the haggard lines on his face and the uneasy creases of his clothes.

"Daddy!" Justin kicked off his slippers and rushed inside.

Ying realised it was the man from the photograph on the wall, the one with Auntie Yoke Lin in the park. He was heavier set now, with the kind of rounded belly that in Ying's storybooks was invariably associated with jolly characters. His hair was unfashionably parted on the right side, emphasising the squareness of his jaw. A bold jade oval, set within a sulky circumference of gold, gleamed from a finger on his right hand, the hand resting on Justin's head.

"Daddy!" Justin chirped. "So long you never come. Are you

eating dinner with us?"

The man grunted, his eyes resting on Ying. Auntie Yoke Lin gestured her forward. "My sister Wai Ling's girl. Her name is Hui Ying, we call her Ying. Ying, say hello to Uncle Robert."

Ying didn't know who Wai Ling was; it wasn't her mother's name. Only the last part made sense. "Hello . . . Hello, Uncle Robert."

"Staying how long?" Uncle Robert's question was directed at Auntie Yoke Lin, who said, "She goes back every Friday night, comes here on Sunday night."

"I thought you said Wai Ling was the one the most upset, the one who told you get out of the house."

Auntie Yoke Lin demurred. "That was a long time ago. Now she ask for help . . . Still family, what."

Ying had removed her slippers and waited in the doorway, her bare feet cool against the speckled terrazzo floor tile. It was as if the adults didn't see her at all.

After a long look at Auntie Yoke Lin, Uncle Robert steered Justin into the living room. "Daddy staying for a few days. Tomorrow we go and buy new toys, okay?"

Tomorrow is a school day, Ying wanted to interrupt, but Auntie Yoke Lin laid a stiff hand on her shoulder and squeezed it. "Ying, good girl," she said with soft urgency, "Wai Ling is the name of my sister. Pretend you're her daughter, okay? Like what you did just now. Her husband's name, we call him Chan. If *he* says Chan," she meant Uncle Robert, she was watching him entertain Justin with silly hand gestures, "pretend it's your father."

Ying nodded with a confidence she didn't feel. "Why he . . ."

"Go and play in your room until dinner time. I call you."

At dinner, Auntie Yoke Lin's focus was on Uncle Robert, serving him the chicken drumstick and refilling his rice bowl before he asked. Justin recited stories from school that Ying and Auntie Yoke Lin had heard before; they seemed to amuse Uncle Robert. The only time Ying was drawn in was when Justin excitedly reported their visit to the 24th floor. "We thought can see the lighthouse."

"What lighthouse?" Uncle Robert mused, leaning back in his chair.

"The light on top of the block," Auntie Yoke Lin interjected. "That's where you all went just now?"

Ying and Justin nodded in unison. Justin described the door and then looked to Ying for help, but before she could chime in, Uncle Robert waved his chopsticks dismissively. "Don't kaypoh so much. Locked door, not allowed to go inside, means don't go—understand? Wait police catch you, then you know."

Ying was old enough that the folksy admonition didn't scare her, but Justin quietened. After dinner Auntie Yoke Lin excused her from helping with the dishes as she usually did, and told her again to play in her room. Before bed she had her usual cup of Milo, but the routine of the home felt different. The next day, Uncle Robert let Justin skip school and took him to the enormous Toys 'R' Us store that had recently opened nearby, at Marine Parade. They came home with three shopping bags of toys, including the newest He-Man action figure that Ying had heard the boys at the playground talking about. Uncle Robert wanted to take Justin to the zoo the day after but Auntie Yoke

Lin intervened, saying he had an English test on Friday and shouldn't miss school again.

When the children came home from school that day, after lunch Auntie Yoke Lin seated both of them at the dining table, Ying with her homework and Justin with some English worksheets Auntie Yoke Lin had prepared. Uncle Robert sat at the other end of the table, his back to the wall of paintings and photographs. He was smoking and shuffling through some papers, periodically tapping numbers into a calculator or flicking his cigarette against a clear glass ashtray.

Auntie Yoke Lin did two worksheets with Justin, then told him to do the third one himself while she went into the kitchen to check on the soup. After a few attempts, Justin pushed his worksheet over to Ying. "Je Je, I donno how to do."

Ying glanced over. "You have to match the idiom from the list."

"What is 'idiom'?"

"Phrases, like sayings. Like you know Chinese we got also. My mother always say I talk a lot, ask a lot of questions, *mng tang mng sai*," Ying told Justin rhythmically. "Like that—idiom."

Uncle Robert looked up. "What did you say?"

Ying repeated it, including the Hokkien phrase.

"Why your mother say in Hokkien, not in Cantonese?" Uncle Robert wanted to know, setting down his cigarette. Auntie Yoke Lin had just emerged from the kitchen and his glance swerved to her. "Wai Ling's husband not Hokkien, why she speaking Hokkien like . . ."

Auntie Yoke Lin looked at Ying, the sternest her eyes had ever been. "What did you say?"

"I said . . . my mother said," Ying stammered, "'I was explaining 'idiom'. I said *mng tang mng sai* is a Chinese idiom."

"Je Je just trying to help me," Justin piped up but Uncle Robert's voice drowned him out.

"Say in Cantonese."

Ying could recognise the sounds of Cantonese, especially now that she'd stayed with Auntie Yoke Lin for over a month, but she couldn't speak any. "I donno," she said quietly.

"Donno how to speak Cantonese?" Uncle Robert had gotten up from the table and it was to Auntie Yoke Lin's side that he marched. "How can? What the hell is going on here?"

Auntie Yoke Lin took his arm, turning him away from the children. "Nothing, nothing. She . . ." She sighed. "She's not Wai Ling's child."

Ying and Justin kept to their seats.

"She's my schoolmate Lily's sister's daughter. The parents working, they needed someone to help look after her during the week. They pay me a little bit. You were gone for so long . . . I thought a bit of money would help."

"You anyhow let people's children come into this house?" Uncle Robert thumped a fist on the corner of the table closest to him, also closest to Justin. The boy let go of his pencil. It rolled off the table, rattling onto the terrazzo floor.

"Not anyhow, her parents . . ."

"What did I say about keeping things quiet?" Uncle Robert backed away from the table. "If people in Malaysia find out, this becomes very difficult for me."

"They won't find out," Auntie Yoke Lin tried to reassure him.

"She's just a girl..."

"Not in my house!"

The argument moved into the bedroom, behind closed doors, some of it in Cantonese, though from the raised voices Ying and Justin could pick out scattered English words: *reputation, business, family, difficult, KL* (which Ying told Justin was in Malaysia), *Justin, home, money* (twice), *work, difficult* (again, several times), and finally, *wife*.

"Why they fighting?" Justin asked her. The children were still at the dining table. Justin's pencil was still on the floor.

"Donno," Ying said, feeling sick to her stomach. She had gotten in trouble in school earlier that year for talking too much in class and asking too many questions—*mng tang mng sai*. She imagined Auntie Yoke Lin calling her mother and complaining, like her teacher had.

Auntie Yoke Lin did call her mother, as soon as she came out of the bedroom. Then she came over to Ying. "Come, Ying, not your fault," she began, surprisingly gentle, "but you have to go home. Your mum will pick you after work, in one or two hours' time."

"I'm sorry," Ying blurted. She had heard Auntie Yoke Lin say it on the phone several times; her version was sharper, more desperate as Auntie Yoke Lin guided her to her room. "I'm sorry I made Uncle angry. I'm sorry I made you angry."

Auntie Yoke Lin drifted her hand across Ying's head. "No, I'm not angry. These things..." She sighed. "Justin and I will miss having you around."

Ying started. "Next week cannot come back? After Uncle leaves?"

"I'm sorry, Ying." It sounded wrong that Auntie Yoke Lin

was apologising to her. She opened the small cupboard that Ying used, pulling out her bag, her clothes and her handful of books. "Go and pack your schoolbag. Don't worry, Uncle won't come out."

Ying felt as if she wanted to cry, but that was another thing her parents had told her not to do. "Auntie Yoke Lin," she attempted with a croak in her voice, "is it also because of the lighthouse, because I brought Justin upstairs?"

"No, nothing to do with the lighthouse. Don't think he even remembers." Auntie Yoke Lin continued stuffing clothes into the bag. "Ying, be a good girl, go and pack."

By the time her parents arrived, it was just after dark. Ying's bags were by the door and her father took them without saying anything. "I'm so sorry," Auntie Yoke Lin was repeating to her mother as Ying slid her feet into her sand-dusted slippers.

"No lah, I'm sorry for the trouble," Ying's mother said. "Thank you." She handed a small envelope to Auntie Yoke Lin, who stepped out of the flat, barefoot, to walk them to the lift. Ying lingered to say goodbye to Justin.

"Bye-bye, Je Je." Justin looked small and puzzled in the doorway, one hand gripping the metal grille gate, his head tipped against it. At the lift, Auntie Yoke Lin patted Ying on the head, then stooped down to give her, for the first and last time, a hasty squeeze of a hug.

"Thank you, Auntie Yoke Lin. Bye-bye, Auntie Yoke Lin," Ying said as the lift doors slid closed.

Ying thought her parents would scold her once they were alone, just like the time after her teacher had called them, but they were quiet as they went downstairs to the car. Her mother only asked if Uncle Robert had scolded her, to which Ying replied, "Not really, but he was very angry."

As her father turned the car onto the expressway, heading west, her mother said, "Jenny said she can look after her the next few days, until we find someone else."

"She shouldn't depend on that man so much."

"Already like that, how to change? Justin then how?"

Ying climbed up on the back seat of the car to peer through the rear windscreen, at the tall buildings that were starting to recede towards the horizon. She looked for the one with the beam on top, swivelling round and round as it always did. She counted off ten seconds, again and again and again.

Seascrapers

Stephanie Ye

Today

SHE WAKES AT dawn and watches his face. She imagines the dreams rippling beneath the calm, stark planes. Dreams are what help perpetuate memory, she remembers, or misremembers, reading once, subsurface currents that weave through and animate the detritus floating in the ocean of the mind.

But what about someone who is losing his memories? What has happened to his dreams? She imagines him swimming in a boundless ocean, but as he raises and lowers his arms she sees that they are made of sand. They unglue and crumble and fall into the silent waters.

Two months ago

It was his new girlfriend who told her. She'd already heard he was sick, of course, but she didn't know how badly. They weren't hostile towards each other, but they hadn't seen the point of keeping in touch once the divorce papers had come through.

He had included her in an e-mail he'd sent out to friends a year ago, that he'd been diagnosed with brain cancer, but that he was undergoing treatment and that the prognosis was hopeful. She had written a sympathetic letter back, saying to let her know if she could help in any way, but he hadn't replied. She was shocked and concerned, of course, but she also felt it was no longer her place to pry. She'd heard no more from him, or about him, until his girlfriend e-mailed her out of the blue and asked if they could meet. It's a little bit urgent, she wrote, and hard to put in writing. It's better if I say it to you in person.

She said it over an hour at a cafe near neither of their workplaces, as they clutched cardboard coffee cups and a quiche cooled to a waxen sheen on its plate. Every day he wakes up having forgotten more of his life, the girlfriend explained. At first, he would ask when they were going to some event or running some errand, when they had already done it yesterday, a few days ago, last week. Then he kept reading the same few chapters of a book; commenting on how the renovation of the house across the road had finished so quickly; asking why the radio was playing Christmas carols in May.

Five months ago, he forgot he had cancer, and had to be told every morning that he didn't have to go to work. Three months ago, he forgot she was his girlfriend, was puzzled why a mere acquaintance was tasked with taking care of him. Two months ago, he forgot her completely.

He started asking for you about a month ago, the girlfriend said. At first, he didn't react much whenever I told him about the divorce, he just seemed to accept it. But lately, he's started becoming increasingly upset. He even cried, as if I'd told him you'd died. But the last straw was the day I e-mailed you. He'd flown into an absolute rage, his hands were shaking and he was throwing things about. Now, I just tell him you've had to go out of town for work. That's the one good thing about his condition—if you hurt him, he'll forget it soon enough, you return to a blank slate.

The girlfriend took a deep breath. I think it would be better if he starts staying with you, she said quickly. He's obviously at some point in his memories where you're together, he misses you and it would be better for him if he were with you. If it's convenient, of course.

It's not a matter of convenience, she thought, but of conscience. How much lying would she have to do? Would she have to pretend to this sick man that they were still married, still sharing a commitment, a life?

She didn't say any of this to the girlfriend, only: But how long till he forgets me too?

I don't know. He seems to be forgetting at an exponential rate. But, he's also getting physically worse. He'll become more and more uncoordinated and weak and then... the doctors give him only a year or so. For what it's worth.

She wondered what *it* whose *worth* the girlfriend was referring to. How do you feel about this, she asked instead. It can't be easy for you.

Yes it's not, the girlfriend said abruptly, harshly, before biting her lip. There were suddenly tears in her eyes. Sorry, she said. I care about him, a lot. But I really think it would be better at this point if he's with you. She impatiently wiped her cheek with the back of her hand. Frankly, it would be better for me, too. Can you imagine being in love with someone who doesn't remember you and never will?

Today

His eyelids are flickering; he sighs; he turns from the weak light filtering in through the curtains. His fingers brush her stomach. Muscle memory, she thinks. Intellectually, emotionally, she is worlds away from what once was; yet his physical presence next to her, the rhythm of his breathing, the scent of his hair and skin, all these are familiar and comfortable. His clothes hanging next to hers in the wardrobe, his toothbrush in the bathroom. Even the way he always leaves the toilet seat up. What fools humans are, she thinks, to believe that myth of the immutable soul, when so much of one's sense of self is determined by one's corporeal circumstances: gender, skin colour, geographic location. Genetics, beauty. Wealth and health. The proportions of one's face, the sturdiness of one's limbs. When a fiery spirit can be extinguished by the breaking of the body; when identity can be destroyed with the mutation of a few cells in that grey hunk of flesh called the brain.

Yesterday

He opened his eyes and looked up at her. His smile made his cheeks and chin for a moment seem soft and guileless; a strange, almost goofy contrast to his long face and gaunt features. He stretched, and the stretch became an embrace. She rested her head on his warm chest and listened as his heart skipped a beat.

She left him to wash up and get dressed and went to prepare their breakfast, making his coffee on the machine fetched from his place when he moved in. She doesn't drink the stuff herself. She laid out his pills too—painkillers, not treatments; there was no pretence at this point that he would ever be cured. Through the kitchen doorway she could see the worktable where she had placed all the documents and X-rays from the doctor, the first things he'd see upon exiting the bedroom. She had thought at first that maybe they'd be too much for him to take in every morning, but he's always been comfortable with facts and figures, the raw data.

She could see him now in profile, reading attentively like the good student he always was, one elbow propped on the table, his forehead resting on his palm as he leaned over the papers. She had to remind herself that for him this was always the first time, the discovery. Sometimes, he would scribble things in a spiral journal. She'd once taken a peek inside; it wasn't a personal diary but a collection of notes, summarising the cancer and what it was doing to him. He also had a section where he'd written down his bank PINs, insurance numbers, e-mail passwords. Orderly and precise, planning for the end.

Today

He opens his eyes and looks up at her. His pupils constrict swiftly as he scrambles to sit up—or is it to back away? She hears herself say his name. He stops moving, but every muscle in his face, his arms, is tense. She says, You've been sick. You can't remember. Everything's all right. She realises she's babbling, so she tells herself to shut up. His lost expression is child-like in its nakedness, and with an impulse of tenderness she reaches out to brush the hair off his forehead; but he flinches and she puts her hand down without touching him.

One Week Ago

Some days were busy with errands: Groceries, taking him to the barber's, the doctor's. Or, if he felt up to it, they would go out on the town, to a museum or the park or to the shops, even to concerts a few times. She handled the schedules, and the bills. They sometimes did the same thing days in a row if she felt like it, since of course he never remembered what they had already done. These days were pleasant: she had forgotten how similar their aesthetic sensibilities were. Once, they attended all three nights of an all-Mozart programme; and every night during the second movement of the clarinet concerto, at the moment when the orchestra first took up the solo clarinet's theme like the tips of waves catching upon a single sunbeam, he reached over and placed his hand on hers.

Other days they stayed home, drew the curtains, ordered delivery. She had stacked photo albums on the coffee table, old snapshots of themselves that she'd kept out of inertia rather than sentiment. She was on long leave from work, and without the weekly schedule she felt dislocated in time. His condition didn't help. He was in his early 20s that day, shy and earnest. He kept apologising—rather irritatingly, given the numerous apologies they had tossed at each other towards the end of their marriage, the kind that's easy to make when you've stopped actually caring how the other person feels. That old cliché of how the opposite of love isn't hate but indifference; amicable divorces are papered with such light-hearted professions of regret.

This must be so awful for you, he said now. I wish I could remember our wedding . . . I hope we've been happy . . . Looking at the flush in his haggard cheeks, she didn't have the heart to tell him, no, we didn't make it. Our love didn't last. Too bad, this is all a lie! Instead, she let him take her in his arms and she told him again about the night he proposed, on a beach under the stars. It wasn't a nice beach—it was a city beach, smoky from the barbecue pits being manned by pot-bellied middle-aged men, as their wives sipped spiked lemonade and occasionally shouted at the children who wriggled underfoot, engaged in their own complex negotiations. As for the stars, cloud cover and the reflection of the city lights obscured those ancient fires. Only the sea looked anywhere near romantic, swollen at high tide, the waves rippling like the scales of an elusive creature. On the horizon was a string of lights, ships lining up to enter the port some ways down. Solid yet shimmering, they looked from this distance like a fantastic city of their own. He called them seascrapers as they sat on a blanket, their shoes slumped on the sand like toppled Easter Island statues. She sat behind him and rested her cheek on his back. The waters surged upwards, shuddering in their effort to obey the invisible moon; when he turned around and asked her to be his wife, what she felt most of all was a sense of inevitability.

Today

She watches him from the kitchen as he sits at the table studying an X-ray. The tumours aren't round, like how she'd always pictured tumours to be, but tree-shaped: branches creeping into the cracks and crevices of the brain, vines clenching themselves round a ruin. She makes the coffee, prepares the pills, lingering a little longer than she needs to on each step. It's a simple routine but it feels contextless today, like a religious ritual whose origins have been erased by time.

She starts as she hears him call her name in a low voice. He's standing at the kitchen doorway, one thin hand on the doorframe, as if waiting to be invited in. He must have prepared for the eventuality and studiously written her name down in his journal. She wonders if he's going to start apologising again, but instead he says, Can I ask you a question.

When she doesn't say no, he continues, Is today the first day?

First day?

First day that I've . . . forgotten you.

She nods, suddenly afraid of where this is going. I see, he says. He purses his lips. Thank you. He adds, I'm sorry. She consciously holds her breathing steady as he slowly walks towards her. She supposes that if she were still in love with him, she would start crying when he draws her into his arms. Instead, she counts to ten, then asks him if he wants his coffee.

47 Days Ago

It was on one of their stay-in days that he'd laid out his plan. He was in his mid-30s that day, sarcastic and a bit brutal.

It's for your own good, he said. Do you still want to be taking care of me when I'm drooling on my pillow and pooping in my bed? By that point, I doubt I'll remember your name to thank you.

She answered coolly, trying to match his tone: And how do you propose to do it? Pills? Slitting your wrists? Hanging? Jumping from a window? Driving off a cliff? It would be great if it were a method where I didn't have to clean up afterwards.

Drowning, he said. It's easy to make it look like an accident. And I've heard it's actually very peaceful, and quiet. There's none of that waving your arms and shouting business, because at that point your body's simply incapable of any voluntary action. Water replaces air; one element replaces another.

And when would you like to do this?

Let's go with the day I forget you, he said evenly, and started writing in his journal.

Today

He tells her he wants to go to the beach that evening. She asks, not very hopefully, if he's sure. I'm quite sure, he replies. There's a mulishness in his expression that she hasn't seen for a long time; she recognises it from when he took business calls at home, wearing down the other party until he got what he wanted.

The sky is edged pink and orange over the rooftops as they set off. She drives. She hasn't been to this beach in ages, but she finds she knows the way, doesn't get any of the turn-offs wrong. He sits beside her gazing out the window; the shadows sliding across his wan face from passing headlights look like cracks, ghostly renderings of the growth beneath his skull.

The city beach, as it turns out, has become even more tawdry in the intervening years. A small funfair has sprouted like an alien colony on a nearby field, lights and colours whirling ceaselessly according to some impenetrable purpose. The air smells of meat and melted sugar. Stumbling about are hysterical groups of teenagers and strained families, dazed children and defeated parents.

He says he wants a hamburger from a stand. Do you want one, he asks, and she automatically says no, I'm a vegetarian, before wishing she hadn't. He stands awkwardly with his hands in his pockets as she digs in her bag for her wallet.

I'm sorry, it just smelt really good, he says, cradling the oily packet like a wounded bird.

Oh, it really doesn't matter, she snaps. Then she sees his face and unsets her jaw. I'm sorry, she says. God, I'm sorry about everything. She's said that word too many times, yet somehow she now feels she's never said it enough.

They walk in silence down to the water. Oddly, the beach is more generous than she'd remembered; the sounds of the fair eventually fade out and soon they're alone in the dark. The starless sky has the sheen of an aubergine. All they can hear is the splash of the waves and, farther out, the humming of the ships. She spreads out the blanket she's brought and they sit and look at the beads of light on the horizon. Seascrapers, she says, pointing at them, and he looks searchingly at her, as if sensing the echo.

I'm ready, he says softly. I'm going soon.

I'll go with you. I won't stop you, but I'll be with you. She feels a deep sense of calm settle in her bones. And I'll bring you back.

Thank you, he says. He smiles. She realises that this is the first time he has smiled at her today.

She rests her head on his chest. She can hear his heart, the thrumming of that robust, blithe muscle. It is the beating of a fantastic sea monster ascending from the depths, still innocent of the knowledge that it is the only one of its kind that survives. She thinks of their broken marriage vow, *till death do us part*, and how perversely they were ending up fulfilling it after all.

Is it all right if I kiss you now, he says.

There are myriad kisses in a relationship: desperate ones as involuntary as breathing, stolen ones on crowded trains, ceremonial ones at the front door, routine ones as dispassionate as licking an envelope. It takes two to kiss, but does it take two to hold the memory?

His fingers trace her brow, ears, eyelids, nose, chin, as if he's hoping their topography will map out for him what his extinguished self found dear in this stranger. She puts her hands to his face and draws him close. His mouth tastes of blood, though it could just be the burger. In that moment, she has never loved anyone else. Or maybe it is just muscle memory; after all, the heart is a muscle, too.

They walk into the sea, and when the waves are lapping at their throats they turn to face each other and he grasps her hands. She inhales, he exhales, and they plunge beneath the surface. The salt stings and the water is black and she can't see anything. She can only feel his hands gripping hers with unexpected strength; but he's right, he doesn't struggle. Afterwards, she holds him, his head to her heart, as they float between the city and the seascrapers.

Because I Tell

Felix Cheong

WHERE I HIDE, I see stars. So many, many twinkle, twinkle little stars. How I wonder what they are. Mama says they are God's eyes. I say that is why God sees everything because he has so many eyes. Mama laughs loud and kisses my head. I remember because she does not kiss me for a long time.

I count the stars. I finish counting at fifteen yesterday. Now I start at sixteen. I think they are my birthday candles. I am sixteen years old today! Happy birthday to Ben, happy birthday to me! I make a wish. Then I close my eyes slowly, blowing one candle, one candle, one candle. I must keep secret my wish. If I tell, I will not get my wish. That is why Cheche says Dada will not come home. Because I tell.

Where I hide, I am cold. I have many, many leaves like a blanket up to my face. I sleep on brown grass. The dry leaves tickle my backside like I remember how Dada tickles me one time. He holds me on the floor and I pee in my dark blue shorts. He laughs loud and says I must go and wash myself before Mama comes home.

My yellow Brazil T-shirt is dirty. Dada gives it one time to me. He likes football very much. When he finishes work, he takes me to the green grass downstairs to play football. I kick the ball to him and he kicks it back to me. He says this is father-and-son talk. Sometimes he kicks the ball very far and I run to find it. I bring it back and we start talk again.

Dada takes me one time to the National Stadium to watch a football game. So many, many people sit, side by side, like taking a test. They shout "Goal!" I think football is a fun game because people can shout. When I play with Cheche at home one time and we shout, Mama scolds. She says, "You shout so loud for what? You want to wake up the dead?" I hear many, many people shout in the National Stadium and I think they must wake up the dead.

I ask Dada where are the dead. He laughs and says, "The team that cannot score goals." I shout "Goal!" but people look at me. Dada laughs loud and says, "Not yet. That was only an offside." I shout "Goal!" only when Dada shouts "Goal!" He kisses my head.

When the football game finishes, the man next to Dada shakes his hand. I see he gives Dada money. I am scared of this man. He is short with yellow hair and he has painting of dragons on his right arm. The dragons grow bigger when he moves his arm. He smokes many, many times and comes to my house many times. He says to Dada, "Next week, more."

Dada tells me to keep a secret. Then we take bus number 16 to Lucky Plaza and he buys me a yellow Brazil T-shirt. He also has a Brazil T-shirt. I wear number 11 and he wears number 10. He says Brazil is his favourite team because he makes money one time when they win the World Cup. I ask who drinks from the World Cup. He laughs loud and says, "Only God and Brazil can drink from the World Cup." I think God must be very thirsty because he has to share the cup with Brazil.

When we get home, Mama asks Dada where he gets money to buy Ben a Brazil T-shirt. I say the dragon man gives Dada money. Then Mama shouts at Dada and he shouts back. They shout for a long time. They throw things on the floor. Mama throws his favourite cup. Dada throws my favourite cup. I am scared and I cry. Now I cannot drink from my cup.

Cheche takes me to the bedroom and closes the door. She says, "Why do you have to tell Mama? See what you did?" I say I forget it is a secret. Cheche says, "You always forget. You know this is not the first time they fight over money. Yet, you purposely told Mama. You want Mama and Dada to break up, is it?"

I say I do not want Mama and Dada to break up. Cheche says, "Then why can't you keep your big mouth shut? Why didn't you say your friend in school gave you the T-shirt?" I say my friend in school does not have money to buy a Brazil T-shirt for me.

Cheche says, "I do not know what to do with you. You were born stupid. You will always be stupid."

I say I am not stupid. I keep secrets. I never tell Mama Cheche takes Terence one time to her bedroom. I never tell Mama Terence kisses Cheche and holds her on the bed. I never tell Mama Terence tickles Cheche and they wear no clothes and they laugh loud.

Cheche hits my face. She shouts, "You have been peeping at me? You pervert!" She goes out of the house but forgets to take her keys. She must go to Terence's house. I cry and I put a pillow on my pain. Too many, many secrets to keep!

When I wake up, I want to say sorry to Dada. I want to tell him I do not know why I am born stupid and I will always be stupid. Many, many days, I wait at the green grass downstairs with the football. I kick it very far and I run to find it. I wait at home. I ask Cheche where is Dada. She says, "Do not come anywhere near me, you pervert."

I ask Mama where is Dada. She says he is dead. I cry I want Dada for father-and-son talk with the football downstairs. Mama scolds, "I take care of you and you only want that useless man? You are ungrateful! Do you know who pays for your meals, your clothes and your school fees? Your useless father is only good at gambling. What has he ever done for us? He is dead for all I care!"

When Mama goes to work, I shout "Dada!" many, many times at home to wake up the dead. I want to have father-and-son talk. But I do not see him.

My Brazil T-shirt is very dirty now. My dark blue shorts is also dirty. I see mud and ants everywhere on my legs and my body. I do not want to go home now. I am scared Mama scolds when she sees me. She says, "You think I do not have anything to do? Can't you keep yourself clean? I have to hand-wash your clothes everyday. Look at my hands. They are bleeding!"

I do not want Mama's hands to bleed. I am scared she dies like Jesus. His hands bleed all the time in church. I am scared to look at him. I ask Mama one time if Jesus hand-washes many, many clothes. She scolds, "Stop talking rubbish. Jesus is God.

He does not have to wash clothes." She wants me to kneel in front of Jesus and say sorry. I kneel down and I say Jesus, sorry I talk rubbish. I do not know why I am born stupid. I do not know why I cannot keep secrets. I want Dada to come home. Jesus looks at me and bleeds.

I keep myself clean because I do not want Mama to hand-wash many, many clothes and her hands bleed like Jesus. I wash myself many, many times everyday. After I wake up, I wash my face and my body. After I go to the toilet, I wash my hands. After I have my dinner, I wash my face and my body.

But now, I smell bad like the drains in Geylang. We go there one time to eat clay pot rice. Me, Dada, Mama and Cheche. I cannot finish the clay pot rice because of the smell from the drains. I remember the bad smell like old eggs from our old fridge. One time, I break three old eggs to let the chickens come out. Cheche says, "The baby chickens are locked up because they are naughty. Like how Mama locked you up once because you were naughty? So you have to open the eggs to rescue the baby chickens. Don't you want to do that?" When I open up the three eggs, I see no baby chickens. Only uncooked omelette. Mama scolds when she comes home. She says I waste food. Then she scolds Cheche but she laughs loud.

I ask Mama why the drains in Geylang smell bad like old eggs from our old fridge. She says, "It is because Geylang hides many people's dirty secrets. Many people go to Geylang to do things they cannot do in the day. That is why it smells bad." After that, I stop eating old eggs. I do not want to smell bad like I hide secrets. If I smell bad and I wash myself many, many times everyday, Mama scolds. She says, "You waste water like that, Bedok Reservoir will run dry tomorrow morning."

I do not want Bedok Reservoir to run dry. I like it here. I walk here with Dada many times after dinner. I ask Uncle Timmy to take me to Bedok Reservoir for a walk. Uncle Timmy says, "You are old enough to walk there yourself."

He comes to our house many, many times after Dada never comes home. He is tall and big like Dada. He smokes many, many times like the dragon man. He does not go to work like Dada. He sits at home and watches football on TV. He does not shout "Goal!" to wake up the dead. I ask can we go to the National Stadium to watch football. He says, "Why go there when you can watch it 'live' on TV? It is free and you can watch replays." I say I want to play football at the green grass downstairs. He says, "You are old enough to play by yourself. Or find your own friends."

Uncle Timmy sleeps in Mama's bedroom now. He is Mama's boyfriend, like Terence is Cheche's boyfriend. Cheche does not bring Terence home anymore. I ask Cheche where is Terence. Cheche scolds, "You dare to ask, you little peeping Tom?" I say my name is Ben, not Tom. Tom is my friend in school. Cheche looks at me a long time and laughs. I say I know how to keep secrets. I keep Cheche's secret and I do not tell Mama about Terence. Cheche says, "Make sure you do not. Otherwise, Terence will come here and beat you up."

I hear noise one time in Mama's bedroom. I think Uncle Timmy beats up Mama. I want to see. I open the door and see Uncle Timmy holds Mama on the bed. He tickles her like how Terence tickles Cheche. They wear no clothes and they laugh loud. I pull down my dark blue shorts and I say I want to pee. Mama pulls blanket to her neck and shouts, "Why didn't you knock? Why can't you use the toilet in the kitchen?"

I say I am scared. "Scared of what? Ghosts? I cannot even have privacy in my own house. I do not know what I did to give birth to a stupid boy like you." I say Mama does not love me anymore. She shouts, "I do not love you? What are you talking about, Ben? If I did not love you, I would have kicked you out long ago and put you in a home. You do not understand anything! You were born stupid and you will always be stupid. Useless like your good-for-nothing father. Now get out of my room! Better still, get out of my house! Go drown yourself in Bedok Reservoir, for all I care!"

Uncle Timmy looks at me and does not say anything. Cheche is not home. I want to pee but I go out of the house. I am scared. I cry but I walk and I walk to Bedok Reservoir.

Where I hide, I lie down on the dry grass and I count the stars. I think God has many, many eyes and he sees everything. He must see everybody's secrets. He must keep many, many secrets. He must smell like old eggs because he keeps many, many secrets.

I am sixteen today and I make a wish now. But I will not tell. I know how to keep secrets.

Sleeping

O Thiam Chin

IT HAS BEEN a week since the accident, and my wife is sleeping soundly on the bed. Her eyes are closed and I kiss them lightly. She doesn't stir; I brush her hair with my hand. I have just washed it with her favourite shampoo and conditioner—she doesn't believe in two-in-one shampoos. Her hair falls through my fingers in soft silky threads. I arrange her hair on the pillow, keeping it straight, brushing the strays from her face. She doesn't move, and the heart-rate monitor beside the bed beeps. I stand back from the bed and take in her sleeping form, her body tucked under the thick blanket.

The doctor said she may wake up anytime now; he has seen cases where the patients just opened their eyes one day and resumed their lives. He put his hand on my shoulder when he said this, and told me not to worry. I cast his words aside, and after spending three nights in the hospital, I decided to bring my wife home. I have not gone out much since then. The flat is my entire world; everything else is unnecessary, trivial. I spend most of my time by the bed, holding my wife's hand, keeping her company, hoping. Sometimes I talk to her and check her face for any response, for any signs of movement. I know she's still there, inside her sleeping body, her mind alive and ticking, sending signals all over the body, keeping it functioning, intact. It amazes me to no end, coming round to this truth: the human body as a thriving underground city, hidden, pulsating with secrets and intentions and meanings. Life is resilient and my wife's a tough woman; she will survive this. I imagine the life we will have when she wakes up, finally.

Sitting by the bedside, I pore through her journals and letters that had been locked in the lower drawer of her study table. Thankfully I have a spare key she doesn't know about. In one of the earliest letters: "Love is an unpredictable thing. You never know how it's born, or what it's made of, or where it's going." My heart jumps at these words, each time, no matter how many times I have read it.

"Maybe it's easy to explain love in this way, to give it a quality that is hard to pin down, unpredictability as its nature, its workings as the way of nature. Maybe it's the easiest way to explain how I have grown to love you. Can you see how difficult it's for me to do this, to put down these words, to create a reality out of something that is unseen or unreal?" I drop the letter in my lap, hit with a blow of conflicted emotions, and reach for my wife's hand, gripping.

In another letter: "Every day you would sit at your desk, typing, drinking your coffee, chatting with the other secretaries. You look contented, even happy. You would smile at me whenever I walked past your desk, and I would hold your smile in my mind, like a precious gift. I know you are friendly with everyone in the office, and there is no way to know whether the smile you bestowed on me is the same one you gave to the rest, but it doesn't matter. I hold it dearly to me, it's mine."

My eyes burn from reading these words, but I hold back. I clench my wife's hand; it's soft, baby-like smooth and doesn't return my grip. When I release her hand, it drops to her side, her palm facing up, her fingers bent slightly inward. I kiss it and put it under the blanket. The machine beeps once, and the numbers on the monitor screen drop and stabilise again.

I put my head on her chest and listen. Her heart sounds like a little dark creature pounding inside her, trapped, surviving but with little hope. I count her heartbeats against the time on my watch, one minute, then five, ten and twenty. The creature moans and moves, never missing a single beat. I want to reach in, pull it out and hold it up to the light. I want to see what my wife's heart looks like, to see the very thing that's keeping her alive.

I unplugged the phone in the flat just before the accident; I have no idea where I left my mobile phone. I don't need to be distracted now. The flat is silent, like a mausoleum, and when I talk to my wife, my voice carries through the air, calm and soothing; it doesn't sound at all like me. It's the voice of a man who has accepted his lot in life, a man in control of himself. I wonder whether my wife would like this kind of man, one with a confident, stable and uncomplicated outlook on life.

Once or twice, someone knocked on the front door. I kept very still and listened. "Just wait," I whispered. "They will leave soon. Nobody will bother us again." When the sounds behind the door died away, I looked through the peephole, checking, making sure. I throw away the pamphlets that have been slipped through the bottom gap of the door, advertising pizza delivery or rental of flat units. I stuff a large torn towel into the gap, but still they litter the doorsteps with these unwanted pamphlets. I make it a point to clear them so that the neighbours will not make a fuss or grow suspicious about our whereabouts; it's always important to keep up appearances and act like nothing's out of the norm.

I love my wife, as a husband should, but she's a stranger to me. The long untried years passed swiftly, then she was no longer the woman I knew, changed, and evolving under her skin, out of sight; though, of course, it's hard to tell when I have gotten so used to her—her presence, her moods, her ways—and taken everything for granted. A person changes constantly, in quiet unassuming ways; the light shifts just a bit, and suddenly she's revealed, a different woman, alive in ways you never knew possible, and it's hard to take your eyes off her, awed and fascinated. Before I found the stack of letters, I rarely gave much thought to my wife's life; but now, it's all I want to do, to read everything she has kept, though the revelations of what I have discovered bring its own hurt and pain.

"A most mediocre person can be the object of a love which is wild, extravagant, and beautiful as the poison lilies of the swamp. A good man may be the stimulus for a love both violent and debased, or a jabbering madman may bring about in the soul of someone a tender and simple idyll. Therefore, the value and quality of any love is determined solely by the lover himself."

I came across this note, jutting out from the cluster of letters, and read it to my wife. I enunciate each word slowly, as if I were an actor on a stage giving a soliloquy, composed, unruffled by the commotion happening around him, trying to undo him, to distract him from the task. I throw out the words, like stones, at my sleeping wife.

"That was from Carson McCullers; I'm sure you know this passage well. You had it printed out on a slip of paper, tacked to your work cubicle wall. I memorised it when I sat at your table at night when everyone had left the office. Forgive me, if you can, but I know you love it when I whisper these words to you when we make love. You don't say it but I can tell. From the way you hold your body to mine, pressing your ears to my mouth, whispering the words back to me, into me."

I search the bookshelf in the living room and find the book. *The Collected Stories of Carson McCullers*. I read every story in the book, almost finishing it, till I found the exact quote. I tear out the page and stick it to the wall, memorising the words. I imagine my wife's voice as she would have read it, the clarity and pitch of it. I hold her voice inside me, a tiny voice in the wilderness of my heart. The words dance in my mind, slipping in and out of consciousness, dangling their meanings—faint, strange and elusive—before me, always out of reach, incomprehensible.

I recite everything to my wife. I want to know whether they would have any effect on her. I breathe the words on her skin, massaging them in with my hands. Can she feel it, this pleasure of words and touch?

"Can you hear what I'm saying? Can you understand what I've said?" I whisper, but nothing stirs in her, her posture remains rigid and aloof.

Sometimes the long monologues tire me out. I talk to her about everything: her life, mine, our courtship. I'm not sure whether I remember all the details correctly, but still it's important that she knows, though she can't hear me. It's the telling that matters. Even as I'm telling the story of our lives, I'm also aware that she, too, has her own version of it, one where she stands in the heart of her story, the omniscient narrator.

I change her clothes every day: a T-shirt, a pair of black slacks, and beige-coloured bra and panties. The T-shirts are all white, size small; I bought a dozen of them at the supermarket, ten dollars for three. Life's so much easier when you don't have to decide what clothes to wear, or what colour suits you; you take what's given, no questions asked. Instead of waiting for the laundry basket to fill up, I wash everything with my own hands. I sprinkle a dusting of washing powder on each piece, wet it slightly, and work up a lather by giving it a few rough rubs. Then I wash the clothes under a running tap of hot water, wring them dry, and hang them up on the bamboo poles in the kitchen. Sometimes when the breeze goes through the hanging laundry—flapping a bra strap or lifting the shirt hem—I'd stop and stare, caught off guard by these little gestures.

I like the smell of dry, clean laundry, the lingering scent of the washing powder. I put my face into the chest of the shirt, taking long breaths, and feel the softness of its texture. I have cried into them on a few occasions, and now I'm learning to control my mood swings, to know when they are turning for the worse. I smooth out the creases and fold the clothes into small, compact shapes, straightening out the corners. The sight of the neat, tidy stacks of clean clothes never fails to lighten me up. Even as I put away the clothes into the respective drawers in the wardrobe, I can't help but take glances at my sleeping wife lying on the bed, hoping maybe she can see what I'm doing, keeping everything in order.

Every day, I clean my wife with a damp towel. I start from her face and slowly make my way down her body. I wipe her jawline from ear to ear, then her neck with a vein pulsating visibly under the skin, and down her collarbone. I rinse the towel and move to her hands, arms and armpits where a light fuzz of hair is starting to grow. It's strange to see and touch my wife's body in such closeness—how long has it been since I took time to study every part of her, before the accident?

Gently I wipe the underside of her breasts, down her pale stomach, and into the dark region of her crotch. I watch her face as I move the towel between her legs, waiting for something to stir in her expression, a flick of desire. Her eyes remain closed, her face placid. When I clean her back, I lift her upper body and lean it onto mine, her head on my shoulder. Sometimes I drop the towel and wrap my arms around her unresponsive body, hugging her tight. After I'm done, I powder her with J&J's baby powder and put a fresh set of clothes on her.

As she sleeps, I continue to read the letters I found hidden among her belongings.

"I often wonder how he's like, this man you claimed to love.

You said you love him, but your face tells a different thing. I have seen you with him several times, once when he picked you up from work, and another time at the shopping mall near your place. You look distracted, distant when you're with him. I know you're unhappy, but you can't leave him. You said you have loved him once, and it'll be wrong to leave him. I know it's your guilt talking, this lie you tried to convince yourself. You tell me this, and I don't know how to react. And then you would turn to me and kiss me, and all I can do is to give in to you, to take hold of something that isn't mine to possess in the first place. I used to hate you for what you're doing to yourself, and to me. How can love and hate be so similar, the intensity, the madness?"

I pause at this point in the letter and stare at the red numbers on the monitor display. I fold the letter, putting it back in the envelope, and then, in the flick of a terrible moment, I tear it up. The ripping sound fills the silence of the room for a brief moment; yet it brings no relief whatsoever.

With time on my hands, I begin to clear the clutter from the flat. I start with the storeroom. The rusty exercise bike, the faulty rice cooker, the shoes my wife couldn't bear to throw away, the smudgy watercolour posters done during her spare time—these are the first things to go. It gets easier after a while. I don't bother to check the contents, tied up in pink plastic bags or packed in small parcels; I simply throw them out. I don't want to disrupt the momentum, to stop and assess the value or importance of any of these items. What I don't see doesn't affect me, this dusty accumulation of my marriage, our shared history. I want to strip my life down to the core, the bare essentials, and I have grown to abhor the mess I have allowed my life to slip into. It seems like with each item I throw out, I'm getting back missing pieces of my life, a sense of control. If it's possible—how I long and work towards it—I want my life to start on a clean, blank slate: just me and my sleeping wife.

Before throwing the watercolour posters out, I bring one—her favourite, I recalled, of a Sunday dusk scene at the Botanic Gardens—to her, placing it on the bed. I put an extra pillow under her head and arrange her body in an upright position; her body feels bony—all edges now—and lighter. "You painted this, remember?" I say, and guide her finger across the cracked surface of the poster. "You always love painting the end of a day, its gradual passing, the dying lights."

I remember the day she painted this poster. She had packed her brushes, her tubes of paint and the empty canvas, and asked me to drive her to the Botanic Gardens. "You don't have to stay and wait, if you don't want to," she said. I stayed and waited for her to finish her painting. We sat near the swan pond, near the entrance of the Garden, under the shade of the spreading rain tree, watching the sun bleed itself out in the sky. She didn't say anything while she painted, her body rigid, her eyes focused. "This is good," I said. She ignored my comment, a quick gesture of annoyance evident in her expression. She took about two hours to complete it; by then, night had descended and the noisy hordes of families gone.

When I run out of food—no fresh produce, no perishables, only canned food—I head down to the Shop & Save supermarket in the next block and buy another week of groceries. I try not to spend too much time, grabbing only the things I need: a one-kg pack of rice, canned sardines, luncheon meat, preserved cabbage, salted peanuts, black-sauce beans. I pay the exact amount each time—no need for small talk with the cashiers—and rush back home.

Once I enter the flat, I drop the grocery bags on the kitchen table and head into the bedroom to check on my wife. Of course, she's still lying there, silent, immobile, sleeping; I have tied the cloth restraints on her wrists to the side bars of the bed frame, just in case she moves in her sleep and falls off the bed. I study her statistics on the monitor and check the drip tube attached to her left arm. Only when I'm sure everything's in order would I leave her alone, again.

I put the cans of food away and prepare a simple meal: porridge with soy sauce and salted peanuts. I cook enough porridge for two people, eating the second share for dinner if I'm hungry. Sometimes I eat beside the bed, bring tiny scoops of porridge to my wife's lips, leaving flecks of rice on them. When I finish my meal, I wipe away the untouched rice on her lips with a face towel. It worries me to see my wife slowly fading away before me, becoming thinner by the day. I may have to bring in a doctor soon, but until it's absolutely necessary, I will hold out against it, my last resort.

At night, I sleep beside my wife, putting my body close to her, my nose in her hair. I move my forefinger across her face, tracing the outline of her features, trying to imagine the dream she's having. I hug her too, fitting my body to hers, assuring her of my presence. Some nights, when I dream too wildly, I'd wake up screaming and feeling in the dark for the tangible proof of my wife's body, that she has not disappeared. On those nights, I would watch her intensely, not daring to move away from the bed, wrestling with the cruel, unwanted thoughts in my head.

The human body never stops functioning, even when the mind's gone. The heart continues to pump, and the hair and nails continue to grow. Now that my wife is incapacitated, I have to take care of the primping and upkeep of her body. I trim her toenails and fingernails slowly, careful not to clip too close to the skin. I wiped them with a cold towel, applying hand cream to her slender fingers, massaging. When I feel she wants a doll-up, I put a coat of fire-red nail polish on her nails, and blow them dry. I hold up her hands and kiss each finger. I put her hands on my face, and try to remember the last time she held me in this way.

"You have a premonition, a fear you can't shake off," the email begins. I have taken over my wife's laptop, and have been looking through her emails. She's careless about her password, jotting it down on a piece of Post-it note—striking it off, writing down a new password whenever she changed it—and leaving it under her desk calendar. Now that she is unable to check her account, I do it on her behalf.

"I know you said that the way he looked at you, the words he used, it's as if he knew something. But I want to assure you that it's just your fear working its way through you, the needless guilt you feel for doing the right thing. Don't overreact; don't let your fear get to you."

I go through every single one of her emails, reading each email two to three times. I delete everything from her account. Everything starts anew for her now. I don't want any unhappy history to blight her current blameless state. She has suffered enough, and now I know she's ready to begin a new phase with me beside her all the time, watching her, taking care of her every need.

During the dead, unguarded hours of the day when my mind slips into a dark, moody trance, I find it hard to focus my thoughts. Strange, violent images fill my head, dragging me down. I stare at my wife—her face a changing mask of innocence, complicity and betrayal—and I have to restrain from putting my hands around her soft neck. Instead I grip her hair with my fist, tilt her face towards me, holding my breath and waiting for the bloodlust to pass. Nothing seems to frazzle her, to break through the surface of her imperturbable composure, her defiance. It takes forever to come around to my usual self, to calm myself down; when my head clears, all I could feel is a deep sense of self-reproach, for not keeping my dark mood in check. Then I kiss my wife's forehead, smooth back her hair and whisper my apologies into her ear. It's comforting to know forgiveness is a give-and-take thing when a couple learns to accept each other's faults, in words and in silence.

Sometimes when I talk to her about our past, my wife would display tiny gestures to let me know she's listening. A slight twitch of her finger, a light flutter of her eyelid, and the slackening of her mouth as if she's about to say something in return. I lean in, anticipating her next gesture. I wait, and I watch. I'm always here for you, I tell her. Her chest rises and falls, another exhalation, the hidden life of her body. Even in her slumber, she's keeping her secrets.

I have cleared out most of my wife's belongings when I stumble upon a note in the front pocket of her dark pants. It's the same pants she was wearing that night. The note is hastily scribbled with wild cursive loops: "Since this is what you want, then we'll do it. Meet me at six this evening. This will all be over soon, I promise you. You'll be safe with me."

I tear up the note and flush it down the toilet. It's dangerous to keep the note around. You never know when another person may read it. I wash my hands at the kitchen sink with Dettol, and set about to prepare my dinner. Once I set the rice to cook, I sit at the kitchen table to wait.

Outside the flat, it's evening, the sky slowly darkening. It looks like that day at the Botanic Gardens—a distant, different time—and the muddling scenes blend into one another, overlapping. Something in the remembrance of the event, or maybe in the hypnotic spread of light and colours in the sky, opens up a dark pit in me, leaving me at the mercy of my memories. I picture my wife's back, her shoulders moving under her white blouse with each stroke of the paintbrush. I used to love to kiss this part of her body, to trace the ridges of her landscape. How she responded to me then—the deep breaths, the sensuous tilt of her head, the perspiration and body heat rising from her body. It makes me ache, madly—a hollow pain ripping me to shreds—to know she may never do this for me again, that I have already lost her, long before I even realised it. The rice cooker clicks, and the rice is cooked, releasing clouds of steam. I halt the train wreck of thoughts, and return to the immediate task of my dinner preparation.

After dinner, I go into the bedroom and sit beside my wife. I don't feel up to any conversation tonight, my mind still troubled with the earlier thoughts. I stroke my wife's hand, touching the wedding ring on her finger. Her hand is pliable, unresponsive. I dig my fingers into her skin, making tiny crescent grooves that disappear after a few seconds; I dig deeper, wanting to break the surface of it, to draw blood.

Then I release her hand. I lift her head and bring her face to me. I run my tongue along the contours of her lips, her nose, her eyebrows, tasting her, filling my mouth with every part of her. I kiss and bite and lick, edging her body to submission. She yields up nothing, only flesh, a hollow shell. I suddenly choke and drop my wife back on the bed; my mind snaps. I run into the kitchen and open the fridge. I dig through the pile of body parts, and finally find what I'm looking for: a pair of hands. I remove them from the storage bag; the fingers are frozen stiff, curling inward, a claw-like grip. I bring them back to my wife.

"This is what you want, right?" I scream into my wife's face, shoving the severed hands at her. I move the cold hard fingers across her face, the dead fingers of her lover. I move them down her body, to her breasts, her stomach, her crotch. I watch her face; her lips part ever so slightly. I throw the pair of hands at the wall, a heavy thud resounding in the quiet room. I turn away from my wife and stand at the window, looking out. Night has fallen, the sky a deep shade of ink-blue, and down below on the streets, the rich golden glow of streetlamps. Everything—the moving cars, the human activities, the flight of birds—seems unreal, small and insignificant, from high above.

Once the darkness ebbs away, I pick up the hands and bring them back to the kitchen. They are starting to thaw, softening. I put them back into the freezer compartment of the fridge. I catch the sight of my wife's lover's head—the half-shut sleepy eyelids, the straight line of his mouth—behind the frosted, translucent storage bag, and push it to the back of freezer, behind the bags of limbs, arms and chopped up torso.

I slip into the bed and lie beside my wife. I can feel the warmth of her body, frail and weak. I place my head on her chest, listening to the secret sounds of her interior, echoing with life. I wish to slip in, to go straight into the heart of her. She lets out a sigh. I hold my breath. But there's nothing more. I hold her hand to me, and I put my weeping face into her palm. My sleeping wife, the woman I love—I almost lost her once, but now I have her, beside me, and I'll never let her out of my sight. She will never leave me again, not even when she wakes up and realises what I have done for her, how I have taken care of her, how I have loved her. I bring my body closer to her, to keep her warm and tight in my grip. Nothing, not even the threat of the darkness that lies around us, is able to separate us, from this moment, from this very night, as long as we hold on to each other like this.

Agnes Joaquim, Bioterrorist

Ng Yi-Sheng

HISTORY WOULD FOREVER remember 2 July 1899 as one of the darkest days of the British Empire, for it was on that day that disaster smote that most precious jewel in the Crown's possessions, the Oriental colony of Singapore.

The city's most loyal subjects were gathered on the Padang that morning, sweltering in their finest dress jackets, hoop skirts, sarongs and mandarins' robes upon the grounds of the Singapore Cricket Club. Regiments of sepoys in khaki uniforms stood at attention, overseen by mounted officers from the Service. Hordes of Asiatic schoolchildren played hymns on oversized bagpipes. An engineer from the Hokkien Clan Association directed a crew of coolies in the manipulation of their hydraulic dragon dance machine.

All were assembled to greet their guest: no less a figure than Her Majesty Victoria, Queen of the United Kingdom of Great Britain and Ireland, Defender of the Faith and Empress of India. Following her Golden Jubilee, at the age of eighty, the monarch had resolved to make a grand tour of her territories, cruising from London to Cape Town to Nova Scotia by means of her gilded zeppelin.

She had disembarked but two days before, leaving her airship moored over the newly completed Raffles Hotel, where she was accommodated in a customized luxury suite. In her honour, colourful streamers dangled from bamboo poles across the island: every shophouse and every kampung hovel displayed the hues of the Union Flag—even the rickshaw coolies had taken to emblazoning their vehicles with penny black stamps as a display of their devotion to the profile of the Queen.

There was, ultimately, only one problem. The Queen was late.

The officers and merchants on the Padang checked their pocket watches, shaking their heads, as the memsahibs fanned themselves with increasingly impatient vigour. She should have emerged at half eight, and now it was well nigh twenty past ten. Whatever could be the matter?

Then, suddenly, a peon came running onto the field: a young Chinese man with his pigtail flying behind him, an expression of acute distress on his face. "Sound the alarm!" he exclaimed, as he prostrated himself before the podium of the Governor. "Her Majesty is under attack!"

Almost as one, the assembly leapt to their horses, their coaches, their sedan chairs and their feet. Walking canes, umbrellas and young children were lost in the mêlée of hooves and wheels as the crowd rushed to the Raffles. As they dismounted, each visage was touched with horror as they beheld the great calamity that had befallen.

For indeed, not only was their Queen in peril: the very building she had been housed within had been taken prisoner by an explosive growth of giant purple orchids. These botanic horrors penetrated every storey of the edifice with an excrescence of creeping tendrils. Guardsmen openly wept as they attempted to penetrate the foliage, hacking with their parangs at the greenery.

At the centre it all, the Governor stood agape, a single name quivering on his dumbstruck lips.

"Agnes," he finally whispered. "Agnes Joaquim."

• • •

By all accounts, young Agnes had had no initial inclination to become a terrorist. Born in 1854 into a wealthy Armenian immigrant family, she grew up in a splendid mansion on the undulating lands near the New Harbour, an area vulgarly known as Tanjong Pagar.

As the eldest daughter among eleven siblings, she assumed the role of housekeeper at an early age. Her girlish voice would often be heard supervising the Cantonese servants and urging her mother to purchase the latest imported domestic gadgets, such as the microwave eggbeater and the orgone-powered Frigidaire.

Then in 1889, everything changed. One summer afternoon, while promenading in the family estate, she discovered the flower. It budded amidst the bamboo thickets, its handsome sepals opening in the shape of a pentacle. She dug it up with her hands, entranced by its delicate form and its strange, subtle scent. Hurriedly, she moved it to the potting shed, bedded it in fertile soil and rushed back to the kitchen, unable to understand the sense of thrill that had been planted in her heart, nor the pounding noises that had begun in the drums of her ears.

A month later, she paid a call on Henry Ridley, the Director of the Botanical Gardens. He received her in his laboratory, built as a vast terrarium, thriving with bromeliads, epiphytes, rubber-tree pods and foolish butterflies that fluttered next to the jaws of carnivorous plants.

"My dear Miss Joaquim!" he exclaimed with a bow. He had reason enough to be courteous, for her family had supported his recent research with not insignificant donations.

"Ah, and I see you've brought a little friend." He examined the flower, pausing to admire its rosy hue and elaborate column, which had been formed from a fused stamen and stigma, almost in the shape of an angel robed in mauve. "Extraordinary," he declared. "A cross between *Vanda teres* and *Vanda hookeriana*, unless I'm much mistaken. Wherever did you find it?"

She described the circumstances of her discovery.

"By Jove, you deserve a reward! Tell you what: I hereby christen this blossom the *Vanda Miss Joaquim*. There's immortality for you!"

Agnes took a deep breath. She had prepared what she was about to say for the past two weeks, and she was not going to make a hash of it. Patiently, she explained that while she was very grateful for Mr Ridley's kindness in bestowing the flower with her name, she sought a more mutually productive form of reward: that of working within the Botanical Gardens' experimental greenhouses, aiding him in his research and perhaps even pursuing her own.

She further assured him that she expected no financial compensation: rather, she was certain that her family would continue to sponsor his research as they had in the past, on the sole condition that she be granted access to his experimental facilities. She paused for breath. Ridley stood blinking, amidst the circling butterflies.

Throughout the rickshaw ride back to her mansion, her face burned with triumph. She had succeeded. In her hands, she clutched her own personal set of keys to the terrarium.

This was what the flower wanted of her; she knew it. For she had heard its commands over the last month, even as she scolded the cook or folded the bedclothes of her nieces and nephews. She stroked the petals of the specimen that sat on her lap, remembering that in her veins ran its fiery sap, transferred via the touch of its spongy roots, its slender stalk, and its gossamer labellum. And in her ears rang the flower's words, over and over like a malfunctioning gramophone: "Only you can change the world."

• • •

Five years later, in 1894, the Joaquim household was alarmed by the arrival of a horse-drawn police carriage at their door, containing a flustered English constable, two inscrutable Sikh sepoys and their maiden aunt Agnes, handcuffed and furious. The constable, whose name was Edmunds, was profusely apologetic. He knew it was terribly bad form to arrest a member of the local aristocracy, but, as he explained, circumstances had rendered such a course of action more than necessary.

While the Sikh guards escorted Agnes upstairs and bolted her into her room, he went over the details of the unfortunate incident. It appeared that Miss Joaquim had entered Government House, elbowed her way past the armed bodyguards, then barged into the chambers of the Governor himself, whereupon she had thrown a pot of fertilizer into his face.

"She'd wrote 'is 'onour 'undreds of these 'ere letters," he said, bringing out a thick sheaf of correspondence. "She were certain 'e could do somethin'."

Her letters were petitions for intervention in the Hamidian massacres: the widespread slaughter of tens of thousands of Armenians in the Ottoman Empire by the crazed Sultan Abdul Hamid II. For despite the horrific news of the genocide and the pleas of their own ethnic Armenian subjects, the British had done nothing to stop the bloodshed, continuing their trade with the Ottomans for the sake of economic expediency.

Agnes's mother parsed one or two of her daughter's letters. "Goodness," she said. "Whatever do these words mean?"

"They're words in the Fukienese dialect, missus. The meanin' ain't fit for a lady's ears."

Mrs Joaquim nodded slowly. She'd understood, even sympathized with her daughter's recent activist work: after all, the entire congregation of the Church of St Gregory the Illuminator prayed for an end to the reign of the bloodthirsty tyrant who had caused their people such suffering. Yet she fretted over the company Agnes kept. The silly girl had made numerous friends amongst the local Orientals. She'd even become familiar with the servants, persistently quizzing them on their knowledge of local herbal remedies. Rumour had it that she'd even ventured into their distant villages, seeking out sinsehs, bomohs and Ayurvedic healers to glean their botanic wisdom.

"Methinks—and the Chief of Police, 'e thinks too—that mayhap Miss Joaquim'd be more comfortable in a sanatorium of some sort. There's an asylum in the north of the island, just past the wooden bridge."

Mrs Joaquim had had quite enough. "Thank you, Constable," she proclaimed. "The servants will see you out."

Over a rather unsavoury supper (meals had become less palatable since Agnes had lost her interest in housework), the family debated the issue of the rebel amongst them. Some were resolved on expelling her from the household; others were quite content to let her carry on harmlessly with her experiments with Mr Ridley, which had caused no harm up till now.

Naturally, all assembled cringed at the thought of sending her to the asylum, but, as a younger Joaquim pointed out, she might well have a disease. What other means was there to cure it? The sun set without a resolution to their conference. But in the morning, Mrs Joaquim decided to check on her wayward daughter. She fetched a tray of hot scones and pressure-cooked coconut jam from the larder, ventured upstairs and drew back the lock.

Agnes was gone, and the room was overgrown with orchids, their creepers extending out the window, through the garden and into the wilderness.

Later, the family would learn that Ridley's terrarium had been plundered the same night. All Agnes's notes and specimens had vanished, leaving only a few puzzling diagrams and fragments of research amidst the rubber seeds and butterflies. Ridley claimed he knew nothing of these studies—particularly not the studies that appeared to use botany for the purposes of warfare.

Then in early 1895, celebrations broke out amongst the Armenians across the world. The Hamidian massacres had ended, for Sultan Abdul Hamid II had been found dead in his palace. Officials claimed he had choked on a fishbone, but the people knew better. They said he had collapsed across his chamber pot, mysteriously asphyxiated by a creeper that had slowly grown throughout the interior of his body, a sprig of purple blossoms sprouting from his mouth.

Agnes's reign of terror had begun.

• • •

One might have assumed that Agnes would cease operations once the oppressor of her race had been wiped from the face of the Earth. No such luck. Her run-in with the Governor in Singapore had given her a profound distaste for all Empires, be they British, Ottoman, Manchu or Nipponese. Clandestinely, she travelled across the planet, making contact with local radicals who fought against the powers of centralized government. Thus, in continent after continent, she spread her seeds of dissension and chaos.

In 1896, the Empress Dowager Cixi went missing in the Summer Palace. After much searching, she was discovered in the pleasure gardens, half-dissolved in a massive pitcher plant.

In 1897, Tsar Nicholas II was struck with paralysis in his private chapel. His attendants discovered him collapsed on his knees, roots shooting through his trousers, his flesh turned into mango wood.

In 1898, US President McKinley and Maria Christina, Regent of Spain, were both snatched from their boudoirs in a single night. They washed up in a lifeboat, miserably fused together through a fretwork of bougainvillea, having been forced to sign away the American and Spanish claims to the territories of Cuba, the Philippines, Guam and Puerto Rico.

Meanwhile, in Singapore, the colonial administration grew skittish. The downtrodden had lately begun to eschew their habit of taking government-taxed opium to dull their pains, opting instead for a cheap, plentiful drug they called Joaquimine, or else simply "Joe".

Joaquimine was especially dangerous for the British Empire, as it worked not only as an anaesthetic and a hallucinogen, but also as a stimulant. It sharpened one's sense of focus, driving its abusers towards new purpose in life. It soon became common to see dockyard coolies in Clifford Pier arguing over their plans for constructing hybrid electric steamships, or else pipa girls in Chinatown, huddled over the writings of Karl Marx in the original German. Shadow universities began to crop up, run by secret societies and mosques, where gangsters and farmers' daughters discussed every branch of the sciences and the arts in a motley creole based on English, Arabic, Mandarin, Tamil, Teochew and Malay.

The government did what it could to stem this burgeoning tide of intellect. They conducted violent raids of farms and shophouse cellars where crops of the magenta flowers were secretly grown, to be dried and processed into orchid cigarettes. Well-publicized trials took place, such as that of the young medical student Lim Boon Keng, who had been caught red-handed prescribing the drug to coolie labourers. And of course, campaigners such as Bishop Oldham and Sophia Blackmore lent their voices to the cause, alarmed as they were that their schoolchildren were puffing Joaquimine to aid their studies.

Such measures, however, worked to no avail. Rather than diminishing, the epidemic expanded its scope, as Singaporean sailors smuggled Joaquimine in their luggage, allowing its dissemination throughout the world. It was speedily adopted by other nations of people, including the Formosans, the Kashmiris, the Ashkenazi Jews, the Coreans, the Zulus, the Boers and the Apache.

And across the Earth, each smoker heard the flower's words pounding in his head: "Only you can change the world."

• • •

A fire sprang up amidst the orchid-choked Raffles Hotel, scorching its white façade a ghastly black. Some thoughtless officer had started it, believing it to be the fastest way to prevent further growth of the monster plant.

The Governor had been apoplectic. "You fool!" he cried. "The Queen's in there!"

There probably ain't much of her left, the officer thought, but did not say.

The crowd still milled about at the scene of the tragedy, hampering the rescue efforts. Chambermaids, barmen and guests wailed as the blaze grew higher, mourning the loss of their possessions and their livelihood. Yet every now and again, a sigh rippled through the masses as a cluster of purple blossoms went up in a psychedelic blaze of colour, scattering their cinders across the darkening sky.

Eventually, a crew of fire fighters arrived. But before they could direct a single hose towards the inferno, the heavens opened up and rain gushed forth from the clouds, drenching the *sahibs* in their Sunday best, ruining the coiffures and cosmetics of the cultural dancers, washing the sweat from the bodies of the horses and rickshaw pullers.

The civilians scattered, and the fire fighters proceeded to assist the rescue team, clearing away the burnt vegetation in the building, for the flames had cleared a way through the ruins, and the downpour was quenching the flames. They clambered through stairways and broken ceilings, braving the smoke and smouldering vines. With luck, they might reach the Royal Suite yet.

Finally, they came to the rosewood doors, now reduced to charcoal and scrap timber by the fire and the orchids. After hacking away a curtain of vines, they beheld an amazing sight. On a four-poster bed strewn with orchids lay the two women, Victoria and Agnes, side by side. Both were motionless and apparently unharmed. The rescuers rushed to the bodies. The Queen, once woken, was in fine condition, though somewhat weak and bewildered about the commotion.

Agnes was dead. An autopsy later indicated that she had passed on mere minutes before the team's appearance. An enormous tumour was also revealed in her uterus, which had been killing her slowly since her discovery of the flower ten years before.

The Joaquim clan took charge of her body, and arranged to have her buried the next day in a quiet ceremony in Bukit Timah Cemetery. Yet, as the priest grudgingly read a psalm over her coffin, the cortege was stunned by the sight of a sea of humanity rising across the hill. Approaching them were men, women and children drawn from every class and race known to Singapore society. Some wore black, some wore white, some wore sackcloth, and some wore sarongs of blue and turquoise.

But each of them held something in common, a token of farewell to their heroine: a single flower.

• • •

After a barrage of medical examinations, the Queen was pronounced fit to return to London, though with doctor's orders to spend the majority of her waking hours in convalescence. Victoria obediently boarded the zeppelin. Yet as soon as her physicians' backs were turned, she summoned her secretary and began issuing a memorandum to the Cabinet to examine the issue of de-colonization.

Once in Buckingham Palace, she caused a scandal with her newfound opinions. She insisted that her subjects—or, as she called them now, her citizens—deserved greater liberty than they experienced at present under their imperial regime. She wrote essays for *The Daily Telegraph* and the *Times*, insisting on the need to equalize opportunities for the working classes.

In the year 1900 she resumed her travels throughout her Empire, armed with a vigour quite uncharacteristic of an octogenarian. She conversed passionately with citizens in Delhi and Rangoon and Cairo, often advising them on how to revive their own pre-colonial governments on a more egalitarian footing, even bequeathing considerable gifts of the Crown to help fund such efforts at nation-building. Such actions were much to the chagrin of her government, her administrators and the rest of the royal family, who watched with dismay as their inheritance dwindled daily. Yet when questioned about her actions, she had but this to say: "Only I can change the world."

Regardless, or perhaps because of the controversy she caused, the Queen remained beloved by her people. Thus it was that she rose on 22 January 1901 quite refreshed and eager to appear in a scheduled street parade from Westminster Abbey to Leicester Square.

Though it was a wintry day, she insisted on riding in an uncovered coach. "I feel so light," she remarked, to no-one in particular. Then, without warning, her body burst into blossom.

The Londoners marvelled at their Queen. And as they gazed upon her, the seeds blew from her body, taking root instantly in the cobblestoned streets of snow.

And across the city, a million orchids bloomed.

The Dispossessed

Karen Kwek

YESTERDAY I WENT back to Leith Road. I had intended only to drive through the neighbourhood and wait outside Lin's school gates until the students were dismissed, but I found I had half an hour to spare. So, on a whim, I parked the car at the top of the road and walked down the gentle slope, taking in the sedate, whitewashed terrace and semi-detached units. The houses seemed to have sprouted second, even third storeys in the long years since I'd lived nearby. Only one or two low-roofed originals were as I remembered. They seemed out of place and embarrassed now, sandwiched between giants and skulking a generation or two behind.

I spotted the old gap between numbers 11 and 13 without too much trouble, but only because I knew where to look. It was easily missed, even in the old days. Now, with the shadows lengthening in the late afternoon sun, the entrance just about vanished between the two houses that towered on either side, bursting at their seams. Stepping off the pavement, I found myself in a neat concrete passage barely two metres across. I moved almost unconsciously, driven by memory. The houses melted and the path seemed to un-form, un-smoothing itself and un-filling, so that soon my nimble feet were straddling a damp old drain and trying not to slip on pockmarked, algae-blackened concrete.

The shortcut emerged on the fringe of unkempt, open land. Familiar organic odours of grass and manure hit me, making me stop to catch my breath. I was standing in a sandy swathe cut in the lalang by foot traffic. The path led to chicken coops and some vegetable plots clustered near a handful of attap houses and dwarf coconut trees in the distance . . .

"Lame dog!" I heard a shout, followed by raucous laughter, coming from the houses.

"Shut up!" I retaliated, quickening my pace in case the speaker was armed with his catapult. My school satchel thudded against my thigh.

"Been studying hard again?" Siong slouched into view from behind the nearest attap hut. We were only a few months apart in age, but he had always been taller and broader. I noticed the cigarette as he put it back into his mouth.

"No," I said defensively. "It's not primary school any more, you know. Potato Tan was asking why you were absent the whole week. Prelims coming up some more." He ran a hand through his hair and ignored me. "They told you to cut it last week," I recalled. "Why you suddenly want to grow long hair? You scared she'll see your ear?"

He bristled, then gave me a withering stare. "She *likes* the ear, okay," he said proudly, "and guess what, *she* has a name."

Suddenly I was fed up with him, the show-off. With his floppy fringe and the silly tail growing down the nape of his neck, and a *cigarette* for heaven's sake. I suspected he'd started weights training, too. I'd seen protein supplements in huge white plastic canisters in his house. I'd waited eagerly for him to share the secret, but he hadn't said a word—no doubt deliberately, and so pride forbade my asking.

I was dying to know her name but forced myself to say instead, as nonchalantly as I could, "Where's your grandpa?"

Siong jerked his head in the direction of the nearest attap hut. "Ah Kong!" he yelled.

"Ah Kong," I echoed loudly, going through the doorway. Inside, the small dark space held a bamboo-framed settee and a wooden dining table with some stools. Against the furthest wall an altar glowered, smoke curling wistfully from the joss sticks placed behind a small bowl of oranges. A familiar sense of unease crept over me. Even as a child I had been grateful when the niceties were done and my parents let Siong and me play outside. Ah Kong's health was now rapidly deteriorating, and I felt more oppressed than ever by the hut, which seemed to shrink even as my eyes grew accustomed to the dim interior. It was crammed with assorted valueless bric-a-brac, from old newspapers to kitschy ornaments to faded clothes. It was a karung guni's paradise but I, spoilt by a different lifestyle, felt only crowded by meagreness in this place.

Pieces of light cotton fabric in a faded print were suspended from a clothesline running overhead, cordoning off the 'bedrooms'. Loud coughing, followed by retching and the sound of sputum being expelled, came from the larger room. Siong's grandfather then drew the curtain aside from within, revealing a wooden dais, the traditional Chinese bed on which he slept. As a child, on my very first visit with my parents, I had never seen anything like it, although much later, as an adult, I observed more ornate antique varieties in museums. Ah Kong's was not elaborate by the standards of old. I imagined coolies carting it off a Chinese junk. It would have been a wedding present, what, sixty or seventy years back, from his family in China. Slightly raised from the ground on four curved legs, it resembled more a low platform stage than a modern bed. It was closed on three sides, carved with simple friezes and in-laid with mother-of-pearl. There was, incredibly, no mattress. Ah Kong sat down on the bed, gave me a toothless grin of acknowledgement, motioned for me to help myself to the titbits on the dining table and returned to his coughing.

"Ma is out," Siong said, turning around and going out.

"No need, Ah Kong, I'm just leaving," I said, somewhat relieved, and followed Siong back out into the afternoon. "Your Ma knows you skipped school?" I asked him.

"No," he sneered, and then added, just to annoy me, "Yours?"

Our mothers were friends of sorts. Siong's mother hand-washed our clothes (those were days before washing machines became commonplace). My mother, unaccustomed to domestic help, always treated her kindly, less as an employee than as someone doing her a favour. My father, too, was good to their family. Ah Kong got bananas and rambutans from our trees, and we got fresh eggs in return.

Siong had been born when I was six months old, inheriting my hand-me-downs until he'd started growing bigger than me, and faster. An old photograph shows us together as babies. Turned towards the camera is his right ear, and I appear to be staring directly at it. Against his bald baby head and captured in stark black and white, the ear looks even more unusual than it really was. The ridge in its upper half is raised and flattened, forming an unnatural space resembling a finger-mark. My parents often discussed this curious anomaly. Siong's mother, they said, had a favourite punishment. If her husband omitted a chore or misbehaved by drinking or gambling, she would grasp his upper ear between her thumb and index finger and give it a sharp twist. During her pregnancy, my parents concluded, this frequent action had imprinted itself on her unborn baby. Siong's left ear was perfectly formed, but his right bore a strange indentation, exactly as if someone had turned the upper part inside out. The ear passed into neighbourhood legend, filed in the old wives' tales under "pregnancy dos and don'ts". The conversation always ended with one of my parents saying something about the sins of fathers visited on sons.

Not that anyone knew much about Siong's father. He had performed odd jobs around the neighbourhood and, if he did nurse a fondness for drink, mahjong and the occasional hand of blackjack, the word was that he good-naturedly put up with his wife's nagging and ear twisting until his sudden death when Siong was just three.

Nor was Siong blighted in any real way. He quickly learned to flaunt his unusual ear and claim it as an asset. It was true that he cut a unique figure. We could spot him without waiting for him to turn around. He invented a history that involved being touched on the ear by a deity. He became faster, smarter and stronger than the other kids, so that when he boasted he had superhuman hearing, half of us believed him. The neighbourhood kids soon lost interest in teasing him, especially when the menagerie of local freaks expanded with the appearance of a girl with a cleft palate scar and a boy with glasses so thick that they resembled jam jars cupped over his eyes.

Added to his resourcefulness, Siong possessed an easy charm. As a child he was open and affable whereas I was cautious and quiet. Although his features were not especially handsome—he had small, single-lidded eyes and his mother's broad nose and mouth—his was a trustworthy face. It worked magic on the provision shopkeepers, for whenever we raided their shops we enjoyed a ready supply of sweets and snacks. I shared all my toys with him, and he taught me how to make catapults, catch tadpoles from the ponds and throw sticks up into the trees to harvest ripe mangoes.

When we were older he walked from the squatter settlement, up Leith Road to the top of the slope, I walked down Glasgow Road from our house, and we went to school together, beating the roadside grass and trees with sticks hand cut from branches. When one of us was late, the other waited faithfully. We whispered about first crushes on schoolteachers, we ambushed unsuspecting lower-primary boys, we punctured the principal's car tyre and lied to protect each other. We went to catechism—I begged his mother to let him come—and confessed our lapses to each other. When Siong said he was renouncing his newfound Catholic faith because Ah Kong objected to it, I tore my clothes and beat my breast. I made him take it all back and covered his folly with a thousand Hail Marys. We knew all each other's secrets.

But things were changing. I like to think it began with the girl, but really, it's more like she simply stepped into the outline we both created, the space he had started to keep from me and that I, resentful and proud, vacated. The truth was, as much as I hoped she might catalyse the sort of catastrophic confrontation and resolution I saw in the movies and read in books, she was nothing mysterious—a lanky neighbourhood schoolgirl always in long skirts, pigtails and glasses, on the pretty side of plain, hardly a femme fatale. I hoped for some explanation for his erratic behaviour towards me, that the cigarettes might hint of darker leanings, but again I was thwarted. There was no taking up with gangsters or being caught with drugs, no detention classes or drunken bad behaviour. No, the girl was not the problem.

"Forget school," Siong said calmly, kicking the sand near the chicken coop. Ah Kong's coughs reached us from within the attap hut. "In less than a year we'll be moving. Who knows which school I'll be going to then."

"What do you mean moving? 'O' levels is end of the year. Where you going?"

"Why don't you ask your dad?" He threw up his hands in annoyance. "You blind and deaf, ah? The surveyors were here again last week. The first time was after the eviction letters came, some months ago. This time they came with a bunch of contractors. One of them was your dad. Don't tell me at home he never say anything. They spent the whole day measuring up the land, dividing here and there, talking to Ah Kong and all the neighbours, Fatty Loh, Ah Gek, the pig farmer, Old Man Seetoh, everybody."

"What eviction letters?"

He stared at me, then spat his cigarette butt into the sand and crushed it with his shoe. When he spoke again, he formed the words deliberately, as if speaking to a child. "This land you see here, these houses," motioning towards the attap huts, "unlike for your dad and you, this land doesn't belong to us."

"Who owns it, then?"

"The government. My family and our neighbours, we've been here a long time, but we don't have title deeds. Last year it seems a big developer bought the land. They got the papers and all. Going to build private housing. Terrace houses and semi-detached houses, bigger, newer than yours."

"You knew since last year?"

"Don't tell me your father never say." He sounded scornful.

The truth was, my father rarely talked about his work when he got home. He was only a small-time contractor. Most of his jobs had been raising single units on single plots. Being awarded the Leith Park project would change all that in less than a couple of years, and we would move to a much wealthier district before the houses were even completed. But I had little understanding of all this back then. Siong's news hit me with an awful reality. I wanted to run home and persuade my father to change the plans. But then something in me hardened, reared up in defence.

"It's not my father's fault, what."

For a moment Siong seemed about to argue. Then he shrugged and turned away. I couldn't see his expression. From the attap hut came another fit of coughing and retching. "Siong ah! Siong, I need your help!" Ah Kong was calling in Hokkien.

"Forget it," Siong said to me. "I got to go. Don't come inside."

Things must have become busy at school after that because it was the last real conversation with him that I can remember. I went with my mother to visit Ah Kong once or twice more, but each time Siong was not at home. His mother mentioned he had found a job and was working hard. My mother didn't ask doing what. Several times I saw him from a distance but had time only to wave. Some afternoons I followed the girl inconspicuously for a while, but I heard that they had quarrelled; I no longer saw them together. Soon after that, Siong had his hair razored brutally close to his scalp. It gave him a mean, hungry look.

The second half of that year, my parents helped Siong's family move their belongings to their new flat in Ang Mo Kio. Ah Kong was the last of the squatters to leave. By then his gait had slowed to a shuffle and he coughed almost non-stop. The old wooden bed, impossible to dismantle, was too unwieldy to move. Siong's mother had packed her kitchen utensils, pots, pans and crockery into boxes and sold all the newspaper, old clothing and useless ornaments to the karung guni. One by one over the weeks, the chickens had been slaughtered for dinner. A couple of chicks left behind grew up as strays. My father driving, Siong and I bundled Ah Kong into our station wagon. Bereft of his clutter, he seemed confused and uncertain. Only the altar, demystified and powerless without its joss sticks, and an old Chinese trunk containing his clothes went with him. The car pulled into an empty lot facing a pristine 22-storey block of flats. Siong and I carried the trunk into the lift, alighted on the seventh floor and walked in silence down an interminable length of corridor, past flat upon identical flat, to their new home.

The bamboo-framed settee and a coffee table now stood on the ceramic-tiled floor of the square-shaped living room. The windows, shuttered and fastened with grilles, gazed blindly out onto the corridor. Ah Kong, shrunken and bewildered, peered into his bedroom and asked for his old wooden bed and his chickens.

In the months that followed, it seems I was always late and running to school in the morning, so I told myself I was in too great a hurry to wait for Siong at the junction of Leith and Glasgow any more. Potato Tan, marking the daily attendance, stopped questioning his absenteeism. Siong's metal desk and chair at the back of the classroom remained unoccupied for the rest of the year. On the morning of the first O-Level paper, and every morning for a week after that, the stack of examination questions on his assigned desk in the school hall remained facedown, untouched, collected blank by the invigilator. On the last day of the exams, I noticed that the name label on the top right-hand corner of the desk had been cut into and ripped out. I thought I recognised the pen-knife marks etched into the otherwise pristine desktop.

The day the earth-moving machines arrived, it was as if aliens had invaded Earth. Overnight they appeared, diggers with huge scoops, plodding their slow and ancient ways across the landscape. By the next week they had multiplied and evolved into diverse forms—cranes with long arms, bulldozers and levellers, an assortment of lorries. All day they worked towards some unseen design, creating and removing debris, their latticework of tracks remaking and writing over the space. Untenanted and vulnerable, the attap huts offered no resistance.

On the pretext of going for a walk one night, I visited the construction site. It was officially off limits to the public, fenced in by gigantic wooden boards, but economy had found a way to overcome this obstacle. The old shortcut was not easily given up, and someone had pried one of the smaller boards loose so that it could be pushed open and shut, like a secret door. When dusk settled here, the noise and dust of the day retreated and the great machines stood dormant, outlined by the beam of a single floodlight that left most of the expanse still dark. I climbed into the seat of one of the diggers in the shadows and slouched low comfortably. Whether minutes or hours passed I had no idea, until my reverie was broken by a series of ear-splitting sounds. Motionless, I stared in their direction.

A figure stood nearby, repeatedly swinging something high above his head and bringing it down with great force. The cracks were the sound of wood being broken. In a flash I realised I was close to the hut that had belonged to Siong's grandfather. All that I could make out of it in the darkness were two pillars that remained erect but leaning. Between them, like a man possessed, the figure was attacking something. I don't know why I remained silent, concealed in the digger. Perhaps I felt, not for the first time, like an intruder on the scene. Only cricket-song and an occasional muffled sob accompanied the terrible rhythm of the axe thudding down on Ah Kong's bed. In horror I realised that the bed's three tall sides were already gone, either destroyed by construction workers or by this same figure on previous visits. Now the person was hacking apart the base. Only partially lit, his silhouette was visible and not his face, but even bathed in half-light his ear was unmistakeable in profile. I lingered in the darkness long after he left, until the first rays of the morning revealed the disfigured bed, horribly gaping and splintered. Then, as if guilty, I fled before the machines awoke.

And so, word of Ah Kong's passing did not in the least surprise me when it reached us. My parents, however, were upset that the wake, funeral and cremation were all long over by the time they found out. "I don't understand why she didn't tell us. Could have phoned," was my mother's response. I had said nothing about the hacking up of the bed. If anyone noticed it at all, they put the act down to vandals.

My father's business drew investors and we soon moved to a handsome property close to my new school. By some bizarre rule of protocol, my parents never contacted Siong or his mother again. Borne along by the tide of junior college and the worlds that soon opened up to me, I had little curiosity for my father's projects, and little time to dwell on the past.

Now, the ringing of a distant bell jolted me back to the present. I was standing in a little cul-de-sac with the shortcut, clean and paved, behind me. A well-maintained road looped around a small grassy circus in front of me. On either side of the road, stretching into the distance, massive terrace and semi-detached houses lined up like silent sentinels. So this was Leith Park. Here, too, the original houses had acquired extra levels and lofts over the years, straining ever upwards while the remains of an extinct settlement receded deeper beneath the surface.

By the time I hurried back along the shortcut and up the slope, Lin was waiting for me by the car, her backpack slung over her shoulder. "Where did you go, Dad?" she asked impatiently.

"Just down the road to look at some houses."

"Why? Are we moving here?"

Slowly I started the engine. "No," I said finally, turning the car around and pulling into the main road that led home. "There's no place for us here now."

Harmonious Residences

Jeremy Tiang

THEY FOUND HIS decapitated body on the forty-first floor. Earlier, his head had travelled down in the lift and rolled out to meet two startled showroom girls, come in early to preen themselves before the first customers. They became understandably hysterical and had to be given the rest of the day off, which would have been quite inconvenient if police hadn't closed off the site.

Foul play was suspected until closed-circuit footage from inside the lift showed no one present apart from the man himself, staying back late to finish a particular job—nobody knew what, there were so many things to be taken care of every day. His hands full, he tried to stop the lift doors with his head, but a sensor was faulty and the doors kept closing, trapping and then severing his neck.

I was on secondment to the Housing Development Board at the time, and had been sent down to the site as a kind of floating officer. These placements were usually uneventful, but

I knew this incident would be seen as a test for me. Harmonious Residences was supposed to be a flagship project, an Executive Condominium with the kind of sleek, imposing design that wins architectural awards. It was in nobody's interest for the new buildings to seem unsafe.

Mercifully, press reception the next day was sombre rather than outraged. The blood had been cleaned up as soon as the police left, so the photographs showed nothing more gruesome than an ordinary lift landing—even if it was, as *The New Paper* insisted on calling it, "An Elevator to Death."

The deceased was a construction worker from China, surname Chen. Not much was known about him; we don't keep files on these people. "At least there's no family to make a fuss," said Li Hsia. When I pointed out he must have one somewhere, she amended that to "No family with access to the media."

Li Hsia was also a scholar. The HDB had sent her to Oxford to read geography, and now she was on a fast-track to the top. She would clearly not be spending much longer hanging around construction sites, but the Party always make you spend a bit of time getting to know people on the ground before you leave them behind, so if you do well enough to stand for election you can claim to have grassroots support.

She was quick off the mark, as expected, and arrived at work having already drafted a press statement on her blackberry. Meanwhile, I was showing the police around and trying to get things back to normal. It was agreed that the chain of unfortunate events was clear enough and, there being nothing to investigate, we would start work again the next day. Of course, no one would use the lift until it had been safety-inspected.

None of us wanted to talk to the workers, until finally Soong volunteered. They seemed to like him—some evenings he kicked a football around the site with them, not something I could imagine myself doing. He spoke to them in his disjointed English, a pidgin simple enough for them to understand, reassuring them this was no more than a freak accident. They probably didn't miss Chen, he was too new to have made friends yet.

Things had just got back to normal when Mr Seetoh phoned, ordering me to meet the widow. "Your Chinese is not too bad, right? It's okay, you won't have to say much." I imagined his round face with the phone clamped under one ear, ticking my name off his list of tasks. Before I could say yes or no, he had hung up, my assent assumed.

I was reluctant to go through something so potentially awkward, and tried to persuade Li Hsia to take my place, but she was busy dealing with Minister. There were bound to be more questions asked, in parliament and by the press, and he had to have all the facts at his fingertips, as well as reassurances that the launch would not be delayed. She waved me away, preoccupied with the dossier she was compiling.

Mrs Chen turned out to be older than I imagined, or perhaps she hadn't slept since hearing the news. She had come directly from the airport and was still clutching her luggage, an old trolley bag and various parcels. I hadn't had time to prepare for this, and found myself running through my repertoire of condolences far too quickly. My Mandarin vocabulary was mostly culled from local TV serials, fortunately replete with many death scenes.

In the face of her eerie silence, my monologue sputtered and stammered to a halt. Had she even understood me? People talk differently in China. In desperation, I started to ask if she wanted a glass of water when she said, not looking at me, "I want to see his body."

"I'm sure that can be arranged," I said unsteadily, then remembered we were supposed to promise nothing. "I mean, possibly. I don't know if they'll need to carry out an inquest."

"Where did he die?"

I mechanically pointed at the block where it happened, and described the circumstances in some detail. Fault couldn't possibly be attributed to our organisation, we operated under the most stringent safety regulations and he should never have been up there on his own. Searching for a positive note to end on, I managed, "He died without any pain."

"How do you know? Were you there?"

"No, of course not, Mrs Chen, no one was. That's why it happened."

"So he died all alone."

"Unfortunately."

"What will happen next?"

Glad to be on safer ground, I began to explain about the compensation structure. He hadn't been working very long for us, so it wouldn't be as high as it could be, but there would be some provision for his family.

She interrupted me. "I'm talking about his body."

I blinked, finding this in bad taste. "He'll be burnt"—I was momentarily unable to remember the Mandarin for 'cremated'—"in the next few days, once the coroner is satisfied."

"No."

"We have to follow the procedure."

"He will come with me."

"Mrs Chen," I tried to soften my tone by imagining she was my mother. "You can't possibly bring the body back to China. It would cost far too much. Let us deal with this, and you can take the ashes back with you."

"You can't do this to him."

"It's out of our hands." And that seemed to be the end of it. Once the conversation moved onto ascribing blame, it was relatively simple for me to deflect it in other directions. The lift manufacturers, the various Ministries with a hand in this—though I stopped short of pointing the finger at Chen himself, even though to my mind he was every bit the author of his own misfortune.

She continued to be silent, and I considered that enough time had passed for our interview to come to a natural end. I stood up and headed purposefully for the door. "It was good of you to come and see us, Mrs Chen. I'm glad I had the chance to speak with you. Do you know where you're putting up?"

Without answering, she walked through the door I was holding open for her. I said something to cover the silence, and watched as she marched into the blazing sun, her bag trailing on the uneven ground. I thought of shouting goodbye, but it was far too noisy—all the machinery was once more going full pelt, the pile-driving for Phases 3 and 4 thump-thumping away even as we put the finishing glosses on the first two blocks.

"How was it?" While I was preoccupied, Li Hsia had come up behind me. I knew it was her before she spoke—unlike the sweaty bodies on site, she smelt faintly of oleander all day. When I turned, she was looking at me with an expression halfway between amusement and concern.

"Not too bad. She's upset, of course."

"I'm sure it's all right. We just needed to meet her, to show we care."

"I guess I'm not used to dealing with members of the public."

"Public?" She smiled. "Wait till you're really dealing with the public, then you'll know the meaning of the word 'difficult.' Foreign workers don't count. Who are they going to complain to?"

"I don't think I was very helpful, though."

"What are you going to do, bring her husband back to life?" She looked narrowly at me. "Calvin, you mustn't care so much. You didn't cause the accident, I don't understand why you're feeling so guilty. These things happen."

Her callousness was bracing. I found myself wanting to be like her, with her certainty and confidence. Everything she said was true—I couldn't argue with her. It wasn't my fault.

"So what if she's not happy? Do you think she's going to *blog* about it?"

"Her husband's dead," I protested.

"That's very sad, but we can't stop everything because of one man."

"Do you want to have lunch with me?"

A defensive colour entered her eyes, and I knew I had mistimed this somehow. Asked her at the wrong point in the conversation, or sounded too keen. Perhaps, as a pretty girl, she was always on the alert for invitations that carried too much meaning.

"I'm just going to eat at my desk. They want the revised schedule breakdown by this afternoon." She smiled, softening the blow, and touched my forearm. "But another time, okay?"

I watched as she walked away. She was a few years younger than me, and already so sure of herself that the last few moments had felt completely natural, as if nothing at all awkward had taken place. I already knew that the next time I saw her, neither of us would mention this, and her manner to me would be as cheerful as ever.

My head badly needed clearing, so I decided not to seek out anyone else but to go for lunch on my own. There were a few food courts and coffee-shops nearby—one of the estate's selling points was its proximity to these outlets—and I knew if I left now, it was unlikely I would run into any of my colleagues. As I walked through the gates, I noticed Mrs Chen across the road, struggling to get all of her bags onto a bus. She did not look in my direction.

• • •

Soong's distorted face looked pained as he shouted rather than sang into the microphone, but his audience seemed to appreciate it. He was gripping the mike in both hands, his hair floppy with sweat. I have never seen the appeal of karaoke, but on this occasion had agreed to go with the flow because everyone from the office would be there. Although usually self-sufficient, on days like this one I felt the need of company.

The funeral had been earlier that afternoon. As a mark of respect, the site was closed so all the workers who wanted to could go—and of course, those of us in the office had to turn up as well. No one had thought to bring clothes to change into afterwards, and we must have made a strange group, turning up to the bar all in dark colours, the men in ties and the women with hair slicked demurely back.

Nobody was feeling good after the proceedings of that afternoon. We had filed into a vast wooden hall in Mandai crematorium, and it was immediately clear that someone had booked the wrong room. This was far too big for the dozen or so of us, defensively clumped together on just a couple of the benches, making the space look even more dauntingly empty. Mrs Chen sat some distance off, ostentatiously alone. Some of the workers spoke to her afterwards in their rough, kind way, and Mr Seetoh said something during the ceremony, but she knew no one in this country and made us all feel it.

Later, in the viewing gallery, I couldn't shake off the feeling that we were somewhere unnatural, like an alien church. The high ceilings and sheer granite walls of the building loomed in all directions, presumably intended to give the occasion stature, vast and comfortless. I drew an involuntary breath when the doors opened and the coffin glided cleanly into the aperture behind it.

"'Cause we might not—be the young ones—for long," sang Soong, heartbreakingly out of tune, his discordant voice dragging me from my thoughts. His last note, hoarse and flat, stretched out longer than the music. He got a respectable round of applause as he sauntered back to his seat, and a couple of the sillier showroom girls simpered at him. He had the casual swagger of the man who knows it is in the delivery and not the tune that hearts are won.

Li Hsia, I was glad to see, appeared indifferent to these antics, and was speaking soberly to Mr Seetoh about whether the office ought to send flowers to the widow, as a gesture of goodwill. I approached to ask what they wanted to drink, and then slipped outside to order. When I came back, Mr Seetoh was at the mike belting out something in Cantonese. I took the opportunity to slip into his seat.

"You're not singing?" said Li Hsia. She herself had been one of the first up, drifting tunefully through "Steal My Sunshine" before declaring she knew no other songs.

"I can't sing," I responded. She seemed to accept this, and I knew for sure she was different from the other girls, the ones who would have urged me to try, be a sport, have a go—Li Hsia left me to myself, and sipped at the dregs of her orange juice.

"What made you choose geography? To study, I mean," I said, after the silence had grown dense. I was on my third bottle of beer and fuzzy around the edges.

She shrugged. "No reason. It was my best A-Level subject."

"Did you expect to end up here?"

"In a karaoke bar?"

"On a construction site."

"I don't mind it. I've met a lot of interesting people." She flashed a smile at one of the better-looking sales staff, squeezing past us on his way to the toilet.

I leaned in as if I couldn't hear her above the noise of the singing. Casually, my hand found her forearm. She didn't react, apart from just as casually angling her body a little away.

"Harmonious Residences," I said.

"What about it?"

"I like the name."

"I don't think it's anything special."

I was saved from having to explain by the waitress arriving. She bent herself expertly to fit into the tight space, and laid our drinks out just so—the coasters parallel to each other, not spilling a drop of the icy liquid. I murmured thanks but she seemed not to hear me, focussing entirely upon her task. She was thin and very young, I realised, and looked utterly exhausted.

Li Hsia toyed with her straw, and I decided it was up to me to ask another question. "Do you like working with us?" She smiled vaguely, not bothering to answer. "With me," I should have said.

"What books do you like reading?"

"What?"

"Books. You."

She shrugged, still smiling. I couldn't work out if she still hadn't heard me, or thought this was too odd a question. I took a pull from my beer bottle, wishing one of us was close to finishing so I could offer to go to the bar again.

"He's quite good." I indicated Mr Seetoh, currently bobbing along with his eyes shut, unfazed by a long instrumental interlude. "I didn't know he spoke Cantonese."

"Do you know him well?"

"No, I only met him on this project."

She nodded again, graceful and contained. The room was not large, and all around us I was aware, despite the gloom, of the other warm bodies contained in it. One of the girls had actually fallen asleep. For all the people just a few inches from us, I felt enveloped in something claustrophobic and sticky, thickening in the air between Li Hsia and me.

"We should come out and have a drink sometime. I mean, just us. The two of us." The English language was growing clumsy on my tongue. I thought how much more elegantly I could have put that in German. *Uns beide*. Or even in Chinese.

She nodded, vaguely, non-committal enough to avoid rudeness without giving anything away. She seemed to be scanning the air to the left of my head, hoping something would turn up, and it was from there that I heard Mr Seetoh's voice.

I jumped up. "I'm in your seat," I began automatically to apologise, relieved someone else had flattened the jagged silence between us.

"Hock," said Li Hsia, looking at him. "I think we should go."

"So soon?"

"I'm tired."

He grunted and, without taking his eyes off me, tossed her the keys. "You drive." A breath of perfume as she stood up. He continued to stare, but his tone was friendly. "Lucky she doesn't drink. Such a good girl. Useful to have someone to take me home."

My throat was too dry to construct a useful reply, but I think I managed to nod fitfully.

"See you at work, Calvin." He patted me on the shoulder. "Bright and early."

I watched them walk away, wondering if she would turn back and smile at me. Not a meaningful smile, just something kind to take the sting out of the evening. She didn't, of course, she looked only at him. As they slipped through the door, I saw the tired waitress leaning against the corridor wall, her broom and tray beside her. As soon as we left, she would swoop in to erase the night's mess as quickly as possible.

As the door closed, I noticed Soong glancing slyly at me. He whispered something to the girls beside him, and they giggled like monkeys. I ignored them as best I could, sat back down and picked up my beer. I would give them time to get clear, and then leave. It wouldn't take long, the car park was only one floor up. Five minutes. I began counting to three hundred in my head.

• • •

Mrs Chen came back to Harmonious Residences the night of the funeral. Dressed in old clothes and carrying a large Styrofoam box, she convinced the night watchman she was a drinks seller, and he let her in. This would cost him his job, because the site was meant to be secure at night—but the men wanted food and drink, and were often too tired to go out to get it. As soon as she was out of sight of the entrance, she slipped round the side of the building, and punched in the security code she must have watched me entering that other day. The office had no alarm, and she was able to walk right in with no trouble. We found all this out much later, at the trial.

By the time the site supervisor called me, it was just after five and pitch black. I was lying face down on my bed, fully dressed. I briefly considered leaving just as I was, but that was too disgusting even for the way I felt, and I stopped to shower and change. The dull throbbing in my head would certainly become unbearable by lunchtime. I slipped some paracetamol in my pocket and left the flat, careful not to wake anyone else.

I have never had a reason to take the MRT so early in the morning—I got on the first train, the sky just lightening, and was surprised how few people were about. At some stations no one got on or off, and the doors did no more than a perfunctory shuffle. Everyone looked cold and tired, although no one quite as ill as I felt. I began working out the quickest way I could get hold of some coffee.

When I arrived at the construction site, everything was still, almost peaceful. With the great machines at rest, without noise and dust swirling around everything, it was possible to see the buildings as their true selves, magnificent. In a few months, defiled by human habitation, they would become commonplace: stained by polluted rain, sprouting laundry on bamboo poles and unmatched curtains from every window. But now, the first motes of sun just landing on their long glass surfaces, they stood proud of their surroundings like monuments, like tall and silent gods.

The security post was empty and I walked straight in, mechanically making a mental note to mention it later. They had told me where Mrs Chen was, but I felt the need to go to my office first, if only as a matter of routine. Entering the showroom, it became clear that Mrs Chen's visit had not been a peaceful one. She had smashed everything breakable in the room—and there were many things, many mirrored surfaces intended to make the space look bigger. Because Minister insisted on creating a gracious ambience to reflect our cultured society and sophisticated clientele, we'd engaged a local interior design firm to dot delicate lamps and vases about the room, now so much crushed coloured glass.

Picking my way through the scarred furniture, I was struck by how little this mattered. I would make some phone calls, and in half a day everything would be put to rights. Perhaps not all the *objets* would be replaced, but the debris would be expertly cleared, and we would be able to admit members of the public by lunchtime. For all her destructive efforts (achieved, we later found out, with no more than a hammer from a stray toolbox), Mrs Chen had gained nothing permanent.

There was nothing to be done here, for the time being, and I made my way up the tallest tower, the one they were holding her in. The lift glided up the outside of the building on smooth treads, until I was clear of the surrounding clutter and could see the view our lucky residents would be paying a premium for, as yet unimpeded by other buildings. I never grew tired of this, the green sweep of East Coast Park and the sea beyond. It was a fine thing in Singapore to look out and see only earth and water, not people.

When the doors opened on the forty-first floor, I saw Mrs Chen on a plastic stool, the security guard's hand firmly on her shoulder. It hardly seemed a necessary precaution, she clearly had no fight left. She was slumped, barely upright, her hands and head limp as though her neck were broken. All around her was chaos, the walls defiled and the floor thick with debris. The guard nodded at me, as did the short Malay policewoman just putting her notebook away.

"She doesn't want to tell us anything. Do you know why she did this?"

"Her husband," I said.

"Yes, I know, sir, we read the papers too," she had a patient voice, but was clearly very tired, perhaps at the end of her shift. "But it was an accident, right? And she's getting compensation?"

"Maybe. We still have to have a tribunal to prove it wasn't his own negligence." Suddenly I was tired of my voice. How could anyone possibly explain why this had happened? Mrs Chen would say nothing all the way through her trial, and remain silent as they sent her to prison. She'd already said all she possibly could.

"She refused to move from here. We're waiting for another officer to assist."

"Her husband died here," I explained. "On this floor."

She nodded. "Do you know what this means, sir?" She was pointing at the walls, which were covered with wild slashes of paint (the Styrofoam box, it emerged, had been full of spray paint—the guard had heard the clanking metal, but assumed it was drink cans). They were Chinese characters, not all of which I recognised. Chen's name. Something about retribution. Some dates. It was a statement of something, or maybe her story. I would have to ask Soong about it later.

Thinking of Soong brought me back to what was in store

for me later, after last night. Soong was incapable of subtlety, and what he thought of as innuendo would no doubt be crude and broad enough to ensure the whole office knew what had happened in the bar. I would deny it, of course, but people notice things, and I had been looking at Li Hsia a certain way all week.

"Sir?" said the policewoman. She was waiting for me to translate the writing for her. I didn't want to admit my Mandarin wasn't good enough to decipher the rant of the woman from China, and took a guess. It was about the circumstances of her husband's death, I told her. It was about a man who came this country to earn money and ended up dead.

The policewoman nodded. "But we heard all that at the inquest, sir. I remember reading about it. My colleague gave evidence. It was very sad, but these things happen." She gestured around her. "I don't understand people like this. Why would you do such a thing? How will she remember him now?"

It was then that I realised the dust we were standing in was not dust. We were in a pool of small grey particles, dotted with charred white lumps. She had tipped her husband's ashes out onto the very spot where he met his end, and when the lift doors opened for me, some of it had blown in. We would never get all of it out, it was so fine. There would always be a little of him here.

"She must be crazy," the policewoman was saying. "Why do these people behave like this? When my father died I was sad, but I didn't behave like this. These people don't understand."

And it made sense to me, just at that moment, why you would want to leave your husband here, in this strange land, and not bring any of him back with you. I understood, but there was no way I could have told her any of this, I didn't have the right words. Already I was thinking: I am in the wrong place. There is nothing for me to do here. I should go downstairs, where there is coffee, and normalcy, and the day can begin as usual. It will be a difficult morning, but the fuss over the destroyed showroom will distract Soong from mischief. Li Hsia, graceful as always, will pretend nothing happened last night. I will be all right, I thought. Everything will be all right.

I told the policewoman I needed to get the clear-up underway. She nodded. She had the situation under control. I pressed the button for the lift and we waited, awkwardly, until it arrived. At the faint ding of the bell, Mrs Chen's head jerked up, her lips silently twitching. She looked straight at me with the wild stare of a cornered animal, trapped and furious, bright with helpless energy. Her eyes were no longer human. I backed slowly into the lift, but could not break her gaze until the doors slid shut between us.

Randy's Rotisserie

Amanda Lee Koe

DINNER'S BEEN UPSET across the kitchen floor; she flipped the casserole and then the roast chicken. Obviously this doesn't make her feel better, because she's still barking. I'm so hungry I actually make a ludicrous lunge to save the chicken, groaning in spite of myself when it hits the floor.

At work they sometimes asked me, What happened to your face, these bruises, and I'd say, football scuffle at the bar, or, jujitsu training, injecting elements of masculinity to salve my pride.

Every time she hits me, I wish I were a woman too, so I could hit back. She comes towards me now, and I grab her right wrist, but she strikes me with the other fist.

I don't believe you love me, I say, and walk away. She doesn't follow.

I rev the car up and drive out of the garage, an aimless, defeated sort of drive, idly contemplating car crashes and emergency rooms: idly, because they require the sort of certainty and adrenaline that elude me, on and on and on, till—

Randy's Rotisserie, it says in red curling neon.

These girls are standing outside in spiffy uniforms—yellow shirts and short white skirts—black girls, white girls, yellow girls, brown girls, all cast from the same mould with perfect teeth and alluring eyes, hands on their hips like race queens at a car show.

I park and cut the engine.

Walking closer, I see that the spits of the rotisserie, rotating lazily, are empty. Completely overstaffed with no roast chicken—good luck to you. I make to head back to my car, wondering where the nearest fast-food joint is, when one of the girls touches me on the arm.

Her hand is hot, sticky with a light glaze. As she presses her fingers down on me, it becomes obvious to me that none of them are girls, and all of them are chickens. They are menu items—they don't have to have feathers to be birds. They don't have to be on the spit to be roasted, nor poultry-sized and dead to be consumed. I breathe in her savoury fragrance and begin to salivate.

She sees that I've understood. She nods encouragingly and ushers me in. We go over to the cashier, an oily man with a cowlick, the heft of his belly showing under a greasy apron. He wipes his hands on the apron before extending them to me.

I'm Randy, he says in a baritone just one note too slick. This is my rotisserie.

Nice place, I say, cocking my head to the left slightly at the chicken. Pretty birds.

Randy gives me a hard look. Right then a man steps in. Say, you got any roast chicken left?

Randy walks out from behind the counter and claps a hammy hand on the man. I'm not sure, mate, he says, Why don't you go check the spits?

Well, I already saw them on my way in, and they're empty. Thought I'd come in to ask.

Then I guess we don't have any, eh? Randy says. Sorry 'bout that, mate. Next time.

The fellow walks out and Randy's beady eyes flicker to me. Well, he says, rubbing his hands together. What seasonings do you favour, sir?

The chicken sits me down with soft gestures, bringing over a menu hardbound in brocade. As she moves, I watch her plump bottom wiggle under the tight white skirt.

The menu reads:

Hickory Southern Belle

African Spice

Chinese Imperial Treasure

Traditional Roast

Siamese Delight (seasonal)

I've got myself a Southern Belle here, don't I? I say, glancing appreciatively at the girl, making her feel self-conscious, making her feel good. She titters.

Yeah, that's right, Randy says. That float your boat?

I think we'll do just fine.

Randy turns behind the counter, buzzes an intercom to say, Hickory in 402, and passes me a set of keys.

He leads me and the chicken to the back of the shop, narrow and dark, where there is an old-fashioned gated elevator. A grinning man stands by the buttons, dressed in a yellow shirt and white pants. He looks like a carcass, and smells mildly of food rot. He jabs at the fourth floor button twice, then looks at me as if he wishes I could give him more things to press, the grin never leaving his face.

The elevator takes a long time to move. I catch a glimpse of the second floor: an old windowpane at the end of the corridor casting stained light on heavy dust, a stray feather spiralling slowly downwards.

Sometimes when she was ranting, when she was coming at me, I applied this stillness onto my being, made myself numb to all the nasty things coming out of her mouth, pretended it was street vaudeville. Tossed her an invisible penny in my mind's eye, made it land in her cleavage, stifled a chuckle.

Was this ever a motel? I ask. No one answers me. The Southern Belle chicken looks a tad nervous, whilst the elevator operator grins right on. The smell he is giving off is becoming unbearable, and I breathe through my mouth instead. The chicken hears the raspy sound of my breath, and responds to it as if I were whispering her name privately. She puts her hands into my back pockets, and presses her ample breasts against my back.

I deserve better, I remember saying to her once, thinking I was ready to leave. She looked at me and said: Don't you know anything? It's not about what you deserve. It's about what you want, and what you can or cannot get.

We hang in the balance between the third and fourth floors. The third floor corridor is pitch dark, the air weighted. When I close my eyes, the colour behind my lids appears a lighter, friendlier grey. The heaviness of the air feels like the weight of every decision—inconsequential choices; life-changing ones—I have had to make, in the moment before it was made.

When I met her, it was one of those foolish, lovely things, where I knew I wanted to marry her right off the bat, and I made it crystal clear, and she was flattered. "You haven't seen my other side," she said, and I just smiled broadly. I couldn't stop smiling. I was so sure that anything she could lay on me would be worth its while by merely being with her.

I feel myself going—where I am going I am unaware of, but surely if I pass through the gated aluminium and into that corridor of black, there is something of consequence waiting for me, a shape fashioned out of a lifetime of opportunity costs— but it is the warm hand in my back pocket that tethers me. She grabs my ass tightly, presses her hot breasts hard into my back, reminding me of reality with sensation. The thought that flashes by is: How rude it is for a man to press his hard-on against the tailbone of a stranger in a night club, or a peak-hour train, but how wonderfully soft these breasts are.

As the thought passes, we reach the fourth floor. I feel travel-weary, as if we've been on the road for a long time. There is good artificial lighting on the fourth floor, warm and low, and the window at the end of the corridor is boarded up. The elevator operator pries open the gates, the same smile intact. He shows us to our room, then shrinks away as I slip the key in.

Room 402: an old bed with white sheets, a silver tray, one large carving knife, a quality linen napkin with a handsome napkin ring around it, a condiment bowl of hickory sauce, a fork and a knife on either side of a serving plate. I sit on the edge of the bed and remove my shoes and socks. The chicken props herself against the fluffy pillows, the very picture of docility. I think of my wife, and tuck the napkin neatly into the neck of my shirt.

I carve her up and eat, bit by bit. She is succulent, delicious. The hickory is a good pairing, we're just missing a matured red wine. I carve slowly, and she doesn't flinch, not once, just looks at me good-naturedly, cooing occasionally, digging her nails into my upper arms as if to steady herself as I eat. I start off with decorum, bringing her meat to my mouth with the fine cutlery, but soon dispense with them and take to using my hands. I resist the urge to ask her to scream and writhe for me, taking a break in the middle to wipe my mouth and undo my belt buckle.

It takes me hours, but I'm a very clean eater; I hate to leave meat on the bones. When she's just a carcass, I kiss her mouth and slide her eyelids downwards. Then I remove the linen napkin from my collar and lay it over as much of her as I can, as a courtesy to the cleaner.

I leave the room, walking towards the elevator. The grinning man welcomes me in. The elevator descends much faster than it ascended.

Back out in the rotisserie, Randy is seated with his legs propped up on the table of a booth seat. I walk to him and he passes me the bill. The figures are befitting of a gourmand experience, and

I am happy to pay up, leaving a handsome tip in cash.

I ask what his opening hours are. He laughs and wiggles his eyebrows. Randy rustles the bills between his fingers, then gives me a sidelong look. Y'know, it's uncommon for us to have walk-in customers at all, he says. I like you—you're a sharp chap. He gives me a pat on the back and waddles away.

In the car I belch, and it is redolent of hickory chicken. I turn off the A/C, roll down my windows. I pull into the driveway, and she runs out to meet me. Her eyes are swollen and she puts her arms around me. Where did you go, she says. I missed you.

I try to pull away from her, but she won't let go. You're mad at me, she says, beginning to cry. Don't be mad at me. She looks up into my face, the way she always does, as she says, I'm sorry. I'll change—for us. You'll see. Her eyes are so soft.

She arranges my arms around her and I let her. I start rubbing her back slowly and she says, You smell like chicken.

I had some, I say. It made me feel better.

She comes away from me and takes my hand as we cross the lawn. I see her backlit against the light from inside our house and for one shining moment I think of divorce papers. Then she turns to kiss me on the cheek and as I bend to smell her hair I can't begin to imagine a life without her.

Is that blood on your shirt? she says, alarmed, as she pushes the door open.

No, I say. That's hickory sauce.

We go in, and the mess is still on the kitchen floor. The cheese-smeared broccoli bits and bread-mix, the smashed porcelain deep-dish, the roast chicken; just like the scene of a crime.

It makes me, at once, lose faith in her apology completely, as well as believe, renewed, in just how much I love her. I reach out for the dustpan, wet a rag, and get down on my knees.

The Protocol Wars of Laundry and Coexistence

Koh Choon Hwee

CITING THE ROMAN orator Marcus Tullius Cicero, Rui Wen, the bookish, youngest daughter of the Tan family, quipped that an unjust peace was better than a just war.

To this Rui Xuan, the middle sibling, snapped that "this Marcus Doofus Syphilis dude" didn't have to live with their eldest sister in a tiny five-room flat in land-starved, space-scarce Singapore. Rui Wen pointed out that five-room flats could hardly be called *tiny*, and would have continued to preach the virtues of peace, as well as the existence of one-room rental flats, if not for the wrathful glares and popping beads of angry perspiration she observed forming on Rui Xuan's forehead.

The two younger Tan daughters were standing in the part of the flat referred to as the 'yard'—a sliver of space where the washing machine was shoved and where the laundry was done—looking with much frustration at all the clothes around them. The morning sun was cheerful and the birds in the neighbourhood were mirthful, but the mood in this section of the Tan household was dreadful.

To the unacquainted outsider, all the laundry would have seemed to be in its proper place. Jeans and pants, clipped securely to bamboo poles, languidly stretched out their legs from the ceiling. Long-sleeved shirts hung all over the window grids, like little alien creatures with their arms outstretched, asking for hugs and cuddles. Panties were clipped at two ends, at the hips, and dangled like disembodied, Cheshire-grins from the same mobile-hanger, swaying sanguinely. In the corner, stacks of already-dry clothes sat comfortably; a blue chiffon dress, however, had accidentally slipped off the pile and lay on the floor, splayed like a concussed girl who had drunk too much at a party the previous night.

Rui Na, the eldest sister, had indeed drunk too much at a party the previous night. And, in keeping with her normal dressing ritual in preparation for any party, she had brought her entire wardrobe for washing prior to the big night out, before finally deciding upon her desired outfit, which was then dried and ironed. Hence, all the clothes that Rui Xuan and Rui Wen were contemplating now, all the clothes in the yard that were fighting for a space to air, to dry, to hang, to sun: *they were all Rui Na's*.

Rui Xuan was outraged. "She *knows* I give tuition on Fridays and Saturdays. She *knows* I only have time to do my laundry on Sundays. And now she's gone and taken up the whole damn yard!"

"You can hang your laundry in your room, or the living room right?" Rui Wen ventured timidly.

"And have them drip water *all* over the floor, the sofas, my

THE PROTOCOL WARS OF LAUNDRY AND COEXISTENCE

bed?" Rui Xuan hollered. "No, I've had *enough*." She stormed off.

Rui Na woke up, groggy, an hour or so later. She tumbled out of bed, head still heavy with a hangover, and stumbled into the toilet, where she saw Rui Xuan, who was sitting on the toilet bowl and reading *The Straits Times*.

"Mooorning, my dear," Rui Na said sleepily, rubbing her eyes and arranging her hair.

"I sent you an email. It is important," Rui Xuan replied, clipped and cold, not once looking up from the papers.

"Oh, how sweet of you, Xuan!" Rui Na exclaimed, and brushed her teeth excitedly. She then rushed to her laptop, logged into her email account, and saw, as promised, a new message from Tan Rui Xuan, subject: "The New Laundry Protocol". *How interesting*, she thought, and opened it.

Dear family,

I am drafting a new laundry protocol for better and more considerate usage of the washing machine:

Firstly, one should not wash his/her whole cupboard full of clothes all at once. There are limited hanging and drying spaces, and there are five of us who need to wash our clothes.

Secondly, one should only wash the clothes that he/she needs, and keep the amount to a minimum on weekends.

Any violations of the two rules above will result in the forced removal of already-hung laundry items.

Thank you.

Best regards,

Xuan

Rui Na thought her sister most eccentric, but adorably so. She happily clicked on Reply All.

Dear all,
How adorable this is! Of course I agree.
Much love, hugs and kisses,
Nana-bear

• • •

When Rui Na arrived to work the next morning, her immediate supervisor, Ms Yeo, summoned her to her office. "Rui Na, you need to spend more time familiarizing yourself with Indian and Chinese names."

"Oh no," Rui Na said, chastened. "Have I done something wrong again?"

Rui Na was a fresh graduate only two weeks into her new job. She felt confident about her career prospects, enthusiastic about her job scope, and appreciated by her immediate bosses. Unfortunately, her positive feelings and attitudes were not always reciprocated, and her rosy impression of her own life did not really corroborate with reality.

Her immediate bosses indeed appreciated Rui Na's cheerfulness and bubbly character, but were rather frustrated by her bouts of carelessness. Their firm dealt with important clients, yet in her short time there, Rui Na had managed to mix up several case files with others that possessed similar but distinct names, damaging the firm's reputation for reliability and efficiency.

For example, the talent file for Manju Chattopadhyay, the award-winning graphic designer, had been sent via email to Company X instead of the talent file for Manoj Chaturvedi, the esteemed financier. However, Rui Na had been lucky that time; in the end, after reviewing the two portfolios, Company X decided to hire both Chattopadhyay *and* Chaturvedi, using the former's designs for a rebranding campaign, and engaging the latter for his skills as a financier – which had been their motivation in engaging the headhunting firm in the first place.

Rui Na had been delighted that she'd brought extra business to the firm, but her immediate bosses, who had panicked from the first point of discovery all the way up to Company X's unexpected positive decision, were not. They were all too aware that things could have easily gone the other way, and feared more mistakes from their new hire – and true to expectations, Rui Na had slipped up again.

"Yes, Rui Na," Ms Yeo sighed behind her desk, "you have mixed up the files for Chen Li and Li Chen." She held the two talents' files up, rapidly running through the differences between the nature of their advanced education and their publications. Chen Li was a mathematician with two PhDs who had published a book on triangles; Li Chen was a fund manager who also had two PhDs as well as a published book to his name, but on investment strategies. Fortunately, Ms Yeo had spotted the error in the internal emails and had moved quickly to contain the potential disaster.

"Sorry, Ms Yeo," Rui Na said. "I don't know what is wrong with me. I've had many Indian and Chinese friends since primary school, and I never mix their names up."

"Just don't do this again, okay?"

With that, Rui Na was dismissed. At the end of the work day, Rui Na entered the lift with a heavy sigh. The old man who swept and mopped the office stepped into the lift next to her, and noted her gloomy disposition. With a kindly tone, he nodded towards her and asked, in Chinese, "You miss home?"

Rui Na looked at him, mildly surprised, and replied, also in Chinese, "Not really, but yes, a bit."

The old man nodded like he understood, and asked, "So you come from which part of China?"

Rui Na gaped at him in horror. What was going on? She said, quite crossly, "Un-*kel*, I am Singaporean lah."

The old man nodded with a chuckle, "Oh. You look like you come from China."

The lift door opened, and the old man stepped out before it occurred to Rui Na to ask him if he meant that her clothes, or her face, or her hair looked like it had "come from China".

And just when she thought that things could not get any worse, Rui Na returned home to find all her damp laundry summarily dumped into a basket, with some items spilling over and trailing onto the floor. Not all of her clothes were completely dry, and her sisters' things now populated the yard. Their jeans and shirts hung from the ceiling, the window grids and the mobile-hangers, swaying blissfully in the light wind. Rui Na's clothes on the other hand had been cruelly squeezed into a tiny basket, like how (she imagined) Chinese immigrants used to be squashed in those huge, leaky Chinese junks centuries ago,

THE PROTOCOL WARS OF LAUNDRY AND COEXISTENCE

with barely enough fresh air to breathe. Rui Na felt *very* sorry for herself, and burst into the living room to confront her sisters.

"How could you do *this*?" Rui Na demanded.

"Well, you agreed to the new protocol," Rui Xuan replied coolly. "Remember the email I sent?" Rui Wen eyed them both warily from the side.

"I had a *horrible* day at work. And I come home to *this*?" Voice cracking, Rui Na gestured towards the overflowing basket and the tortured, writhing agony of her clothes within it.

"I had a pretty messed-up day at school too," Rui Xuan folded her arms and tapped her foot impatiently. "But that has nothing to do with our laundry and the protocol agreement."

"The sweeper uncle thought I was from *China*. He thought I *dressed* like I was from China." Tears streamed down Rui Na's unhappy cheeks.

"Uhh... so?" Rui Xuan said, genuinely bewildered at the irrelevance of this *non sequitur*.

Rui Na did not reply—her face was covered with tears and mucus, and she was too busy grabbing tissues from a nearby tissue box and stuffing her face with them to answer.

"Look, I'm sorry he said that," Rui Xuan said, glancing around and scratching her head. Rui Na had always been very self-conscious and sensitive to what other people said, but the point here was laundry and Rui Xuan wanted the confrontation to stay on topic. "Deal with it. Get over it. And don't wash so many clothes next time." When Rui Na still didn't answer, she added, "People think I look Malay, okay? They ask me if my mother or father is Malay, if I'm half."

"People think I look Korean," Rui Wen added helpfully, her book open on her lap.

"*Korean* is . . . hic, hic . . . *cool*, and mixed . . . hic, hic . . . Chinese-Malay is *Peranakan*, which is . . . *also* . . . *cool*." Rui Na hiccupped through her sobs. "But to look like a *P-R-C* . . ." She dissolved into tears again.

"You're such a racist you know," Rui Xuan said, disgusted, and went into her bedroom.

Rui Wen watched Rui Na from afar, and with some consternation. The girl who looked like she came from China was now sneezing repeatedly into a clump of tissue paper, and rummaging half-heartedly through her basketful of clothes. Rui Wen ventured to console her eldest sister. "Well, *dajie*, Gong Li and Fan Bing Bing are from China too, right? And they are very pretty!"

"Mmm..." Rui Na mumbled, eyes downcast. "Isn't Gong Li now Singaporean though?" She looked confusedly at Rui Wen, then, sniffling, she dragged the basketful of clothes back to her room.

• • •

The next morning, Rui Xuan was the first to discover that a tree had appeared on a wall in the living room. It was short, and green, and had three branches. There were also two birds— or rather, two round blobs with spindly wings—on one of the branches.

"What's this?" Rui Xuan asked Rui Wen.

"Hmm." Rui Wen scrutinized the picture. "Looks like a tree."

Rui Xuan smacked Rui Wen on the back of the head. "I know

it's a tree, stupid. But why is it there? Who painted it?"

Rui Na had painted it, and Mrs Tan was very displeased. The tree had 'devalued' their flat, and now potential buyers would be put off. Mr Tan thought it would be nicer with more birds, but Mrs Tan yelled at him, and the only male in the house promptly held his peace. Rui Xuan added to the general fury, commenting loudly that she felt Rui Na's actions were inappropriate, selfish and breached all sense of propriety. Rui Wen didn't see what the big deal was. At six-thirty in the morning, just when everyone was about to head to school or to work, the whole Tan household was up in arms.

In response to all the angry comments, Rui Na only said, "I've sent all of you an email. It explains things," before picking up the morning papers and heading towards the door.

There was little trace of the sobbing girl they had seen the night before. In her place was a determined, serious-looking woman who had inexplicably stayed up all night to paint a little tree with branches and birds on the living room wall. It did not make sense, but if there was any consistency in this whole affair, it was that Rui Na rarely made sense anyway.

The email that Rui Na had sent was titled, "The New Painting Protocol":

Dear family,

In the same spirit of the previous laundry protocol, I am now drafting a new protocol with regards to painting in our household. As many of you know, I find painting very therapeutic. I also find looking at my own paintings very therapeutic.

Hence, I am informing you all that I will begin to paint on the walls of our house, since there is so much empty space on them anyway.

You all are free to do so as well.

Thank you.

Best regards,

Nana-bear

"She is completely unreasonable. She's being a bitch," Rui Xuan fumed upon returning home from school that afternoon.

"Well, you are free to paint on the walls as well, you know," Rui Wen said lazily, looking up briefly from her book.

"What if I don't want the walls to be painted? What if I like them just the way they are?" Rui Xuan kicked off her shoe, which flew out and struck against the offending, newly-painted, little green tree on the wall.

"Hey! Be nice to Mr Java!" Rui Wen sat up straight, frowning at her elder sister.

"What the... The tree has a *name* now?"

"*Dajie* said I could name *any* of her paintings *anything* I want!"

"Oooooh," Rui Xuan said, nodding her head in a menacing manner. "I see what's going on. You're on her side now."

"No I'm not on anybody's side," Rui Wen protested.

"But guess what, *you* can't name the tree just whatever *you* want," Rui Xuan yelled, pointing her index finger aggressively at Rui Wen.

"And why not?"

"Because *you* didn't draft a *naming protocol*. Those are the rules now." Rui Xuan smiled, hands on waist.

"You're freaking *bo liao* can." Rui Wen leaned back on the sofa and held up her book in front of her face so that it blocked Rui Xuan from her view.

• • •

The next morning a purple giraffe had appeared next to the tree. The morning after that, an elephant with five earrings and a nose stud. By the weekend, a pink penguin and a man reading a broadsheet edition of *The Online Citizen* had joined the happy group on the living room wall.

"Who's that man?" Rui Xuan asked on Saturday morning, scowling.

"It's daddy," Rui Wen replied.

Mrs Tan spent a long while fussing over and analysing the portrait of her husband, from different angles and from different positions in the living room. "You gave him too much hair," she said suddenly to Rui Na at one point over breakfast, and burst out laughing.

Rui Na and Rui Wen laughed too, but Rui Xuan's face only darkened. Despite the seeming rapprochement between Mrs Tan and her eldest daughter, the sisterly tensions were not about to subside anytime soon.

Later that day Rui Xuan dumped another damp basketful of clothes at Rui Na's feet. "You're taking up too much space in the yard again."

"What? Again? But I washed only what I needed!" Rui Na's voice was shrill. "I was taking up less than half of the bamboo poles and the windows. What's wrong with you?"

"Yeah, you took up less than half, like maybe forty-nine per cent. Look at how many clothes you've washed!" Rui Xuan gestured towards the overflowing basket, which, to be fair, did contain a lot of clothes. Sleeves spilled over the basket rim, like arms trying to lift themselves out of a fix.

"But in the stupid protocol that you wrote, you said we could wash all the clothes that we *need*. I *need* all these clothes," Rui Na protested.

"I am *sorry* that you *need* so many clothes, but you will just have to learn to *need less clothes*. God!" Rui Xuan turned away, throwing her arms up in exasperation. Before she knew it, a pair of jeans came flying and slammed hard into the back of her head.

She whirled around, and saw Rui Na getting ready to throw another bundle of shirts at her. "Seriously, *dajie*, what the fuck do you think you're doing?" The bundle of shirts caught her straight in the mouth, preventing Rui Xuan from saying anything more.

The catfight that ensued was so utterly senseless and petty in nature that it behooves us to turn our attentions now to something less mortifying. Just a few metres away from the sparring sisters for example was a window, and through the window one could see two cars, with their windows wound down, and both drivers conversing animatedly. The first was telling the second that he was blocking his way, whilst the second was telling the first that he was blocking *his* way.

A little further up the road two maids were walking back to their block of flats, arms laden with grocery shopping. As they neared the void deck, they began hurrying towards the lift, hoping to get in before the doors closed. However, the woman inside it was too busy preventing her young son from hitting his younger sister, and so she let the door close. The two maids reached the lift, disappointed, shrugging and waggling their eyebrows at each other as if to say, "Was it on purpose? But what can we do?" They broke into giggles at the futility of the situation and resumed their girly chat.

Back in the Tan household, the Tan parents and Rui Wen had, by now, successfully intervened in the petty brawl, only just preventing the occurrence of any major injuries. In a five-room flat, one is generally aware of any commotion that takes place in any part of the house. Now that the two warring sisters had been separated and pinned down, and everyone was trying to catch their breath, Mr Tan took the opportunity to launch into a long speech, expressing his great disappointment with his daughters.

He began by saying that they may not be a rich family, but they were a dignified family, and no member of his family had ever fought physically with any other member—not even when his elder brother had gambled away all the family's savings, not even when his elder sister's children were desperately trying to convert her to Christianity on her deathbed in order to 'save her soul', and not even when his father sold his house and all the proceeds had gone to *one-of-his-siblings-whom-he-shall-not-name*. Anyway, girls must behave like girls, and it was saddening to see his two elder daughters pulling each other's hair and rolling about on the floor like boys. And all this drama, all this for what? Was their house too small for all five of them? Was it so hard to live together happily, in peace? Were his daughters complaining that he was not good enough a father for them, for he could not earn enough money to buy them a bigger house? *Were they?*

Rui Wen was weeping by now, crying out, "No daddy!" and "Sorry daddy!" at each appropriate juncture. Rui Na and Rui Xuan, their hair and clothes all out of place, looked at the floor guiltily. Mrs Tan sat solemnly to the side, staring into space. Mr Tan sighed, and retreated into his room gloomily.

There were no more fights between Rui Na and Rui Xuan after this scuffle, and peace soon reigned again in the Tan household—not an unjust peace, though it depended on how one defined the concept of 'just'. Rui Na greatly reduced her laundry load, but as if to compensate for that sacrifice, the walls of their five-room flat erupted in even more brightly coloured, wobbly portraits of animals and people. Rui Xuan grudgingly accepted these paintings, warning Rui Na not to let them come within a metre of her own room. They eventually did, but Rui Xuan just gritted her teeth and ignored them the best she could.

When she ran out of space on the walls, Rui Na decided to turn to the windows. The first windows she painted were those in the living room; she painted a large face on them, big ugly eyes with long spaghetti-eyelashes and voluptuous, bulging lips. She painted them symmetrically along the divider, so that when she pushed them open every morning, the windows would blow a kiss to the world, or so she imagined.

One Sunday morning, the whole Tan family was sitting in the living room as usual, reading, working and enjoying each other's company. Rui Na pushed open the windows happily,

THE PROTOCOL WARS OF LAUNDRY AND COEXISTENCE

mentally visualizing a kiss of joy to the world, but at that moment Rui Xuan complained loudly that people were staring into their house. She continued crossly that because all the flats were built so close to each other, people could look right into their living room from the next block. Indeed, the Tan family could discern two maids in the near distance; they were waiting at the lift lobby and staring right into their flat, perhaps trying to make out what was painted on the windows.

To Rui Xuan's dismay, Rui Na waved at them. "What the...?" Rui Xuan groaned and held her head.

Mrs Tan looked at her eldest daughter as if she were crazy, and told her to stop waving at strangers; who knows, they might remember where the flat was and then come and rob it when nobody was at home. Rui Wen, who could no longer concentrate on her reading, cried out, "AIYOH!" and told everyone to stop being grumpy. She proposed that there should be gracious protocols guiding communal living in their land-starved, space-scarce city—she could draft one tonight, if anybody insisted upon it.

Zero Hour

Cyril Wong

AISHAH COULD NOT wait to get out of bed. She rushed through her morning shower, but did not forget to take the required amount of time to condition her hair. She liked it that her hair was soft and fragrant after every shower. The conditioner she applied, before she washed it off, filled the bathroom with the smell of fresh flowers. After she came out from the bathroom, she picked out a white blouse from her cupboard and decided to couple this with a pair of black jeans. Then after blow-drying her hair, which had grown too long and was slowly becoming unmanageable, she tucked it all back with a dark hair band, and delicately put on her tudung—pale blue, her favourite colour. It was a Saturday and she had planned to meet her friends at Bugis Junction for breakfast. They would then shop until lunch, and after that she would meet Khairul—it would be their fourth date today—for a movie. They had not yet agreed on whether they would watch the latest Bollywood romance, or some Hollywood film about Greek gods and hunky mortal-heroes at war with each other; they would probably argue a little about it before he would give in to her preference for American movies and even offer to pay for the tickets. He was sweet like that. She met him in her second year of university, during which they had both decided to major in political science after taking a few modules together. She knew he found her attractive, and was intrigued by the seeming contradictions in her personality, such as the contrast between her argumentative nature during tutorials, and her pious, religious self outside of school. She just thought he was hot. The fact that he was gentlemanly, kind, and a smooth-talker, merely added to his appeal.

Just as she stepped out of her flat and walked to the lift, she wondered if perhaps the jeans she had chosen were too tight for her waistline, or too uncomfortably snug around her butt; she really had to watch her weight if she wanted to keep herself attractive for Khairul. When the lift door opened, a sudden sense of foreboding crept into her, followed by an unexpected chill. It was a bright morning in Bedok North and the air was predictably humid; there was no reason for such a chill to enter her body. The empty lift stayed open, waiting. *What was that about?* Shrugging off any lingering sense of unease, she rode the lift all the way down to the ground floor. When she arrived at the void deck downstairs, the feelings of uneasiness returned. She looked around the neighbourhood and wondered where everybody was. There were similarly tall flats on either side of her but nobody was hanging out in the void decks or heading out. Even the nearby streets were empty of vehicles. It was a clear day and she was the only one here—not that this was really anything in particular to be worried about. Maybe everyone was still asleep. It was a weekend morning, after all.

As she walked to the Bedok train station, her uncomfortable feelings became harder to suppress. It was not possible that nobody else was up at this time of the day! That playground where annoying children would play, while their maids or grandparents watched, was deserted. The two familiar swings were not even moving, even though she distinctly felt a mild breeze. She looked up at the flats in the distance, and saw no one standing at the windows, hanging laundry or just peering blankly out into the sky. There was not even the faint sound of children laughing, crying or being reprimanded by their parents. It was all very still and way too quiet. Judging from the slight perspiration gathering at the edge of her forehead, made warm by the tudung hanging slightly over her eyes, Aishah decided that this could not be a dream. Surely one did not perspire in dreams, right? She kept on walking, but a little faster this time. It was not that she was in any hurry, yet instinct buoyed her along.

She walked and walked until the train station came into view. It crouched like a frightened animal astride a twin pair of roads leading in opposite directions; a mall squatted impassively beside it. The closer she walked to the station, the more she knew that something was not right. Usually, from where she stood now, she would be able to see commuters waiting for the train on the elevated, open-air platforms. But nobody was in the station. She turned to look in another direction, whirling a little too violently, in an attempt to affirm an earlier subconscious thought that had been born secretly within her. People were also shockingly absent from inside the bus interchange across the street. This helped explain why the white noise of buses leaving or coming did not penetrate her ears, the grind of their engines that would normally add to a general buzz of activity from commuters restless in their organised queues. The only buses that she saw were all parked in an orderly fashion, without any intention to drive off anywhere. The whole place was impossibly quiet. *Ghostly*, she thought, hating the word instantly.

But how could this be? At the same time, Aishah could not stop herself from walking to what she was now certain to be a deserted station. She stepped tentatively into the station, rode the escalators—even with nobody else riding them along with her, they seemed to be operating just fine—then she moved past the turnstiles, which stood curiously open, and paused, at last, on a deserted platform. She noted that there was no sign of any train arriving or departing. She gazed out and squinted into the distance, hoping that if she stared hard enough, a train would appear. Soon a childhood fantasy—a slightly sick and disturbing one—replayed itself in her mind, about what it would be like to jump off from the platform and play along the railway tracks, even touching the track itself, electricity jumping all the way into her. It would be the best time to play out this fantasy for real, as nobody would see her. Was this some half-buried suicidal tendency that had lingered within her since she was five? Or just a universally-acknowledged, morbid curiosity; one shared by all but denied, or repressed, by everyone? Aishah instinctively folded her arms. She decided to wander up and down along the quiet platform, her body sliding through the heavy stillness like a knife.

Call Nora! a small voice at the back of her mind shouted. She stopped. She had forgotten that she had a mobile phone in her pocket. Nora was one of the friends that she had planned to meet today. She reached into the front pocket of her jeans, which was difficult since her jeans had become too tight for her, and yanked out her iPhone. She touched the numbers on the screen, and placed the phone against her ear, waiting for a ringing tone, instead receiving only a numb silence. She looked at her phone. There was not even any reception. She waved the phone up in the air, half-believing that this might help in catching some phantom wave of connectivity. She brought the phone back down to her face so that she could see the screen again—there was still no reception. "Fuck," she uttered, out loud this time, and before she could stop herself. She seldom used such language, especially not when there were other people watching her. "But there's no one here!" she shouted. Her voice had a strident ring to it. And why shouldn't she shout? Who would care or hear her anyway?

But still she turned around to look, just to make sure no one was there. A frightening thought came, that perhaps there was someone, after all; somewhere in her peripheral vision, hiding perhaps under the bench, watching and waiting. Was she afraid of being heard to swear? Or was it something else altogether that scared her? An image from a movie popped into her head in that instant, a man in a mask crouching under one of the nearby benches; a mask with huge goggles, behind which the man's face would be green, slightly decomposed, or maybe there would be no face at all— *Stop it! How childish and stupid!* Maybe this was an elaborate prank or something. Or had everyone left the country in a state of emergency and all without telling her? But how? And why? Had something happened last night? Why was she utterly unaware? Had there been an announcement on the evening news? And what about her parents? Were they at work or had they left too, leaving their only child behind? She could not call them on her mobile; that was surely out of the question now. But how about a public telephone? They still had those around in the station, right? She always saw Bangladeshi construction workers making overseas calls on those phones, or Burmese and Filipino maids, during the weekends.

Aishah could feel her heart running a little faster. She dug into one of the pockets of her jeans to see if she had any coins. She always left crap in her pockets, sometimes torn movie tickets or leftover scraps of tissue paper. She found a ten-cent coin and immediately ran from the platform area, racing down the escalators, which moved at an eerily steady speed. She quickly found a row of pay phones just to the right of the bottom of the escalators. At the corner of her eye, she noticed that nothing had changed; there was still nobody entering the station, and nobody loitering outside in the brightening sunlight. The morning was already coming to an end and afternoon was slowly closing in. Was there a chance that Nora and the others were still waiting at Bugis Junction for her to show up? Were they going through what she was going through at this present moment? Or had they vanished too? Was she the only one left in this godforsaken country?

But first things first: she picked up the pay phone, pushed in her coin, and dialled her mother's number at the travel agency where she had worked for twenty years. At first she heard a sustained ringing tone, but then the line went swiftly dead. "What the—!" she exclaimed uncontrollably. The same happened with each pay phone on either side of the middle one that she had used. On the left phone, she pressed the number for her father's school where he taught Malay studies, and then on the right phone, she dialled Nora's mobile number again. All the phones refused to work. Still gripping the handset in her fist, Aishah let it rip from inside of her: "What the fuck is going on—you motherfucking *bastards!*"

She was stunned by her outburst. Who was she cursing at anyway? A part of her felt relieved at having shouted, and only for a moment. Another more distant part of her noticed that her voice had echoed from the corners of the empty station in an unsettling way. She let the handset drop from her hand. It swung uselessly on its cord. Aishah took a breath, followed by another. Without knowing why, she peered up at the ceiling. There was no sky above, only the train station ceiling. She started to pray. In her mind, she composed the words haphazardly, "Please help me find my parents! I love them and if they find me missing, they'll be worried sick. Please help me find my friends. And Khairul . . . *won't you stop fucking with me so I can go on my date with Khairul!*"

Not surprisingly, there was no reply. In the past, when she used to pray at the mosque or at home, she would imagine that a deep baritone voice—full of love and warmth—would answer her with reassuring platitudes whenever she was stressed at school or after a fight with her parents. Perhaps that voice was silent because she was too pissed off, even if she was only angry in her own mind, an anger now wildly projected to that anonymous entity which had made this universe, the same entity that was allowing this madness to continue around her. She looked back down from the ceiling, and realised that she had put on the wrong pair of shoes by mistake when she stepped out of her flat this morning. She had wanted to wear the black ones, not this orange pair that clashed with the colour of her head scarf. What would Khairul think if he saw that her clothes and shoes did not match? She closed her eyes and squeezed them shut for as long as she could. Then she opened them again. She looked around—there was still no one around. She sighed. Her heart was no longer beating as quickly as before. What was she to do now? She looked out at the sunlight streaming into the train station entrance, and decided she would wander back out of the station. She stopped when her shoes landed dully on the warm pavement outside. "This is the worst day of my life," she lamented, softly under her breath.

Maybe ugly, green-faced aliens had abducted the whole country's population. Or crazier still: maybe she was dead, and the reason she could see nobody else was that, as a ghost, she was simply not able to? Maybe the dead wandered the planet alone because they were detached from the living and had no more part to play in daily life. Maybe the living were around her now, just that she could not see them, and she could only move through them as though *she* were the only one here. If this was true, then where were the other ghosts? Wouldn't there be others that she would encounter along the way? Or were ghosts destined to drift in complete solitude, in some sadistically-arranged, purgatorial state? Was there some lesson she was supposed to learn by being alone in this phase of her supernatural journey? And then what would happen after this momentary hell (if it was at all momentary)? Heaven? Rebirth? Or just a gnawing, soul-sucking void? No god or even a minor deity to greet her with open, loving arms. Just a relentless fade to black, an endless falling into an infinite nothingness . . .

As these fragmented thoughts wafted in and out of her mind, another angrier and more urgent thought pushed through: if she were dead, why was she still perspiring? She touched her forehead, and her fingers made contact with sweat. In an uncontrollable fit of rage, she grabbed her tudung and tore it off her head. Clutching it for a moment in her fist, she flung it to the ground, and as she stormed away, she made sure that her wrongfully-chosen shoes crushed it further in passing. She also pulled off her hair band and threw it away as she continued to walk on without any direction in mind. Then she began to cry. The tears came forcefully and seemed to have burst through a thick dam that had been built up inside her. With hair falling over her face, she wiped the tears away with the back of both hands, and kept on walking. She was slowly making her way out of Bedok now and entering a different neighbourhood; not that this neighbourhood looked any different from hers. The surrounding flats appeared the same as the flats she had passed before; dull-coloured, with the jarring picture of some national flower half-heartedly painted onto one side. Another identical train station loomed in the distance. As usual, nobody watched her approach from the elevated platforms. No trains arrived or left to break the silence. But Aishah noticed none of these things. She just kept striding forward, crying unstoppably.

Finally, the midday sun wore her down. She had to stop and catch her breath. A low steady hum entered her ears. Her tears subsided. Curiosity made her gaze back up at the sky. What was that sound? Where was it coming from? The hum started from an exceedingly low pitch, then rose ever so slightly, and settled on an even tone. Swelling in volume, the humming seemed to rise out from the very ground beneath her. She even felt it vibrating in her chest. It felt peculiar, but not necessarily discomforting. She turned in a frantic circle and looked around the deserted neighbourhood. There was nothing that alerted her to the potential source of the sound. The hum was growing even louder now; soon it would be deafening. She looked up again. An unexpected breeze caressed her hair. But there was nothing in the sky, even though she half-expected to see something—maybe a plane or a helicopter, even a flying saucer or some crazy shit like that.

Instead, the cloudless sky was brightening. The entire canvas of sky arching above her was turning from blue to white. Yet there was no real change in the level of heat pressing against her face. Maybe whatever had come to claim everyone else was coming back now for her, realising that by some bizarre error during their epic calculations, they had forgotten all about Aishah, the girl who was supposed to grow up to be a schoolteacher like her father, to get married to a handsome and kindly man and have four children with him, to live with her family in one of the newly constructed flats in Tampines, to retire by fifty-five and watch her own children grow up to be lawyers, bankers, even politicians. What else could they do in this country? How else would they be able to support themselves—*and* their aged parents? The light continued to burn up the sky and seemed to erase her surroundings with every second. Although she was becoming blind from all the light, Aishah refused to close her eyes; she wanted them pulled wide open. She wanted to be ready for whatever it was that would take her away from here. The humming sound was truly deafening now. She tossed her head back and flung her arms wide open, without hope— and resolutely without fear. She was not even aware that she was crying again. She had never before felt this alive, or so unspeakably light and free.

Walls

Verena Tay

SHOWING OFF THEIR lean, stockinged legs, the two shop girls, with manga-perfect coifs, lounged against the entrance of the neighbourhood hair salon. In the early afternoon lull, they giggled and smoked away time while waiting for customers.

"*Wah lan*, eh! Two sarongs, like you say!" blurted the apprentice when she saw Hui Luan approach the shop. The hair stylist elbowed her colleague into silence; then she smiled and called out to the old woman, "Hello, Auntie! You want wash, blow and set? Special price!"

Hui Luan did not reply. Her face was red. Uneasy, the two girls could not tell if she had heard them and was offended, or whether she was simply overwhelmed by walking. Their eyes followed Hui Luan as she lurched past the salon. How could someone so huge, who needed two sarongs joined together to cover her body, actually move? Each hip-heave, huff-puff forward caused their jaws to drop further.

What you know, Hui Luan thought, refusing to look at the two hairdressers. It was hard enough getting about; she did not need people staring at her when she did her errands, especially slim, fashionable teens with nothing to do. Hui Luan hated this hellish place next to the ground floor lift lobby leading to her home in the HDB block where she lived. Every time she passed the salon filled with nosy devils, Hui Luan felt ashamed about her over-ample bulk, shapeless clothes, liver-spotted skin and untidy grey hair and longed for the light, happy girl she once was.

No, today cannot think like that, Hui Luan told herself as she entered the lift. She leaned against the lift walls to recover from the palpitations and giddiness she always felt after walking too much, thankful she did not suffer any falls this time. She pressed the tenth floor button and mulled: *Xiao Ming coming home soon from school. He will be hungry. He will love this.* She held the bag of deep-fried chicken and chips even more tightly, as if it was gold.

• • •

How dare you say I treat my mother-in-law badly! You think I don't warn her about diet and nutrition? I tell her, Ma, eat less fried stuff, more fruits and vegetables; go for walks. I buy her all the good stuff, including expensive supplements. What does she do? Throws those pills in the rubbish bin! Waste my money! I prepare her salad and ginseng chicken soup; she won't eat. Instead, she goes downstairs and orders nasi lemak and Hokkien mee, and snacks on cream crackers and sweet Milo. And 24/7, she sits and watches TV. That's why she's so big! The amount we spend on doctors and medication for diabetes, cholesterol, heart trouble, don't know what else! Plus all the time I've to take off to bring her to the GP! And then, she buys my son Big Macs, KFC all the time. What if Xiao Ming ends up like his Ah Ma one day? *Jin gek sim!*

She spends all her money on nonsense food and doesn't care about her flat. No upkeep done, no new furniture bought since she got married and moved into the flat more than thirty years ago. Sentimental value, my foot! Everything was falling apart! And aiyoh, so dirty! Trash up to the ceiling, dust everywhere, mould in the toilet! I kept quiet for the first few years of married life. I wanted to buy our own place, move out and raise our own family there. No, Hong insisted on staying here: must look after Ma, he said. As if . . . Her precious son travels so much on business; so who has to look after her? Me! I told him I will stay only if we buy over this flat and renovate. No way was I going bring up Xiao Ming in a dump!

Convincing Ma to sell and renovate was tough. Even worse was sorting out the flat, moving out, staying in temporary accommodation. Every day, cry. Everything, also cry, even throwing out old Milo cans and dirty smelly blankets. Thank goodness, I insisted on the clearing and renovations. I swear I found cockroach nests in her room! Because of the stress, I lost 5 kg, and she gained more than double the amount!

I give up my job and look after the house? No way! Me and Hong are still paying off our home and renovation loans. Bringing up Xiao Ming costs a bomb with school and all those enrichment classes. And not to mention, Ma's doctor fees. Hire a maid? Even more money! And then Ma will complain: I can still do the housework, I can still look after Xiao Ming. As if... She's the one who needs looking after. Do you know she can anyhow *lau jiao*! Try cleaning someone over 200 kg! Aiyoh! *Bo pian!*

• • •

Hui Luan sighed as she turned the key to enter the flat. Although she still lived at the same address since she was married, it was no longer home. About eight years ago, she caved in to pressure from her son Hong and daughter-in-law Priscilla and sold them the flat that she had inherited when her husband Seng died. She never actually saw the money from the sales proceeds; Hong swore that he was keeping the money in a fixed deposit account for her. Even more disturbing were the changes that came after. Priscilla tore through the entire five-room flat like a demon, threw out all that she claimed was junk (which was practically everything that Hui Luan held dear) and then had the place renovated into a white-chrome-mirror-glass-steel palace, a far cry from the previous jumble of cheap wooden furniture and bags of clutter.

Hui Luan no longer felt welcome in her own home. She was always terrified that she would spoil the new decor and anger Priscilla. She never sat in the living room anymore because the designer white leather settee did not look like it could support her weight and the matching glass-top coffee table, and the glass-fronted cupboards filled with crystalline objects, called to be bumped into and broken. Moreover, the hallway/living-cum-dining area was stuffy as the windows were always closed: keeping the windows open would allow dust to settle on

Priscilla's expensive furniture and keeping the air-conditioner switched on all the time was too expensive. In particular, she hated the walls of the common areas of the flat: they were covered from floor to ceiling with mirrors. Priscilla claimed the reflectors made the flat look bigger and brighter. All Hui Luan saw was her image being multiplied and magnified a thousand times, which made her even more uncomfortable.

Beads of sweat rolled down her forehead as Hui Luan gingerly lumbered from the front door to the kitchen, keeping her eyes straight ahead to avoid looking at the mirror-lined walls. She placed the KFC bag and her purse on the counter top and made a beeline for the common bathroom and toilet. *Why they never widen the bathroom door when they renovate this place*, thought Hui Luan for the umpteenth time as she squeezed through the standard-sized entrance, closed the door, shifted her clothes and sat on the loo. *Lucky, just in time*, Hui Luan sighed as she passed urine, *another accident real malu, if Priscilla finds out. Good, Xiao Ming not home yet. I will put the chicken and fries inside the oven to keep warm. And must keep the blanket I left sunning outside before Priscilla comes home.*

• • •

Abuse? You're accusing me of hitting my own mother? Are you mad? What kind of son do you think I am? Fuck, since I was seventeen, I've been taking care of her, not taking things out on her!

All I do is for my family, okay? I work damn hard to make sure Mother, my wife and son have a nice home, food on the table, money to spend, good medical care. And for my son, the best education possible.

So I'm on the road all the time, travelling to Vietnam, China, Indonesia on business, even over Christmas and New Year. I'm lucky if I'm home one night a week. I don't even have time to eat dinner with my family, and you say I hit Mother every day?

What? Now you're suggesting my wife beats my mother? Hold on, Mister! You better watch it! My wife is the CEO of the family. I trust her to look after everything at home and she does a damn good job taking care of my mother and our son.

Bruises on my mother's legs? Oh come on, she's always falling! Simple as that! She's so big, poor muscle tone—so she falls, once, twice a month. That's how she gets the blue-blacks. They take a long time to heal. Get her a tongkat? She doesn't want. Stop her from going out? Hey, at least she gets some kind of a workout when she goes to the shops downstairs. Get a maid? As if things were so easy . . .

You really have the nerve to think I abuse my mother or that I let my wife abuse her. I tell you: I swore when I was twelve that I would never lift a hand against any one I loved and I would look after them, especially my mother. I am not my father.

What I'm telling you—you don't talk about in public, you understand? Pa, when he was alive, man, if he got mad at you, you'd better watch out. Every time I got bad marks, skipped school, came home late, or even no reason—*Piak*! *Piak*! Damn, see stars for days after.

For Mother, it was worse. Day in, day out, any little thing she did—scold, fight, *piak*! Her bruises today—nothing like back then. I don't know why she took his nonsense until the day he died. And the more she stayed, the more weight she put on.

Look, I'm not proud of the past. It's not really worth talking about. We put that all behind when Pa died. But I told you so you can get your facts right, and not any old how say that I or Priscilla use Mother as a punch bag! What will my bosses and clients think? I could lose my job and then where would my family be?

• • •

As the kettle boiled, Hui Luan looked at the box of Earl Grey tea and the tin of Milo. If it were any other day, she would spoon out four heaping mounds of Milo powder and pour out an equal amount of condensed milk. Then she remembered Priscilla's latest health lecture about the need to control her diet and weight. Since she already had nasi lemak for lunch from the corner kopitiam, Hui Luan sighed and reached for the tea box and took out a teabag to put in her mug, even though she hated tea because it made her go to the loo more often.

She emptied the chicken and fries onto a Pyrex dish, opened the electric ovenette, placed the dish within, closed the door and pressed 'Warm'. Then she switched on the TV. The kitchen was the only common room in the flat where she felt good. There was space to move about in the open concept plan, there were no floor-to-ceiling mirrors everywhere and the brown colour scheme of the cabinetry was actually more homely than the hall or dining area. She could actually sit on the large sturdy kitchen stools without fear of breaking them. In one corner of the counter top, Hong had installed a small TV, that was much more user friendly than the cinema-sized LCD screen in the living room. She usually had the TV on while she did her chores in the kitchen, allowing the sound to fill up the emptiness of the flat.

The kettle was ready. She poured the hot water into her mug and let the tea steep. She shuffled to the kitchen window and brought in the pole on which she had placed her old patchwork blanket to sun. She lifted the blanket off the pole and folded it. Wrapping her arms around and burying her face into the warm cloth, Hui Luan, for a moment, remembered when she was a kampung girl, running and playing with other children, her long-dead grandmother calling her to come see the new blanket she was making for her from whatever scraps of cloth she had, how beautiful it was turning out as her grandmother carefully hand-sewed each uneven patch together, how it kept her warm during cold monsoon nights and comforted her when things with Seng, Priscilla and Hong got too much.

To Hui Luan, the worn blanket was a precious heirloom that she hoped to pass down to Xiao Ming as lovingly as her own grandmother had made it for her. To Priscilla, it was a bed-bug-infested eyesore that did not match the present decor of the flat. It was the source of many quarrels between the two women during the time of Priscilla's purge; in the end, Hui Luan kept it on the condition that other things were thrown away and she stored it in her room, hidden away from Priscilla's sight.

As soon as Priscilla left for work that morning, Hui Luan had aired the blanket, because she wanted at last to give the blanket to Xiao Ming. Lately, Xiao Ming had been complaining that it was too cold for him to play his computer games and sleep in his room where the air conditioner was kept on all the time. As she waddled with the blanket to her grandson's room, she thought: *Aiyah, this boy spends all his time on the computer. Don't know what he does also. Doesn't want to talk to me or his parents. Teenagers! So hard to know what he wants any more. So hard to hug him, like last time when he was a baby. Never mind, this blanket will help him, hug him for me.*

• • •

The dungeon corridor is dark. I walk down, my MX sonic gun ready to shoot. Ah Ma Blob drops from the ceiling, threatening to swallow me. I press the trigger. Sonic beams fire from my gun and burst the monster into green drips. The slime re-gathers. I shoot again. This time, the blob dissolves for good. 500 points!

I walk down the corridor. Travelling Salesman Ninja Dad jumps out in front, flicking one after the other diamond-tipped credit cards that will slice me into strips. I press the trigger. He explodes into a thousand pixels. 200 points!

I walk down the corridor. Crystal Mum Cow springs from the ground. She intends to capture me with her waving lasso. I press the trigger. She dodges. I aim my sonic gun properly and squeeze again. She shatters into a million glass pieces. 1000 . . .

Shh! Leave me alone! Stop disturbing me, okay? I'm winning, can't you see? Aiyah! See, see! Game over! All your fault!

I hate everyone. I hate Ah Ma. I hate Dad. I hate Mum! Ah Ma wants to feed and hug me all the time! I'm 13, okay? Not a baby anymore! Dad thinks he can cut off my allowance so I can't buy any more game cards! Hah! As if . . . I can hack into games anytime and play all I want! Mum? Thinks I should study hard and be a lawyer, doctor AND engineer! Thinks I should play tennis to learn a sport and keep fit! Has she seen me move when I play Wii games? Not *xiong* enough? And does she know what I can already do with computers? Why do I need all those certificates for?

I wish real life was like game life. I'd take a machine gun and *tatatatatatatatat*! Ah Ma, Dad, Mum—gone! As easy as that!

• • •

Gazing at the reality TV show and drinking the last bit of her Earl Grey tea, Hui Luan thought: *Why's Xiao Ming so late? Must be hungry by now. Don't worry, got his favourite all ready. Can't wait for him to come home. I hope he likes the blanket . . .*

At the sound of keys in the front door lock, Hui Luan put down her mug on the kitchen counter, stood up from the stool and hurried to greet her grandson. The front door banged open. Before she could even move from the kitchen to the hall, the gangly teen stormed past the kitchen towards his room without acknowledging Hui Luan. She called out, "Xiao Ming! Come and eat! KFC, your favourite!"

"*Yah, yah!*"

"Hurry up, otherwise the food will spoil!"

"Aiyah, stop bothering me! Who wants to eat your stupid food?"

Hui Luan froze at the kitchen entrance. Dumbstruck and hurt, her face flushed red. Xiao Ming swung his bedroom door open and slammed it shut. Sounds of things being shoved and of things falling could be heard from within.

There was yet another shock. Priscilla, who usually only came home at dinnertime, stepped through the front door, grumbling at Xiao Ming, "You'd better find those exercise books fast! We're late! Stupid boy, specially take time off and pick him up after school for his first Chinese tuition class and then he dare say he forgot to bring his . . . Oh, hi, Ma!"

Before Hui Luan could say a word, Xiao Ming burst out of his room into the hall, holding her blanket at arm's length and accusing Priscilla, "You put this in my room? I don't want it!"

Priscilla marched into the hall, without taking of her high-heeled sandals. She grabbed the blanket from her son and waved it in Hui Luan's face.

"You dare put this dirty old thing in my son's room? What were you thinking of, old woman? I swear, if his room has bed bugs, it's all your fault! Xiao Ming, go and wash your hands!"

"What?"

"I said, wash your hands!"

Xiao Ming dashed past Hui Luan to reach the kitchen sink. Hui Luan protested softly, "It's clean . . ."

"This thing's so old, God knows where it's been! How can it be clean? Xiao Ming, ready? Then grab your books! And don't forget your racquet for tennis later!"

Pushing past Hui Luan again with dripping hands, Xiao Ming returned to his room to fetch his things. Priscilla walked to the flat entrance, still with the blanket in her hands.

"Wait! My blanket!" pleaded Hui Luan.

"I'm throwing it away!"

"You promised . . ."

"So? You broke yours! Xiao Ming! Quick! We're late!"

"But..."

Xiao Ming joined his mother. A second later, the front door was shut. Mother, son and the blanket were gone.

The flat was silent, except for chatter from the kitchen TV. Hui Luan was panting. Her face was purple. Her head and chest were pounding. She felt giddy. She reached for the kitchen counter to steady herself. A thin stream of urine trickled down her right leg, matching the fat tear drop rolling down her left cheek.

Ignoring her damp state, she held onto the counter top and hauled herself to where the kettle was. Like how she had done many times before, she switched on the kettle, grasped a clean mug and spoon, reached for the tin of Milo and dug out four mounds of powder that she placed inside the mug. From the fridge, she took out a jam jar filled with condensed milk and used another spoon to transfer a generous quantity into her mug. As soon as the kettle boiled, she poured the hot water into her Milo mug and stirred. She opened a new tin of cream crackers and sat in front of the TV. Staring at the screen, she sipped her Milo and stuffed cracker after cracker into her mouth.

The throb in both her head and heart still would not go away. To forget herself, she focused on the TV programme. Usually, she liked watching this show every weekday afternoon. In each episode, some woman would get a complete free hair, make-up and wardrobe makeover, sometimes with dental work, new eye ware or Lasik surgery, personal coaching or some other treat thrown in as well. The woman would then be transformed from an ugly, unhappy, lost person to a glamorous-looking star, now upbeat about her future. The show never failed to amaze Hui Luan; as if changing one's looks could solve all of one's troubles within thirty minutes.

Even through the fog of her pain, it was easy for Hui Luan to catch the gist of what was happening in this particular episode. It was the part of the programme when the woman was being helped to overcome her past problems. Hui Luan watched as the woman crossed a bridge. In the middle, the woman was asked to lean over the side of the bridge and shout out her troubles into the emptiness above the river. When she finished screaming, the woman claimed she felt much better. A commercial break followed.

Hui Luan continued to stare at the TV. Then she started to laugh. From small little hiccupy noises as she tried not to choke on the cracker that was half-eaten in her mouth to huge body-shaking snorts that caused the Milo in her mug to jump out and splash down her body onto the floor where it mixed with urine. *What bloody rubbish!* As if yelling for ten seconds of TV time, or one real hour so the show host said, could change a whole lifetime of things going wrong!

Hui Luan grasped her head with her free hand. It felt hot and thumped furiously. The heat and pulse soared as years of pent-up frustration and unacknowledged anger against insults and injuries forced their way to the surface, pushing against the plug of repression. Before she was even aware of it, her body erupted with volcanic wisdom, obliterating all control.

Her increasing blood pressure raised her hand. Her lungs inhaled sharply. Her mouth opened, ejecting an indefinable scream from the very cells of her body. At the same time, her fingers released the mug in a mighty swing across the open plan kitchen. The mug hit a mirrored living room wall in a shatter of glass and Milo.

Further waves of fury cascaded through her. She grabbed the cream cracker tin, spice containers, condiment bottles, utensils, plates, bowls, knives, kettle, ovenette, TV—whatever was handy—and flung them against the surrounding walls. Sonic missiles shot out from her lips, multiplying the destructive force of each physical projectile. All around the old woman, glass, plastic, porcelain, metal, laminate wood and concrete exploded, spreading shrapnel, dust, flames and smoke across Priscilla's precious designer decor.

In her mind's eye, Hui Luan witnessed the devastation she was unleashing and cheered. In reality, she convulsed in pain. The flying debris had not hurt her. Instead, the involuntary effort of discharging her grievances was detonating bombs in her head and body.

Despite the pain, Hui Luan continued her verbal blitz. To Xiao Ming's bedroom door, she let loose volley after volley of disappointment at her grandson who lacked manners and respect for others because he was spoilt rotten by his parents. He had long forgotten that it was she, Hui Luan, not his mother, who babysat, fed and cleaned him since he was a tot when she could have left all these duties to Priscilla and put up her feet to rest as was her right as a grandmother . . .

To the living room, Hui Luan blasted out her woes about Priscilla, the greedy bitch that plotted against her and stole her home away and turned it into a torture chamber, the lazy bum that never lifted a finger to do any housework and expected her mother-in-law to be the maid, the two-faced 'expert' that spitefully criticised Hui Luan's diet and lack of exercise while spending hours herself in the toilet throwing up whatever she ate, the deaf and blind monster who failed to understand Hui Luan and threw away all her precious things into the rubbish...

Against the kitchen wall, Hui Luan machine-gunned Hong down for sweet-talking her into selling her flat away, for stealing from her since she never saw a cent of the money he said he was paying her for the flat, for not speaking to her whenever he was home from his business trips, for failing to protect her from Priscilla and take her side against her daughter-in-law, for never standing up to Seng and stopping him from tying her up with telephone cord and whipping her with his belt before raping her again and again all those years ago...

Hui Luan saved the final bombardment for the kitchen windows. She hurled grenades at Seng, the salesman ten years her senior who charmed her into marrying him, that alcoholic bastard who made twenty years of her life hell on earth. She shot bazookas at her naïve, wilful teenaged self who refused to listen to her parents' warnings that Seng was not trustworthy, and who was disowned when she ran away to marry Seng so that she did not have anyone to turn to when Seng began hitting her and she had to stay with the devil until the day he died. Then at last she nuked each cream cracker and mouthful of Milo that she had ever swallowed to bolster herself against the unfairness of everything that happened to her since she was introduced to Seng at her surprise sixteenth birthday party that her friends gave her at the old Magnolia Bar in Cold Storage and she became infatuated with his worldliness . . .

As Hui Luan ran out of verbal ammunition, she collapsed to the floor and curled up into a foetal, egg-shaped position. With her eyes shut, she lay amidst the debris and breathed in and out slowly. The pain that had wrecked her body disappeared bit by bit with each exhalation. Still with closed eyes, she became aware of her surroundings. Using her mind's eye, she sensed the chaos she had caused around her, she who had tried so hard not to be a trouble to anyone throughout her entire life. Instead of becoming ashamed and agitated about her actions, she felt an intense calm.

Hui Luan smiled. Now she understood how the reality TV woman felt, only that Hui Luan's satisfaction was a million times greater. For the first time since her childhood, Hui Luan was truly happy. Joy and light rippled through her body as she inhaled and exhaled. Joy and light urged her to open her eyes and rise from the ashes of the kitchen. Joy and light caused her to spring to her feet, not lumber up in heavy, ungainly jerks. Joy and light made her spirits fly as she caught a glimpse of her new self in the vertical remains of a wall mirror.

Her double sarong and giant boxer shorts lay at her feet. Her XXXXL t-shirt and oversized bra hung around her frame like flabby skin. Gone were the kilos of stress, anxiety and grief—all convulsed away just moments ago, the fat now feeding the fires that flickered around her. Quickly she pulled the t-shirt and bra away from her body, kicked all of her bulky clothing into the blaze, and gleefully watched the flames engulf the faded cloth. Then she turned back to the mirror and saw to her disbelief her sixteen-year-old self. She stepped unsteadily forwards to touch her reflection. Then she brought her hands to pat her face, breast, belly and thighs. Indeed, her body was now slim and supple, her skin was smooth and tight, and her hair was shiny and jet-black like they used to be before she met Seng. She was more beautiful than those girls at the hair salon downstairs would ever be.

Hui Luan stood for what seemed like an eternity, caressing her naked re-born body and marvelling at the miracle. At last, she had lived up to her name and become the wise phoenix her grandmother had always envisaged her to be and named her after.

In the distance, she heard the sound of sirens and knew that she did not wish to be present when emergency personnel burst into the flat to douse the fires and investigate the cause of the explosions in the flat. Nimbly, she walked to the kitchen window, brought in the sole laundry pole that survived her assault, took off Xiao Ming's t-shirt and shorts and Priscilla's underwear. Dressed, she skipped to the front door of the flat, slipped her feet into Priscilla's Gucci sandals and walked out of the place she had called home for more than forty years, never to return. The lift was waiting for her. She entered. The lift door closed just as the first fireman emerged from the stairwell in search of a blazing flat.

• • •

As a police officer, you see many strange things when you enter people's homes. I was the one in charge of investigating and interviewing people about whether or not the obese old woman in the tenth floor flat died of natural causes. Her case was sort of like the Twilight Zone, generating more questions than answers.

Fact 1: Emergency personnel found the deceased in the middle of her kitchen floor surrounded by a burning apartment. How did the old lady die? Why were there explosions in her home? Did the old lady try to fight off some assailant who then tried to disguise the attack when the old lady succumbed?

Fact 2: The neighbours did not witness anyone breaking into the flat, there were no conclusive signs of forced entry into the home, and no valuables were missing. So if strangers did not enter to steal and then assault the old lady in the process, then what happened? Did relatives cause her death and try to cover up the crime by setting the flat on fire?

Fact 3: The autopsy showed that the immediate cause of death was a massive stroke. There were no defensive wounds, although there were some minor shrapnel injuries from the various explosions. What was more worrisome: the deceased had many bruises on her hips and legs that occurred weeks and months before she died. Was she a victim of maltreatment by her family?

I investigated the whereabouts of the son, the daughter-in-law and the grandson at the time of death and all three had solid alibis. I interviewed the family members and they all claimed they treated the old woman well and that her bruises were the result of frequent falls due to her poor health. I also consulted with the family GP who corroborated on the old lady's medical history.

So if she wasn't fending off strangers or family members, was it possible that an old lady in frail health could suddenly have gone berserk for some reason and started a wild rampage to destroy everything in her family home, but died in the process because the physical exertion was too great for her? The berserk theory seems farfetched as everyone I spoke to claimed the old lady was very mild mannered. But if indeed it is true, then why did she do what she did? Who knows what actually happened in that home. She must have been very satisfied with her last actions for I have never seen anyone die with such a wide smile on her face.

However, the weirdest aspect of the case was when we removed the deceased from the kitchen. Given her huge bulk, I had arranged for four men to lift her body onto the gurney. I needn't have worried. The old woman was as light as a child.

Copies

Eleanor Neo

WE ARE A city that has not forgotten how to dream. Some of us dream in snow globes, according to mall directories, whipping each other soundly round the face with handbags. Some of us dream behind windows and put our fingers onto slick, sliding glass, feeling the cold, looking for another lost-and-raining street, but it is just like our own, anyway. Illusions of otherness. It is the twenty-first century and introversion is fashionable. Coffee, watercolour stills, a pretence to bibliophilism. Windows that open inwards.

Either way, it burns, burns at thirty-four degrees on average.

• • •

She is a city that has not forgotten how to dream. Or at least, that's what she hopes to be, building an inner library of carefully chipped-off prose passages, all of which devoid of geographic specificities, and an inner mazework of romantic sensibilities—which trap and shroud the subject, male or female, according to her will; she gives and takes, all at her own will, and she dreams, in control. She's started building it on her skin already, like a secret passageway from inner to outer—a long rain tattoo skating across her shoulder blades. She took the design off the web. She doesn't realise she's fixed herself.

She buys scarves in summer and dreams of expanses of cracked grey skies. She imagines boots and snow crunching under her feet upon cobbled streets, as if everything is amplified sound, fragments of quiet introspection from a mainstream movie. All digits and buttons, but as usual she is selective, or pre-selects. She's just that kind of person. She reasons with herself: everything about the climate induces one to dream of what they do not have.

She loves it best when lightning splits the sky into a blinding whiteness, which remains, and she is safely indoors to watch nature's amoral impasse with a relentless urban landscape. That has been whitewashed, she notices; all the twenty-four storeys in sight have been slapped across in white, as though they were stripped down instead of having been ravished in paint. Ravished, and an anticipated fertility; she knows she is looking at a painting of that white, Gondor-like city she has always dreamed about as the rain strikes and bounces off these bare surfaces of rooftop deserts. She grabs the camera, sticks it through the grilles as far as she dares, snaps. It isn't enough. And soon enough the storm will be over and soon enough the colours will be returned and soon enough she'll be disoriented again by the same buildings, always there, only in different clothes now . . . Her home is an endless cycle of change, construction, reconstruction.

She laughs. She *deconstructs* all these. And still, dreams. Her home is a tribute to vanity.

(The colours shift over the city. Split it up into ten regions, twelve, if you like, twenty, even. Snap a photograph of each, then do the same, ten years later. The taller ones are still the same but the colours are not. They migrate. They are part of the Colour Wheel. People do not move with them. Instead, inside, their colours change to adapt them. They become chameleons and never know it.)

The weather is dry today, however. She applies colourless lip balm that somehow reddens her lips. She sticks earphones into her ears, accidentally brushes white polish across the knob when her fingernails click the door open. She has left her contacts swimming in a sealed container on her shelf. She goes downstairs in rabbit-faced slippers with a tall book and keys that droop insouciantly out of her pocket.

• • •

To her dismay her usual shop, the one with Miss/Mrs Unhappy and her dingy SingPost sign, is closed. She has to move on to another one that offers photocopying services, all the way down that long stretch of pavement as varied in its attractions of both buildings and plain as a travellator in a glamorous mall; all this with her white tee sticking and melding closer and closer into her skin. She walks slowly, carefully, but the beads are forming readily on her brow and by the time she reaches her destination, she is in need of another shower, barely twenty minutes after her previous one.

KHNG'S SUNDRIES AND PHOTOCOPYING SERVICES PTE LTD, hidden and tucked away, so dim and quiet that most people approaching it from the side assume that it's closed even at a five-foot distance. The place is a dream in itself. Oh, it's easy to dream up big discourses of heritage and preservation here, easy to ruminate, imagine, selfishly (as imagination is always selfish), on the numerous ways in which it is an old curiosity shop, forgotten and hopefully safe, still true to itself, for our time. Many of its items are set under a decade back—national-flag eraser sets, abacuses, those 2B pencils you used in school, the ones that mimicked the honeybee. Classy, though you hated them then. But the real antique, the real attraction of the store, is the old lady herself.

A shock of white hair with a face that's barely lined—the kind of appearance that the young woman finds most unsettling.

She isn't smiling as much as she used to. What's happened to the auntie, chirpy friendliness? Her radio? The cheesy 1940s, 1950s Chinese songs, the perfect BGM to such a deceptively quaint setting, that smelt of cheongsams and rickshaws and sped-up movie reels in grainy brown?

The young woman opens her book, dog-eared and tabbed.

"First page from page 22. This will be the cover page. Then for the rest, it's simple. Just photocopy page 36–41. Then combine the page 22 with the rest and this will make one bundle. One worksheet. 21 copies."

She has to explain it over again in Chinese. She has to repeat the instructions twice for the old lady to understand. And when she finally does, the look on her youngish old face is an inert satisfaction that also almost seems to be unconsciously berating the young woman for not explaining it more clearly the first time around.

She's vague today. She's blank. She takes the book and toddles to the machine, which comes alive with an ancient hum.

The young woman returns with a dutiful "谢谢" and moves away. It is cramped within; only the old lady is supposed to tread upon most of the shop's interior. The young woman opens her eyes wide, takes a long whiff, wanders in and out of the store, up and down the elevated wooden plank that serves as doorstep. She takes in everything, every minute detail, record-collecting with her eyes. What she sees disappoints her—disappoints her romanticisms, though she does not admit it to herself.

Meanwhile the hardy Khng begins her task, one sheet at a time, vaguely, blankly.

• • •

She is a city that has not forgotten how to dream. Or, at least, she isn't aware of what dreaming, controlled dreaming, is all about. To her, dreams are of the stuff you encounter in sleep, threaded through with children's laughter, arms flung wide, grandmotherly chases down fish markets with their inevitable finales and slapstick falls; a morbid death encounter witnessed by the self, of a brother in three-year-old form lying in a pool of blood, or a baby in its cot with a turkey-sized, turkey-shaped dump. Once upon a time she dreamed that. She remembers it again some days, if only for its absurdity. Then it wafts out of her head in a sea of other slippy-slidey images within minutes, even seconds. These days, thoughts do not stay long. They don't even drop in for a cup of coffee anymore—they knock as ice-cream sellers, brighten visibly when the door opens, but slink away upon polite declination. Or they melt in the old lady's hands.

The Holy City of Lamentations; that's where her complaint-king sons live in. Always refined, yet loud; always levelling charges against some MP or bus commuter or other. (Her father, brothers and husband were quieter, but they've been silent for many, many years now; she grew up in a world of men, toughened up by saying 'yes' all the time, and the one time she decided to say 'yes' to herself, she founded a tiny business kingdom selling miscellaneous nothings to the occasional passing shirt-tucked-out student, a shop with a long name that she can barely pronounce now. It's funny how there isn't any Chinese name for it when she doesn't speak English.)

Well, she isn't in *their* city any longer, though—she's long moved on into a golden city of Jerusalem where the walls never peel, the dust never snows and the television never moves on with its glitzy dice-shaking dice-flicking veteran actors and actresses. She loves singing best—lifting one's voice out in harmony with, or against, perhaps, a substandard world of general okay-ness; it is the only transcendence given her, golden and cheery; it isn't that she longs for the past, or for a better future, but that song is a semblance of her own buried youthfulness.

So she continues, spreading, spreading the paper, as if spreading butter... the green laser light moves under her hands, and slowly another sheet of white is spat out. She has been used to this for years. She is the midwife of the machine. Her real mirror, though, is the telly, now. 黄金年华。She's moved on from the radio. Women, an aerial chorus, all her age, in glitzy dresses and bad make-up, singing. The air turns crisp and gold around them. There are her favourite flying frying smells. The telly helps her to dream.

• • •

She moves around the shop's exterior, snapping pictures of noteworthy items with her phone camera:

An empty chair; the last sand playground of that housing estate (there is the shape of a clock, with movable, if crumbling hour-hand and minute-hand and all, embedded on the left of its main structure); tall, rusty, yellow-painted metal shelves that hold nothing behind bars now; a vintage Coca-Cola sign; a shelf anachronistically loaded with Hello Panda, Fisherman's Friend and their contemporaries; an old newspaper cutting, laminated and pasted on a Yakult fridge, on "Anti-Smoking Pictorials from Eighty Years Ago" in Chinese; a row of colourful umbrellas, not for sale, hanging for dear life from the top of the drinks chiller. The air is hot and humid and there is no one else about the shop; all the rest of the world's activity coagulates around the buzzing coffee shop only ten metres away. But Khng is an island, an enclave, the last of her time, and a stronghold for ineffectual antiquity.

The young woman takes the photos, swipes them with new colours. Programmed film filters—a function of algorithms. She feeds all the shots through the same process. Some of them she washes, rinses through, so that they are faded and spotted and old. Some she over-saturates so that their colours are a-glare and lively, a last larger-than-life stand against their own dying-away. She surveys her work on her mobile phone. She is satisfied. The Restorer.

And now she grows increasingly bored and impatient. The old lady is taking too long, and she is running out of time. What she requested to do, she could have done herself quite easily had she been on campus, with a photocopying machine of her own to utilize. She takes a few tentative steps forward to watch the old lady at her ministrations. What she sees appals her. The old lady is carefully photocopying twenty-one copies of each page. It is a long and painstaking process. Use the *feeder technique*! the young woman wants to scream. *Or is your photocopying machine too primitive for all that? Have you forgotten? Did you never know? Which is older? Is age in the eye of the beholder? Are we all old?*

The young woman is far more pragmatic than she realises she is, too practical for her own taste, even if she doesn't know it yet.

• • •

Factsheet:
The old lady lives to the ripe old age of 81.
She's seen snow before. On her first and only trip abroad, with her husband at 20 years old. It is their honeymoon. They are in the States, in winter. The less you see, the less you know. The less you anticipate. So our old lady goes to a new country, and it is all new and wonderful—*everything* is equally new and wonderful. The excitement of everything is flattened out on an even plane. Snow is . . . *good*. As everything is good.

(Snow is okay. As everything is just . . . okay.)

The young woman lives to the age of 75. She never gets to see snow. She visits the States, Canada, Norway, Russia, Australia, Taiwan. The blizzard ends before her flight touches down, or begins after she boards her plane for departure. She is blessed with fine weather, okay weather, all her life, wherever she treads.

Both take many photographs.

• • •

She ends up paying the old lady an amount she does not deserve for her slipshod work. She has to allow herself to be enlisted in organizing the papers, in putting them together from page one to page seven, correcting errors, requesting for reprints of one or two sheets, stapling, biting down on her tongue so that she doesn't mention the drastically-slanted margins, the black outcrops, how the words are all too faint in some instances.

"谢谢," she says anyway, lightly, as a final clemency, a last request for the old lady's old vigour, one small spark of sheepish, apologetic youth. The two words rise in the air and sink. The old lady offers only a shadow of her smile. She turns. She forgets the moment her back is turned. She opens a jar, takes out a pale biscuit. Bites into it and stares blankly into the telly.

The young woman steps out of the shade. Rain falls and crashes.

She has no choice but to borrow an umbrella of resplendent purple polka-dotted glory, which she eventually never remembers to return and which the old lady never remembers to remember.

• • •

That was a rare rain.

The summer continues burning on. Plot a graph of dreams against temperature, with latitude as variable; you'll find that dreams climb with temperature here, at an increasing rate, until it slows and eventually hits a peak. From then on it is a constant decline. It burns. One becomes sluggish. It becomes harder and harder to dream. Dreaming consists of mundane activities, like waiting for the cool bathing baptism of a rattling air-conditioner, which never properly comes. It becomes harder and harder to breathe.

She doesn't take to recording dreams much anymore, then, that season. In one of her idler moods she makes a last stab at creativity. She opens a notebook to a final page and fills it with a host of unevenly spaced, unevenly sized, liquid paper dots. The pictorial depiction, as usual, fails her expectations. She lets out a languid sigh, shuts the book, and walks away.

Welcome to the Pond

Wei Fen Lee

TODAY YOUR EYES are bright like tungsten, inflamed with silence. How did that happen? Glowing outward-bound, luminous at the edges. Did someone paint your sides? Where did the other terrapins go?

• • •

The last time I saw you, you were swimming-pool shiny. Shoulder blades gleaming with chlorine and your head matted from the sun, sweat tattooed into your shell—and what intricate patterns they made. The leader of the terrapin pack, was the title they had introduced you with, but all I could do was stare at emerald inflections on your back.

My job was to interview you, to find out all you knew. I had been told you might be dangerous and your dissidence contagious but all you did was breathe, refusing to speak. I posed question after question, but you were so calm and so poised and so quiet, cooled by water and indifferent to the world of words I work for.

I grew up sandwiched between an academic father and a lawyer for a mother. Grammar was a birthright, expression an obligation. I floated from debate at the dinner table to secondary school composition awards, then stopped gently at journalism, where the dream of presenting relevant and urgent news gradually—and comfortably, I have to admit—sashayed into the easy sell: lifestyle, culture, new novelties. No stray feet to step on, no politicians to be accountable to. No conflicts of interest. There isn't much news to report anyway, I told myself at the end of each day. I live in a world happy without wars, a nation concerned with the weather.

Then I received a tip-off about the pond, about you and your friends. This island had been home to a pond in the botanical gardens for centuries but it had been ignored up till now, merely acting as the singular ornamental feature fit to decorate the island's larger aims of becoming a leading international institution for tropical botany. All I knew was that some news of overcrowding in the pond had broken, and there were now a multitude of terrapins, their numbers unmonitored, murmuring dissent. No one had a straightforward story; no one could explain the lead up to this. Instead, I'd been summoned to do what I used do best: write, research, and question.

So it stunned me, your indifference. My reputation as an influential journalist had demanded up till then at least a show of strained courtesy on the part of interviewees. I was determined to get to know you, to shake you out of your torpor—and failing that, to enter it.

• • •

How do you breathe with that thing on your back?

That was the first question I'd asked you in your box before the camera started rolling, not part of the official set list handed to me. Later, I would find out that you could not hear well. I was curious to know you beyond speech, beyond my duty. You refused to answer though—not the personal questions, not the dispassionate ones, and certainly not the intimate ones. *Where did all the terrapins come from? What were they grumbling about? How did they feel about this new environment?*

In the following weeks, I grew used to your silence. Instead of questioning, I learned about the keratin under your shell, and how melanin created the carvings of light on your back. My hair in you, your patterns under my skin follicles. Reptiles used to make me cringe with their swamp-like bodies and labyrinthine skin, but then I learned that your three-chambered heart continues beating for hours outside your body even after removal. That impressed me.

So I began to study the temperature of your blood, whilst my photojournalist colleague angled shots. You didn't say much, but I guess there wasn't a need to.

• • •

When I'd arrived at the pond, past the joggers and lovers, the journos were in an uproar and excited for the first time about something other than the stock market. Word on the street was that for years, unwanted pet terrapins and their kin had been dumped into this national pond out of plastic tanks, glass aquariums, and in some bad scenarios, biscuit boxes. It was entirely uncoordinated, and more a matter of the tiny flats on the ambitious island having no space for these pets: for where else could an unwanted terrapin go in this city of concrete and glass?

The problem arose, I think, when the terrapin movement grew wildly popular, with millions of citizens joining in secretly but not knowing that their neighbours were doing it too. A few mothers milling about the pond with empty plastic boxes told me—not without guilt—that they had snuck out that early morning to deposit their children's pet terrapins into the pond to shorten their list of chores. It was rumoured, they whispered, that even a Cabinet Minister had been spotted adding his terrapin to the mix (although once splashed in, he became indistinguishable—he no longer looked rich).

This is what they did not need to tell me: that the pond came to contain the dissatisfactions of nuclear families, the secrets of politicians, pubescent girls, long-drawn fights between grandparents and siblings and spouses... together, its inhabitants had absorbed within them the four walls of tiresome tiny flats, the conversations of inter-generational dinners, the clang of chopsticks and the way each door slams shut differently. It had imbibed a nation of antagonism. The pond was an accumulation of intimate knowledge, an underwater mirror of you and me.

By the time I got to the park, there was a buzz in the air so loud with fear and anger bubbling through the water that anyone close by could only close their eyes and bunch their fists in a minimal response of empathy.

• • •

The history of bait lies in the power of a bite.

So it follows that I saw the breadcrumbs before I saw you, the red mark around your ears distinguishing you from your peers. I would later look out for that same flash of blood red amongst identical boxes of terrapins to find you. The park rangers lifted their arms, and hundreds of white crumbs were flung into the pond to cover its surface. For a moment, the park was quiet. Then a head bobbed up and out of the water, nibbling at a crumb. Then another. And another. It took all of thirty seconds before what looked like a multitude of green faces emerged to greet our world, mouths agape for food. A watery army arising to answer the banal call of sustenance. A million eyes dancing to an uncoordinated blink. Then a roar, a tsunami of dissatisfaction breaking across the water's surface so that the rangers had to run back.

Other things I later discovered you could eat: lettuce, clover, grass, chopped liver, tadpoles, bloodworms. A cuttlefish bone is a calcium-rich treat.

• • •

The very next day, news of the overcrowding broke.

When we arrived again at the gardens, the pond was a mess of bodies, a population plague, unstoppable. What happened? I remember shouting at you across the din, even as you slid off the rock and continued speaking to your crowd, swimming solo.

• • •

The specialists say that you cannot hear well. It is typical of your species. You did not hear the early signs of stress, the lowering rates of fertility. You could feel it though, when another terrapin climbed on your back for a better view, and once, another fell asleep under your belly, his head against your plastron. You could not hear it but you could see it, you could feel it swirling besides and around: the orgies in the mud, the clang of bony plates against each other. The murmurs now made tangible in anger.

You could feel the brackish water growing warm.

• • •

In spite of their usual efficiency, it took ten days for the authorities to arrive in order to assess the situation. Some say it was planned to let the mess grow old.

There is no use pretending that anyone cares about what happened next. Disappearance is not to be taken lightly, unless the object of disappearance is inconsequential.

So no one knew when pail after pail of homeless terrapins were loaded onto a waiting truck, parked in a handicapped lot. No one knew when night shrouded the water and missed the scuted bodies it had previously cloaked. No one heard the algae multiplying, the oxygen underwater suddenly and deafeningly free.

You must have blinked, and then you were gone.

• • •

I spent a week chasing the story, ringing the authorities, looking for you. My editor, usually patient, threw up his ink-stained hands and told me to cover something less urgent, more edible, less relevant.

Finally, the authorities sent out exclusive media invitations to the best journalists to talk to the terrapins—they too were growing desperate for some answers—but by then the hype had fizzled out, and only three of us bothered showing up.

We were ushered to an industrial-sized swimming pool where hundreds, maybe thousands, of terrapins were now housed neatly. The tessellation was dizzying. The walls must have been grey, or a colour unmemorable. Each terrapin had a corner, a little box. That was the second time I saw you and when I finally got to interview you, back when you were shiny with chlorine with sweat tattooed into your shell. I spoke to you with my recorder alert but you merely blinked slowly and swam in circles, your tail curled uncomfortably around in a defiant clockwork exercise.

There were whispers, later, about the cold dark rooms you had been plunged into. Cold-blooded, they had said, laughing, when asked for a reason—cold-blooded conspirators should be able to withstand harsher treatment. They should not need to sleep. What they could not distinguish was the metaphorical from the metabolic, had they not seen you before, stretching out on those rocks, basking in the sun? So they matched your body temperature with that of the room in the hope that it would make you speak, desperate for warmth. The quieter rumours conveyed images of being force-fed, of wax worms wriggling down a matchstick tube invading your throat. Co-operation can be difficult to win.

In the absence of sunlight, blindness or deformity in the shell may occur. I didn't want to imagine the instinctive response of hibernation, the thousands of terrapins digging furiously into a tiled ground where the mud of bay waters was supposed to lift and cover and warm. They wanted your tales but instead, silenced your sight.

By the time they lifted you out of your box for an out-of-water inquiry I noticed that the ground beneath you was moss-tiled and smooth, dig marks faded and grown over. I fought the urge to slide my fingers across to find some friction.

• • •

A month passed. I attempted new questions, new angles, but you resolutely answered none of them. I even brought my own chair to park by your corner. The other two journalists gave up after a week, and the authorities eventually revoked my pass, citing that the project had been a failure and that no news coverage would now be permitted.

You had given nothing of yourself away, and the strength of your silence made me doubt my own skills of articulation. How many more dazzling stories could I sell, if I couldn't coax a response from you? How many more people could I cajole and convince, when your refusal to speak was more compelling than my words? I wanted to tell you how I had never tasted failure before, had never held it so gingerly between my tongue and my teeth, that it had only crawled into my mouth the day I met you. I said nothing, of course. I had a reputation to uphold, and I suppose, so did you. The insouciant murmurs of the pond, once deafening, were now contained obediently in the neat geometrics of each self-sufficient box.

I returned to the office only to find a new assignment to

review the new hip brunch place in town. The Pawn, it was called. An old pawn shop, once infamous for housing illegal horse-betting activities, now refurbished and home to the best fish and chips in town. No one seemed to see the irony, or at least if they did they never commented.

• • •

Ladies and gentlemen, welcome to the Pawn. We stand here, on the cusp of a new dawn. Look at the insides of this building, observe how heritage is respected by retaining the stains on each hanging wall, how the rosewood furniture harkens directly back to the nineteenth century. Appreciate how the chambers have been reformatted, the past a room you'll never want to step out of.

Look how the walls are allowed to breathe, and how old signs of paint have been scrapped and retained. Read the stories of an era in the chinaware, and do pick up a name card or two on your way out.

Privacy is guaranteed here, in the midst of this tastefully decorated luxury. Observe not only the carefully restored vintage items and their ornate details, but also the beautiful people here, decked only in carefully crafted designs. Seek shelter here from the lewd hustle of the city, for the traffic passes not this door. Look hard at the carvings on each bench. Remember, it is here that we preserve the past. Our painstakingly treated walls reveal only an architectural history we can be proud of.

Oh, and when you have time, head for the bathroom. You'll find that there's more than natural lighting that shines through.

• • •

The Pawn is located in a Chinese heritage building with high whirring fans and wood-backed chairs, a rarity because wood is difficult to find these days. I enjoy their devilled chicken liver, and find the watercress pasta exceptionally well done. The lack of an aquarium is a nice change.

No one understands why I keep returning, least of all my parents. I tell them that the heady environment is conducive for me to write my assignments—the food, travel, and movie reviews that are thrown my way. Despite that, they have noticed over the dinner table my newfound inability to articulate myself, and are worried about my dying relationship with words, my abstinence from the usual debates, my sparse writing. Even my handwriting has changed: I now pen a chicken scrawl.

• • •

I discovered you again when I stumbled into the restaurant bathroom for the first time in months, on a break between menu presentations and the stammer of high society, drunk on tea-time cocktails and a lack of stories to chase.

There you were, on a toilet cistern, in a jade bowl almost big enough for two. I could almost see the interlock of your bones. I don't think you recognised me—after all, you didn't blink during our first meeting, and you didn't care during the second. I felt like I knew you though; I'd traced those patterns on your back before. I had seen your underbelly. I knew the strokes of fire on your head.

It could have been the sheen from my last mojito, but your eyes were bright. Like tungsten, that secretive shine. Scrubbed like a morning that spills into eyelids, so surprising, but not nearly warm. What did we do to you? Isolated and still deaf, no longer cold but swimming in the shape of an infinity sign, exactly the loops those cubicles conformed your body to. Cleaner than ever, your retina wiped pure. You are mute, you are deaf, and now you are blind. When Oedipus ran pins into his eyes, he escaped and embraced both knowledge and consequence. What knowledge did you have, that you could not share? When the Assyrians put out the eyes of Zedekiah, did they rub salt in for the big heal? What are those black shards doing, sitting in your eyes?

Earlier, speech had been a deafening choice you made. Now, your silence felt like sandpaper; shiny, abrasive, a burst bag sealed shut.

I cried that day, in the bathroom, thinking of the futility of these interviews, those cornerings, that dizzying big-boxed pool, my writing, and how it would all end with me never being able to connect with a terrapin. You looked at me and did not blink.

Later, I told myself it was the alcohol.

• • •

The day you first caught sight of me the sunlight drew shadows of infinity on the water's surface. It would later trap you in its web of angularity, sketching you with those very same paths and patterns. The day after I saw you on the bathroom cistern, I watched the video footage of our interview. There you were, tied to that chair, almost shy. There you were, quiescent, your tail quivering, your shell now soft. The camera shakes a little as I ask, how do you breathe with that thing on your back? I could have sworn I heard you laugh, low.

The day your eyes breathed mute light and the last time I saw you, I stepped out of the Pawn and never returned. I ceased writing; ceased addressing unconcerned ladies and gentlemen, walked down those perfectly preserved steps, and looked up. Have you ever seen the sky lying flat, horizontal above the sun? It is a sand of blue, and I do not know where it goes, only up, only rising.

Scared For What

Ann Ang

I KEEP TELLING my Ah Pa this: "I cannot die, I really cannot die." We are standing at the entrance of the bicycle track at Bukit Timah nature reserve. Mountain bikes leap up the slope and helmeted riders yell, "Good Morning! Excuse me!"

"We are walking this way," Pa says.

Katie is running around the rocks near the visitors' centre about eight metres away. The humid sunlight makes her hat and the ground around her appear luminous, but she's wearing a light, long-sleeved shirt picked out by my wife. She's okay: I've applied mosquito repellent and she's carrying her own water bottle. You don't need to be wearing a Dads for Life badge to know that. Neither do you need a Dads for Life badge to know she shouldn't be walking that near to the rocks.

Pa is already wheezing. He has emphysema but insists on these trail runs. His favourite line to me is, "Why you scared? Why you scared do everything wrong? Everything scared die?"

I tell him, "You can die, no problem."

I cannot die. If I die, no one will pay for the house and the car instalments. If I break a leg, someone may take my place at the accounting firm. Not that my wife doesn't work, but this is an expensive world to live in. Katie needs to go to university.

I have three different insurance policies. I have insurance against car accidents, against fire, against a flu pandemic, against flash floods (we live on the second floor of our block). Each clause on our each policy is a solid tick off an unimaginable, dangerous future. It pins us to life, just in case of loss of sight or hearing, of permanent and total disability, of death.

"Die! Why you only know how to say that word?" Pa says.

It is like finding a thumbtack in the sole of your shoe and somehow it has not pierced your foot.

"I didn't ask you to go and die," I say, "I only say I cannot die."

"Still say that word! Bring bad luck only."

Bad luck makes sense in Pa's world. Once you've reached his age, naturally everything has been paid off. The house is yours, finally, because you were faithful and true to your job for thirty-five years in a universe that let you keep your job for thirty-five years. If anything goes wrong, if the numbers go awry in the log-book he scrawled in with a Chung Hwa 2B pencil as a shipping clerk at Brani, if a man falls from one of the container cranes and dies, then that was bad luck because you did not question the goodness of things and the certainty that the future would be good. That was the seventies.

"Daddy," Katie says, very seriously. No traditional Papa, or outmoded Pa for her. Only the best American-accented phonics for her, or so my wife says.

"Daddy, I want to go down that path."

"No, very dangerous."

"Daddy, please, I want to go there. Please."

It irritates me when she begs in that ang moh accent. 'Please' is just a pretty word—she doesn't mean it. Like all children, she wants what she wants and doesn't know what's good for her. So she needs to learn how to wait.

"Okay, we can go down there if we walk up the hill."

"Why, Daddy, why?"

"Because we must do things the proper way."

And maybe after we go up, she'll forget.

"What's proper way?" She skips over on her mini air-cushioned Nikes and points down the bike path. "Ah Gong is waving to us from down there."

A mountain bike hops up the mud slope just behind Pa. The red-visored rider swerves.

"Pa! Watch out!"

The bike passes, hops neatly to the left. Pa stays still.

"Sorry! Good morning!" The biker yells.

"It's okay! Good morning!" my Pa replies.

I leave Katie safe on the main path and run down.

"What are you doing, Pa?"

"I'm okay."

"Do you want to get injured?"

He looks away, up to the main road.

"You want to die?" I shout.

"If you everything also scared, then bad thing will happen," he says.

I kick a stone. I wipe the back of my mouth with my hand.

He waves and beckons towards the main path.

"Katie is not coming this way."

"Oi Ah Hock! Ah Soon! Ah Leong, down here lah, you blind or what?"

His kakis are here. They are smoking. Ah Soon is shirtless and twirling his yellow singlet. Ah Leong is bald and his heavy gold chain gleams like his head in the sunlight coming through the trees. Ah Hock is shouting. His Hokkien takes a while for me to understand. Meanwhile they are laughing, kicking mud, stamping their feet, slapping Pa. How childish, my wife would say.

"Wait down here for what? Nobody can see you!"

They are red-faced, dark-skinned, skinny, muscled. Ribs show, bellies show.

"Uncle," I say. "Uncle. Uncle."

I wear spectacles and a polo shirt. I'm not as good because I am an accountant. But I went to OCS.

A small hand tugs at my hip. Somehow Katie has made it down.

"Daddy, can we go with all the Uncles?"

"No," I say, tugging her away. "We are going up Bukit Timah the proper way."

Real men don't need to talk. We head towards the visitors' centre.

• • •

The first slope is easy: a wide tar road and plenty of signboards about flora and fauna that give us good educational reasons to pause. "Call-loo-go" Katie recites dutifully. She has never seen the word before. The information panel says that the winged squirrel frequents the canopy before dawn and after dusk.

"Daddy, have you seen a colugo before?"

"No."

"Then how do you know it's really like that?"

"I don't think people will pay money to put up a fake signboard, right? Let's keep going."

Older folks walk backwards down the hill. Two Gurkhas run up. Three girls in sun-hats talk about Chewy Junior and eat Oreos. Their legs are smooth and hairless in denim shorts and protected by an aura of citronella repellent.

Katie is walking by herself.

"Mummy says that if I am good today, you will buy me another Mini Lalaloopsy doll."

I keep walking, gazing away into the mounds of leaf-litter, knee-deep under the trees.

"Daddy?"

"Huh?"

She repeats herself.

"But you need to earn it first, right? You have to do things the proper way, like how you're carrying your own backpack with your own water-bottle and repellent."

Katie nods. She knows the rules and plays by them. She's my daughter, after all. But I wonder about the doll.

"So now we're going to climb the hill."

The next slope is hard—the teenage girls start off on a whooping, screaming run. They collapse against each other one-third into the ordeal—laughing, holding their hands to their chests, losing more air. I hold Katie's hand and we start slowly, regulating our strides, jogging along at a constant pace. One of the girls pulls off her cap and sits down in the middle of the path. We walk around her.

That's how you become a good accountant. You're careful about everything, but you know you've got to keep up the pace, or you won't finish auditing for your client on time. When the customer asks questions about the rows and curtains of numbers you have been dealing with, you explain clearly, concisely and conservatively. You plan ahead and work hard because you're verifying truths about what people do with their money. "Rubbish," Pa would say, "scared again about everything."

Katie is staring at the girl. I pull her a little closer.

"Don't be like those girls," I say.

Pa doesn't know what it's like to feel your heart close shut like a miser's fist when the books don't balance, when money has inexplicably disappeared because the numbers don't add up. That's when I know how the days people have spent slaving away for their company can vanish without such records. For us accountants, the clock turns back as we rush to find out if it was one of us who made the mistake. We waste time going back as time goes forward. But things must be done properly; everything must be accounted for.

"Daddy."

Katie is tired. She needs to stop, she needs a drink of water, but she wants neither.

"Daddy, Mommy told me something."

We are at the top of the slope now. Neither of us is out of breath, but we stop at one of the rest huts to sit down.

"Mommy said that if I was good this whole week, you would

buy me a new Lalaloopsy doll."

I pretend to think about it, but really there is nothing to think about. The Lalaloopsy doll costs forty dollars from Toys R Us. I'm her father and I'm not buying it.

She found her Hello Kitty water bottle from inside her Barbie doll pack and took a sip.

"Today is Sunday, Daddy."

"Let's go," I say, getting up and leaving her to follow. She does.

"On Monday, I came home and instead of watching the Powerpuff Girls, I did my homework straightaway."

The rest of the way up Bukit Timah hill is relatively easy: the tar road curves gently and every now and then exhausted hikers emerge onto the main path.

"On Tuesday, I helped Mommy to take the forks and spoons for dinner. Mommy say I complain too much, so I never complain."

As we walk along the main path, I hear shouting and screaming from among the trees in the valleys below. We are trekking on a raised path. The red, blue and yellow trails are not that far off down.

"Daddy, are you listening?"

"Yeah."

"Wednesday I packed my table and used a rag to clean it."

It occurs to me that she may be making everything up. Or at least the part about the Lalaloopsy doll.

"Thursday, was the most difficult."

"Why?"

"Thursday I mopped (she takes care to pronounce the 'd') the whole house."

"Really?" I am surprised and irritated at my wife. Maybe Katie didn't make up the doll part; maybe Lee Mei did, but I don't believe in these modern, ang moh ideas about taking care of a child's self-esteem.

"I used a rag and tied it to a stick and wet the rag and swept the whole house with it. Mommy said I did very well when she come home from work. But I don't think so. Later she mopped the entire house again at night."

We are on the final bend near the summit.

"Friday, Mommy say I don't have to do anything when she come home early. She want to make spaghetti for dinner but she never buy the correct onions. But she cannot leave me at home to go to NTUC to buy. So last minute she change plans and cook rice and dishes, but then already so late and she haven't wash the windows.

"She say I just sit there and don't cause trouble can already. But when I try to help she shout at me, then she cry."

I don't remember that happening. Was it last Friday or the Friday before? Perhaps that's when my wife brought up the doll as a bribe. Stupid to spoil the child like that.

"Saturday, I so scared I just do my homework and don't dare to say anything."

Probably last Friday. Which was why the house was so peaceful yesterday. Lee Mei was watching TV because as a rule, no housework was done in our home on weekends.

"So Daddy, after this, can we go to Toys R Us and buy the Lalaloopsy doll?"

"No."

"Daddy!" she screams, as only ten-year-old girls can, "Mommy promised me!"

"Have you finished climbing the hill? Where is your mosquito repellent?"

Katie swung her backpack onto the road. Pulling open the Velcro, she dove for the bottle.

"Aren't you supposed to re-apply it every hour?"

She rummages through wet wipes, tissues, takes out a crushed Nature's Valley bar, a comb, a journal.

"Stop blocking the path!" I yell, "Do you know how inconsiderate you are being?"

She drags her bag to the left and continues searching. I notice she's starting to cry, but she needs to learn.

"I told you to be responsible and re-apply it every hour. Now what time is it? You want to get dengue fever?"

"Daddy, I can't find it."

"Look properly."

"Daddy, I really cannot find it."

"Then we are not going to Toys R Us. Continue climbing."

Katie shrieks; she wails. She squeezes her eyes so hard that the tears don't flow convincingly. I pick up her pack, put all her stuff inside and shoulder it. If she can't appreciate what she has, she is not going make me spend $40 for that doll. I'm saving up the money anyway.

She stamps her feet. She isn't going to walk.

"Katie!" I warn. Incredulously, there is the sound of male voices singing on the path below in Hokkien. I take a while to decipher the words, as if we are underwater in the forest:

I walk on this narrow path
In search of someone I can trust.
I know that the road leads to doom,
Yet I still choose this path of no return.

From the yellow exit, Ah Pa and his kakis climb up. They have come up from the steep Seraya Loop.

Please do not reason me with the truth
Or expect to change me with your words of kindness.
I can't offer you an explanation for my life.
Many say it's because of the Brotherhood.

Still singing, they emerge onto the tar road and start laughing.
"Want to run down again or not?" Ah Leong shouts.
"No lah, damn hot, you know!"
Ah Hock strips off his singlet.
"Wah lao, so fast you old already?" Ah Soon taunts.
Ah Hock's sweat-filled singlet hits him in the mouth.
"Yeah lorh, go again lah!"
Why?" It's Pa's turn, "You run like a girl, is it?"

He starts to make little girl wailing sounds. I am at a loss because I have three women in my life. He stops as soon as he sees Katie.

"Ah Girl, what's wrong? What's wrong?"

He rushes over. My daughter is still bawling, her fists crushed against her eyes.

"What happen? Your father bully you?"

I glare at Ah-Pa and make the finger-on-the-lip-to-keep-quiet sign. Katie squalls louder.

My father picks her up.

"Scared for what?" he rocks her about. "Scared for what?'

The other uncles hunker down like full-fed macaques and squat by the Seraya exit. This was going to be a long wait, but they are unembarrassed.

"Ah Gong!" Katie blubbers. "Mommy say that if I am a good girl this week Daddy will buy me another doll! But I cannot find my mosquito repellent."

"Aiyoh, aiyoh, scared for what."

He can buy the doll for her if he wants, I think. I'm not spending the money.

"Ah Gong take you on a roller-coaster ride down the hill, want or not?"

"But Daddy say that I must finish climbing the hill if I want the doll."

Pa lifts Katie on his shoulders and flies her about like an aeroplane.

"Woo! Woo! Scared for what?" he yells.

Ah Hock slaps the ground and laughs.

"Let's go!" Katie giggles. The kakis stand up.

He leaps down the first rock ledge of the Seraya path. It is two and a half feet high. Rocks the size of guavas stud the ledge and shift under Pa's shoe. Katie swings wildly about.

"Stop it! It's too dangerous!" I shout.

Ah Soon slaps me on the shoulder.

"Aiyah, don't scared!"

"Yeah, you scared to spend money to buy the doll, right?" Pa hollers over his shoulder.

They are off, bouncing down the steps, running when the ground is flat. Ah Hock's singlet is tied round his waist. They move like troopers—I can't keep up. I can hear them singing again and the words float up to me:

Young man, why are you always in pain?
Is it because you want to play God?
Why are you still so foolish?
When you know this path leads you nowhere.

Somewhere down in the Seraya Loop Katie shrieks with delight. I want to kill Pa.

• • •

When I finally reach the visitor centre, sweating and hurting in my right knee, the uncles are already hosed down and smoking. Katie is sucking on an ice lime split from the gift shop. Pa wipes down his chest with his shirt, which doubles as a towel and which he has made wet with soap and water from the public toilet.

Ah Hock plants his cigarette in between the wooden slats of the bench he is sitting on, whips off his shoe and lifts it above his head in an arc, before thwacking it hard on the ground to get rid of gravel.

"Very expensive that ice cream," Pa says.

Ah Leong is stretching: his foot is planted flat on a wood

pillar, at a height above his head.

Pa flips open his Camel pack and counts.

"Cigarettes are very expensive, Pa," I say.

He says nothing, takes out one and lights up.

"I'm taking Katie home now."

"Umpf," he says.

All the uncles are smoking in a single cloud-bush. The smoke rises into the tree canopy where a monkey waves it away. I don't understand how they can run their lungs out only to put tar in it. But there they are, squatting, shirtless, smacking their Brookes trainers at squirrels, flies and each other, throwing snake brand powder about like magic. Pa returns to them.

Real men don't need to talk. I tug at Katie's hand. We are heading towards the car park and home, where she would be better off with my wife.

"Are we going to Toys R Us?" she asks.

Note: *The lyrics alluded to in this story originally appeared in* 15: The Movie, *directed by Royston Tan, and are used with permission.*

Joo Chiat and Other Lost Things

Justin Ker

AT THE HOSPITAL'S rooftop garden, Qianqian hobbled as she pushed Zu on a wheelchair. Her neck was sticky with sweat and she wiped it with the collar of her blue hospital *baju*. Qianqian pointed the wheelchair at a glass railing, and then sat down on a wooden bench. The setting sun cast an orange glow on the waters of the artificial lake next to the Yishun hospital. There were people jogging around the edge of the lake, which had once been an abandoned prawn farm.

Qianqian had been admitted three days ago. A car had run over her foot. Zubaidah, the forty-ish Malay woman in the next bed had asked Qianqian to wheel her to the rooftop garden. Qianqian was missing her right big toe. Zu's left leg was amputated up to the knee.

"Eh, you got strength to throw me over the railing or not?" Zu smirked.

Qianqian said nothing. She moved her right foot around.

The dirty, unfurled end of the bandage flapped around in the breeze, like a child who would not let go of her.

Zu let out a sigh. It escaped her pink lips and drifted up into the air.

"You got family or not?" Zu said.

Qianqian shook her head. "I'm from Vietnam."

"Wah. Really, ah? You sound very Singaporean. Eh, so Vietnam why got Chinese name, ah?"

Qianqian looked away and didn't answer.

"I thought you from Ang Mo Kio," Zu said.

"Here two years. Going to get PR already."

"I told the physio he ang moh, so must live in Ang Mo Kio," Zu chuckled. "He don't understand."

• • •

Two weeks ago during the election campaign, some Minister had mistaken Qianqian for a Singaporean and had taken a few photographs with her.

She was eating breakfast on her own at Joo Chiat market. She had just finished work and her muscles ached. Her jaw was sore. She chewed on the carrot cake slowly, using her tongue to flatten the salty, crumbled turnip against the roof of her mouth.

The Minister's minders had grabbed her from the back, lifting her up to her feet. Then suddenly ten people appeared behind her, and the Minister in his gold-rimmed glasses was next to her, shaking her hand. "Good to see young people up so early in the morning on a Sunday. We need hardworking Singaporeans like you."

She did not know how to respond, and just nodded her head.

Someone said, "Okay, one-two-smile," before a camera flash blinded her.

Then they all left.

The photograph appeared in the Joo Chiat Constituency Newsletter a week later. It was a small one, on the second page.

It was the first time she had seen a photograph of herself in two years.

Later at the KTV lounge, the mamasan laughed as she crumpled the newsletter and threw it into a pink, plastic rubbish bin. "Aiyoh, Qianqian, ah. You tell him if he takes photo here with us, we all vote for him!"

After the mamasan left the bar counter, Qianqian retrieved the newsletter from the bin and smoothed it out on the black marble counter top. She looked at her own photograph closely, under the light of the white neon Heineken sign. Her facial expression was exactly like the one in her fake Spanish passport—blank.

The mamasan called from the back: "Qianqian, got customer want you in room seven."

Qianqian left the newsletter on the bar counter and walked towards the back. The muffled sounds of a Jay Chou song escaped the closed door. She pushed the wooden door open. Three smiling men sat on the battered PVC sofa. One of them was singing, and another was drinking a mug of beer. Her friend Hahn was straddling the third. They all looked up as Qianqian entered the room; she took off her top before the door had fully closed.

• • •

"Your son is quite good," Qianqian said. "Always come and visit you."

"Yah lah. His father died long time ago. Just me and him." Zu wheeled herself closer to the glass railing. "You know what 'widow' means?"

Qianqian looked at Zu from the side.

Zu said, "It means 'empty'. Someone told me it comes from a Sanskrit word."

Qianqian touched her abdomen, in the spot over her womb, without meaning to.

She had been smuggled into Spain before coming to Singapore. Five thousand US dollars. She had saved every one of those dollars, so that she could get out of Vietnam. But all that only paid for six months of work in an airless underground clothing factory in Barcelona, before the Immigration police caught and deported her.

On the aeroplane back to Vietnam, she caressed her belly, wondering how beautiful her child would be. He—or she—would be half a Spanish human-smuggler, and half a Vietnamese woman, one who could sew the most perfect pair of Armani blue jeans.

But as her pregnancy began to show back home in Da Nang, her father, an ex-Vietcong Major, ordered her brother to hold her down as he extracted the foetus from her with a metal wire.

"My son ok, lah," said Zu. A pair of sparrows circled each other overhead. "Eh, doctor say I can go home soon. When you discharge, you come my house. I cook for you. My lontong very steady one."

"What is lontong?"

"You here so long you don't know lontong? Anyway got special sauce. Secret."

Secret.

The word caught on Qianqian's mind like the hooked end of a brown lalang seed on her naked forearm.

Qianqian's last memory of her mother: it was during the December monsoon, a few years after the Americans had left. Qianqian was four or five years old then. Her mother stood at the doorway and smiled at her. Qianqian remembered hugging her leg, pressing her cheek against the cold smoothness of her mother's silk *ao dai* dress. Then the world of the silk left her face, turned, shimmered down the wooden stairs, and never came back.

She had gone on a rainy day.

Qianqian had a recurring dream about once a month: Her mother stands at the doorway, smiling at her. Qianqian asks her—where are you going?

Her mother kneels down and cradles Qianqian's face with her hands.

Her answer is always the same.

Secret.

Only years later, the story of her mother emerged, piece by piece, one broken paragraph at a time from the mouth of her father, once again drunk on moonshine.

Qianqian's mother had been a Vietcong spy. One of the best. Qianqian's parents had met while they were digging out one section of the Cu Chi tunnels for the North Vietnamese Army. It was a long, jarring, underground architecture that approached the complexity of an ant colony, with tunnels that branched and re-branched off into sleeping quarters, meeting rooms, kitchens, bomb-shelters, and death-traps. There were numerous storerooms that held different things—artillery shells, potatoes, sacks of rice, and even the corpses of fallen comrades before they could be properly buried.

"The history of our country is the history of her body," her father had said, with equal measures of pride and shame. She had seduced the last Governor-General of French Indochina when she was only fifteen. Then various South Vietnamese ministers of agriculture. She had even gotten a high-ranking American military attaché to reveal the position of an artillery firebase in the jungle. Five hundred young American Marines died in one night as a result of her seduction.

Like mother, like daughter.

After the war ended, they had lived well for a while, before Qianqian's father descended into alcoholism. He said it was the only way to cope with the ghosts of his comrades who visited him, even during the day. They would come, sit down on his bed, look at him, and smoke ethereal cigarettes without uttering a word.

Similarly, Qianqian's mother hardly spoke after the war. She sometimes brought Qianqian and her brother to the few green leafy parks in the city, left behind by the French colonials. One of them had a rectangular maze whose walls were made of hedges, as tall as her father. Qianqian remembered getting lost in the labyrinth, and the desperate feeling of looking for her mother. It was like her body was being turned to ice from the inside. She shouted and cried. In the end, it was her mother who found her. Her mother was good with mazes.

During one particularly drunken night, Qianqian's father spat at Qianqian as she cowered in one corner of their house. "I don't even know if you are mine!"

Qianqian's mother did not say anything. She stood by the window and had a faraway look.

Then she left on the rainy day in December.

No one knew if the Americans had turned her, or assassinated her, or if she was just trying to escape her own silence by disappearing.

• • •

"Oi, Zubaidah!"

Qianqian and Zu turned to see a female Indian nurse call them from the doorway to the roof garden.

"Doctor looking for you," said the sweating nurse as she walked up to them. She wiped her forehead with her hand. "One no leg, the other no toe, still can run everywhere."

Zu and Qianqian smiled at each other.

"The ang moh say must exercise," said Zu. "What ang moh say, we must do." Zu placed one hand on her wheelchair's armrest. Qianqian reached out with her right hand and covered Zu's hand with her own.

• • •

After Qianqian was discharged, the mamasan visited her on her first day home to inspect the foot. She brought a tin of "love letter" wafers and sat down on Qianqian's bed. "Aiyoh, Qianqian. Like that how to work?" said Mummy, holding up the four-toed foot by the heel.

"Mummy, don't worry," said Hahn from across the room, fanning herself with a rattan folding fan. "She can cover it with high heel shoes. Wear stilettos. Even more sexy."

Qianqian looked at her foot with the absent toe. She wished the rest of her could disappear as well. Like her mother.

She was not even sure if the traffic accident that night had been the taxi driver's fault. Five a.m. and the KTV lounge had just closed. She'd been walking home alone, barefoot, still slightly drunk, the straps of her heels twirled around her fingers. She had seen the taxi coming at her just as she was about to cross Joo Chiat Road. She remembered thinking what it would be like if she just stepped in front of the car. And her right foot had lifted off the asphalt.

• • •

A month later, Qianqian knocked on the door to Zu's flat in Pasir Ris. It was nighttime, and the fluorescent lights in the corridor were lit.

A teenaged Malay boy answered the door.

"Oh, you're from the hospital, right?" said the boy.

"Yes. Is Zubaidah in?" said Qianqian. She was holding a rustling NTUC plastic bag of oranges.

The boy kept quiet. The vertical metal bars of the grill door segmented his face into rectangles, the shadows of the bars falling across his face.

He asked her to come in and take a seat; he had some news. Zu had died three weeks earlier, soon after leaving hospital. The doctors had said it was a heart attack.

Qianqian did not know what to say. She mumbled a "sorry" and got up from the wooden sofa to leave. Her mind was not working. She could hear the boy talking as she struggled to put on her shoes outside the flat, but she could not understand what he was saying.

She looked at him, and feared to make the shared connection of pain. So she turned away and left.

Later, he would throw the uneaten bag of oranges down the rubbish chute. He would not taste the sour, crescent-shaped slices of her confusion and the small hard seeds of her pain, of losing another mother figure yet again.

Qianqian walked away from Zu's flat aimlessly. She came to Pasir Ris Park and stopped beneath a line of black rain-trees. She took off her shoes and trod down the short beach to the sea. Under the moonlight, she stood knee-deep in the salty water for a long time. In front of her was the South China Sea, and further away, the coast of Vietnam. A sea breeze blew, lifting up her hair.

When her legs got tired, she turned away and left the sea.

As she crossed the park, she noticed a dark area, in the middle of a sandpit bordered by rain-trees. She walked towards it, and realised that it was a circular maze for children. Wooden planks stuck into the ground formed its curved walls.

Qianqian entered the maze and left nine-toed footprints in the sand.

She reached the centre of the maze and sat down, leaning her back against one of the planked walls, as if she were once again waiting for her mother to find her. Life, Hahn had said, was an accumulation of losses. But Qianqian refused to enumerate the lost things from her thirty years.

She could only imagine her mother hiding underground in the Cu Chi tunnels after her escape. She pictured her mother, huddled in the underground maze, furiously constructing another series of tunnels inside her own head, where, amongst the rooms that held the bodies of betrayed lovers, there was a single indestructible chamber, built deliberately to hold the quivering memory of her five year-old daughter.

Anniversary

Phan Ming Yen

WHEN HE SAW the green light beneath the exit sign on the wall at the end of the other corridor, he realised something had changed.

For the past three days, he was sure that it had been a red light instead. He was sure that it was a red light and that it was an indicator for the fire hose and the extinguisher cabinet just below it. When he and his wife had checked in three days ago, he had noted a similar red light beneath the exit sign and above the fire hose and extinguisher cabinet on their side of the corridor before the passageway ended.

Then suddenly, he saw a figure appear from one of the rooms on the other side of the corridor.

Although both corridors were well lit with overhead and floor lights, he could not make out the face of the figure.

At first, the figure stood motionless, looking at him—he was sure that it was looking at him—and then he saw it raise its hand, as if gesturing for him to walk over. It appeared to him though the figure was either a woman or a girl as it had long hair and he could see, from its outline, that the figure was wearing what looked like a dress.

He was carrying the pot in his right hand and, in his left, the key card to the room. He knew that he could not go into the room to put down the pot and come out again, for his wife would ask why. And he felt ridiculous walking down the corridor with the pot in his hand, dressed only in a t-shirt, a pair of jogging shorts and the light bathrobe provided by the hotel.

The figure remained motionless. It, or she, just stood there with what he perceived to be an outstretched hand, as if asking for him. He was sure it was some mistake. The figure probably mistook him for someone else, perhaps a colleague from another group that was staying in a room on his side of the corridor.

As he walked to the lift lobby, which also served as a pantry, with the snacks and drink-vending machines and the hot water dispenser, he kept his eyes lowered. As he was refilling the pot, he looked out of the wall-high window and he focused on the colourful display on the gigantic LED screen on the building across the road.

He was so engrossed with the display that he had not noticed the overflowing pot in his hand and so as he returned to his room, he walked slowly and carefully and he decided not to turn to see if the figure was still there.

However, as he slotted the key card into the door lock, he could not resist looking up and it was then that he realised he was not at the room he and his wife had been staying in for the past three days. The number on the door was different.

He turned instinctively and saw, behind him, on his right,

above his shoulder, the exit sign, the green light and the fire hose and extinguisher cabinet. He turned to his left and saw, at the far end of the other corridor, the exit sign, a red light below it and the fire hose and extinguisher cabinet.

• • •

There was a soft whirring, as the lock mechanism processed the key card, and then he heard the voice of a young girl, from behind the door as it slowly opened, calling, "Daddy! Daddy!"

The girl held the door for him as he entered the room, and from where he stood, near the wardrobe, he saw a woman sitting on the edge of the bed, her back towards him.

She was still in the clothes she had worn during the day when they had gone out to the theme park: a long grey skirt and a blouse with a matching design, such that from a distance, you would think she was wearing a dress.

He remembered that she wore the same clothes the following day in the car. He remembered her saying that the skirt was comfortable to wear when travelling long distances. Their daughter had been asleep in the back seat and the sun came in bright and strong and he remembered being worried about it being too warm for her. Then, just as he turned again to the road ahead, a car had suddenly shot out from behind the truck in the opposite lane.

Later, as he lay awake during the nights in the hospital, he tried to think about her and he just kept his thoughts on the dream that their daughter would not wake from now.

"I am back," he said, as he put the pot down on the mini-fridge chest. He lifted his daughter, who cried out in surprise, and carried her towards her mother.

The woman turned and smiled. "What took you so long?" she asked, as she rose from the bed.

The Borrowed Boy

Alfian Sa'at

THEY WOULD BORROW the boy for a day. He would be checked out in the morning, after the Aidilfitri prayers, and then sent back in the evening, before his bedtime. During the course of the day he would follow them as they visited their relatives and in all likelihood he would receive some money, just like their other children. People were most generous on the first day of Hari Raya; as the weeks passed the amount placed in those palm-sized paper envelopes would depreciate. Not simply because money is finite but also because the visitors would tend to be more distantly related, people who were encountered once a year. As a matter of fact, the boy would probably receive more than their other children, once it was made known that he was an orphan.

They had already prepared a set of baju kurung for him at home. It was made from dark pink satin, and the collar was in fashion that year—the Telok Blangah cut, where instead of a Mandarin collar the neckline was embroidered with a herringbone stitch. The boy might not like the colour, but what was important was that it was the same colour as the baju kurung for their other two children. It would make him feel like he was one of the family.

Junaidah walked into the orphanage alone, unaccompanied by her husband and son. They had preferred to wait in the car. The orphans were picked at random, but a week earlier Junaidah had called the person in charge and requested for an eight-year-old boy. The reason, she explained, was that the family had decided to purchase a baju kurung for the boy, as a present. Thus it was necessary to know both his gender and age in advance. At the bazaar in Geylang, Junaidah had used her own son as a gauge for the size of the baju kurung; placing it against his back, holding it up with her forefingers and thumbs. For her own son she chose a sky blue baju kurung; for the boy, pale orange.

She prided herself on her choice of pastels; it was a sign of good taste. Some of her relatives seemed fond of garish colours: ruby reds and turmeric yellows, which though festive, betrayed an inability to appreciate subtlety. It struck Junaidah that these choices weren't just aesthetic, but also economic: bright colours took a longer time to fade after repeated washings. But most unpalatable to her were those families which had decided to dress their children in identical colours, as if all their clothes had been cut from the same bale of cloth. She had, on occasion, pointed out families attired in such manner. Looking out from their car window, she had once made the remark that they looked like a Boria troupe, those performing minstrels from Penang that she had seen on Malaysian television.

After she had picked out the baju kurung, her husband had

commented that the colours were too muted for children; they were 'old people' hues. Junaidah sighed in disappointment. She had wanted to say that her husband was an engineer; they had a car and did not have to take public transport for their visiting rounds. As such, it was unlikely for the family to cross roads, and thus unnecessary for the children to be costumed like warning flares. Instead, she asked Haikel whether he liked the baju kurung she had chosen, in a solicitous voice that guaranteed a fearful, though positive response. When the boy nodded, Junaidah triumphantly walked to the shopkeeper and announced, "I'm buying two sets, can give discount or not?"

There had been an incident in the morning with the baju kurung. Haikel had walked into her room as Junaidah laid out the two sets on the Queen-sized bed. The room smelt of the mint shampoo in Junaidah's hair, drying by an electric standing fan, and rose attar, the non-alcoholic perfume that her husband had dabbed on himself before the morning prayers. Because of their new curtains, the light in the room was an underwater turquoise. A brocade jewellery box was opened, its contents twinkling in the dimness of the room.

Haikel was sifting through the box when Junaidah said, "These are women's things. Go and wear your clothes." He then proceeded to reach for the pale orange baju kurung.

"Haikel, that's not yours. Don't you remember?"

"Then whose is it?"

At that moment, Junaidah realised she did not know the boy's name. All this while, she and her husband had referred to him as the 'orphan boy'. Junaidah felt that it was too much trouble to explain what an orphan was to Haikel.

"It's your friend's."

"Who?"

"Don't you remember? Today you're going to have a friend following us around. And that orange one is his baju kurung. Yours is the blue one. Remember how you told Mak that you liked it?"

Haikel looked at the two sets of clothes on the bed. The look on his face told Junaidah that her answer was not satisfactory. He knew, with that eight-year-old intuition of his, that she was hiding something from him. And thus he said, his voice suddenly taking on an adult assertiveness, "But I like the orange one."

"You said you liked the blue one, Haikel."

"I never said so. I want the orange one."

Junaidah looked at her husband. He was using a brush to clean the lint off his velvet songkok. "Look at Haikel, bang. On the morning of Hari Raya he's making a fuss."

"Haikel," her husband said, without looking up from his task. His voice was stern, but the response was so automatic that Junaidah felt insulted. Even if he had not entirely surrendered all parenting duties to her, sometimes she felt as if he was skimping on his share. And there were times, like this, for example, when Junaidah felt as if she was being treated not so much like a wife but a whiny daughter, petitioning a father weary of the melodramatic antics of little girls.

"That's all you can do," Junaidah said. "You didn't even lift your head to look at him."

"Why do I need to look at him? I know what he looks like."

Junaidah rolled her eyes. In this triangle she was suddenly

the petty one, the child. She caught a triumphant smile creeping up on Haikel's face, endorsed by his father's nonchalance. Sometimes Junaidah felt that she would have preferred to have a daughter instead. She was tired of having these two ganging up on her. But weren't daughters supposed to be closer to their fathers, while sons were mummy's boys? Why was it that Haikel rarely took sides with her? She wondered if it might have been better to have asked for a girl from the orphanage instead.

But that would fulfil her own need, instead of the needs of the child. It would have violated a certain spirit of charity. She wondered if there were childless couples who borrowed a child from the orphanage on Hari Raya. No, she decided, it would make too much of a scene, it would highlight the void in their lives, a void to be filled by endless gossip. That poor couple, people would say, playing at being parents for a day, like a bride and groom playing at being king and queen for a day.

Also, she had chosen a boy for Haikel's sake. She knew he was at an age where girls were treated with a mixture of shyness and hostility. And for him to be so ungrateful, to test her with this mischievous amnesia, was unacceptable. They did not know the boy's name yet, but the orange baju kurung had been reserved for him. Her son could not ask for it as if nobody else had claimed ownership. Thus Junaidah said, "Don't be naughty ah, Haikel. This one isn't yours."

Suddenly her husband interjected. "But they're the same size, right? They're just different colours. The orphan boy doesn't know which one you picked for him. If Haikel wants to wear the orange one, let him have it."

Junaidah felt as if she had been elected the sole spokesperson for the boy. She had to stand up for him, to assert his presence. She found herself looking at her husband, and articulating silently: *You can have Haikel today. But the boy is mine. I will not start the day by betraying him.* But she suddenly checked herself; she had not even met this boy, and it would not do to become too attached to him.

She let Haikel have the orange baju kurung, and hoped that his victory marked the end, instead of the beginning of what she now uncomfortably realised were the stirrings of jealousy. They had always talked about having another child, but kept on postponing, because her husband had always insisted that Haikel was not ready. It would be traumatic, he reasoned, for the boy to have his parents distribute their affections at so young an age. But Junaidah sometimes wondered if it was already too late for Haikel to learn to share his life—and his parents' lives—with another sibling.

Thus when Junaidah entered the orphanage, she could not help but feel expectant. It was just as well that her husband and Haikel preferred to remain in the car. She would be the first point of contact into the family, and despite the fact that she was not a man, she hoped that he would somehow stick by her side for the rest of the day. A woman in a cream tudung was waiting at a counter, which was decorated with ketupat woven from shiny light green ribbons. There were children's drawings on the noticeboard, many of them filled with the words 'Selamat Hari Raya'. Junaidah noticed how they were filled mostly with pictures of children, not families. But at least the children were smiling.

After Junaidah had introduced herself, the receptionist

checked a list and said, "You're the one who wanted an eight-year-old boy, right?" Junaidah wondered if her request had been exceptional, and immediately felt apologetic. She did not want to come across as someone prone to unreasonable demands. The receptionist smiled and said, "I'll go and bring him down. They're all upstairs right now. They've just had their breakfast. We had lontong and rendang today. You know lah, once a year. Why don't you take a seat first?"

Junaidah sat down on a leather sofa. There was a crater in one of its armrests, exposing the beige sponge padding inside. Someone, probably a child, had been picking at it, fingernails burrowing through the sponge either out of nervousness or boredom. She did not expect the orphanage to look like a school, with two flags at a quadrangle near the façade, and three storeys of what could have been classrooms—except that they were dormitories. It was a good idea to have them sequestered upstairs. Junaidah had feared having to pass through the faces of children, their hopefulness on her way in, their disappointment on her way out. She wondered if she might have asked for another child, and another, just enough to fit into the car.

Was it not somewhat cruel, to choose one over the rest? Except that the orphanage had chosen for her. Perhaps this was a reward for good behaviour, to be hosted by a family for a day. Junaidah felt comforted by the idea that she was merely a host, and that the child was her guest. Her role today was to be defined by hospitality, not the construction of an intricate fantasy. She was not going to pretend that the boy was her son; neither should the boy believe that this family setup was anything more than temporary.

Junaidah had to admit that she had not always been so circumspect. When she had watched that TV magazine programme during the fasting month, the one that showcased the children at the Darul-Ihsan orphanage, it had affected her so much that she could not sleep properly at night. It made her cry just to relate the story to her husband when he later got home from work: all those children without parents, whose Hari Raya would painfully remind them only of what they lacked, no jars overflowing with cookies and biscuits, no filling their pockets with crisp, folded dollar notes, a festival of absence. Her family members didn't know how fortunate they were, it was an obligation to let others partake of their privilege. The next day, she called the orphanage, asked them about the scheme where families could volunteer to provide selected children with a 'real Hari Raya experience', and signed up. When she put down the phone she was flushed with that superior happiness that comes about from making other people happy.

The receptionist returned five minutes later with the boy. His name was Mydeen, and she spelt it out for Junaidah, a unique English spelling for a name otherwise recognised as 'Maidin' or 'Maideen'. He was dark, a Jawi Peranakan child, of Indian Muslim and Malay extraction. Junaidah did not know many Jawi Peranakans, but it sometimes amused her how the 'i's' in their names became 'ee's': Fateema, Jameelah, Lateef.

Mydeen looked at the floor shyly as the receptionist spoke. She told Junaidah that he was in Primary 2, a badminton player, and that he was quite reserved. He was wearing his pink satin baju kurung, a colour that clashed with his skin tone. Junaidah noticed his thick, well-shaped eyebrows, his high cheekbones, and a sharp, almost hooked nose. He was tall for his age, and while Junaidah believed eight-year-olds were still amorphous, she could already see how this one's features could step out of the haze of youth and solidify; he would turn out to be quite a handsome young man.

"Have you eaten?" Junaidah asked him.

"Yes."

"Was it nice?"

Mydeen nodded. And then he reached out and slipped his hand into Junaidah's. She was shocked by the intimacy of the gesture, and thought to herself: *He must be impatient to get out of here.* Junaidah signed a few forms briskly, thanked the receptionist, and walked out of the building with Mydeen. On her way out, she considered the possibility that the act of taking her hand was something almost reflexive for him, having been fostered out to different Hari Raya families year after year. So she had been mistaken about the automatic handholding, a gesture not of animal instinct or need but habit and perhaps even calculation. *I'm not the first*, Junaidah thought to herself. A moment later she found herself beaming in the direction of the family car, a red Honda whose door had swung open to receive her and her dark-skinned guest.

The first place they would visit was the house of Junaidah's mother-in-law. She lived in Teban Gardens, which despite its name was a working-class housing estate. In the car, the two boys were sitting in the back seat. Mydeen had already changed into his light blue baju kurung; her husband had helped the boy into it at a toilet in the orphanage. Haikel was playing with his handheld game. On the radio, Sudirman was singing the evergreen "From Afar I Ask For Forgiveness".

"Haikel, what are you playing?" Junaidah asked.

"PSP."

"Why don't you ask Mydeen to play along?"

"This game for one player only."

"When you're done, why don't you let him try?"

Haikel did not reply. And Junaidah thought there was little point in forcing him to share his toy. Did she even imagine that the two boys would be able to get along? Junaidah suddenly thought of all the other children who would be present at Teban Gardens. Could Haikel somehow rally his cousins together to exclude the boy from their activities? Was her son capable of such a thing? Suddenly Junaidah felt a certain protectiveness rise within her, a feeling that caught her by surprise. On the radio, Sudirman was winding up his song with the final lines: "I hope for perpetual blessings from Mum and Dad, for your son who is far away."

When they arrived at the house, there were already about a dozen pairs of shoes at the door. While taking the lift up to the eleventh floor, Mydeen had asked to press the floor button. It was the first statement he had made, actively, which was not a response to a question. Junaidah felt a certain sense of reassurance: the boy would know how to conduct himself later. He had just made a desire known, and she would not have to attend to him all the time. Wasn't that what children were essentially, the exhausting mystery they presented to her, as she tried to meet their needs: are you hungry, cold, sleepy, in pain? It was the one thing all mothers said to their children, patting a crying child, or rocking one in her arms, not "I love you" but "what do you want . . . what do you want?"

It was her mother-in-law who greeted them at the door. She was a widow, who had raised four sons on her own. Her husband had passed away at a British shipyard accident when the youngest was still an infant. She had married young, and a popular story they liked to tell was how her late husband had come home one day to find his wife playing hopscotch with her friends outside their kampung house. Junaidah's husband was the eldest and the only one with a degree, and it was no secret that he was his mother's favourite.

"You're finally here," she said. "Why are you late?"

"We had some business to attend to in the morning," her son replied.

"Haikel," she said. "You haven't visited grandma for so long! And who's your friend?"

"He's a boy from Darul-Ihsan," Junaidah replied.

"Oh, Ihsan. Come in, Ihsan."

"His name's not Ihsan. His name is Mydeen."

Haikel's grandmother was hard of hearing, and Junaidah sometimes found conversation with her a draining affair. The old lady, however, always had a smile on her face, and even if she had misheard something, was likely to have heard it in a completely benign way. Mydeen, without any prompting, began to salam her, and then went around the living room, seeking out the hands of all the adults.

"Go and salam everyone, Haikel."

Haikel would usually resist, backing up indulgently against

his father, but this time, he readily complied. He retraced the path that Mydeen had taken, grabbing hands and holding them up to his nose, bowing perfunctorily, but at such speed that he managed to overtake Mydeen. After he was done, he started to seek out the rest of the children. It was not difficult to find them; shrieking and laughter were spilling out from one of the bedrooms.

"Who's the boy?" one of Junaidah's brothers-in-law asked.

"He's from the orphanage," Junaidah replied. "He's following us for the day."

"Just for today? He's such a well-mannered boy. Why don't you keep him for one week?"

Junaidah had not considered it. But why not? Already she was observing the effect the boy's presence had on Haikel—arousing in him a competitive nature, an eagerness to please. She recalled Haikel's demands for the orange baju kurung in the morning, and suddenly the exchange of the clothes between the boys assumed a significance for her. Maybe siblings had a mutually tempering effect on each other: Haikel would learn to be more generous, and Mydeen would be drawn out of his shell. The receptionist had supplied Junaidah very little information about Mydeen. Was he a real orphan, abandoned after birth? Or was he sent to live there because of a broken family? Were his parents in jail? What was life like in the orphanage?

She thought about the routine that they had conducted just before leaving the house—did they have such a thing at the orphanage too? Every Hari Raya, Junaidah's husband would set up a self-timed camera in the living room to take the family portrait. But before that, they would participate in a ritual of forgiveness. Even though Hari Raya did not mark the Muslim New Year, it had always felt that way to Junaidah. In the morning, those who went for the Aidilfitri prayers in the mosques sought clemency from Allah. And then later, the members of her family would solemnly seek the forgiveness from their seniors. Time moves in a single direction. How else could one start anew, other than through absolution by another, an annual clearing of accounts? Hari Raya helped to formalize a necessary moment which might have otherwise been too difficult, too awkward. That remorseful sobbing while clasping another's hand was rescued from theatrics by the fact that it was a scene that happened in every living room across the island on that one morning.

Junaidah looked around her. There were six Tupperware jars on the table, each one placed on a white doily. They were filled with the usual Hari Raya fare: pineapple tarts, layered cake, cashew cookies, almond biscuits, glazed cornflakes, shrimp rolls. She wondered when Mydeen would come out of the room to sample them. The living room was sparsely decorated; two vases of plastic flowers provided some cheer, the curtains, cushions and carpet were new. A wall was painted lime green, which provided Junaidah with yet another example of how some Malay families were colour-blind. They were kampung colours, she thought, their brashness perhaps suitable to mask the drabness of wooden walls, but entirely inappropriate for a HDB flat.

She gazed at the television. Every year, after a few conversations, everybody's eyes would converge on the screen. The Hari Raya Variety Show was something everyone could agree upon; men preferred the news, the women preferred dramas. A new singer, someone probably unearthed during an idol-style competition, would sing a Hari Raya standard. There were cutaways to well-wishes from local personalities, like that singer who started covering up when her age advanced, but in her own flamboyant way: no tudung and long-sleeved baju for her. Instead, she wore a turban, and elbow-length gloves, which made her look like an exotic fortune-teller. There would be comedy sketches, and everyone would agree that P. Ramlee's comedies were better, more unforced, his formidable deadpan leaving these mug-faced exertions in the dust.

Her mother-in-law started serving lunch. She had cooked her specialty: sambal goreng, a Javanese beef and vegetable sauté, in coconut-based gravy. The children were summoned to wash their hands. Haikel was panting when he got out of the room.

"What have you been doing, Haikel?"

"Playing monster-monster."

Junaidah had seen a version of this game played once—one of the older children would adopt a fearful character, while the rest would huddle in a corner, sometimes shielding themselves with pillows or the edge of a mattress. They might sometimes launch futile guerrilla attacks, throwing useless projectiles like balls of paper at their tormentor. Junaidah remembered one of the adults scolding Haikel for playing the game because it would give her child 'nightmares' later on—a euphemism, as Junaidah had later realised, for bedwetting.

"Where's Mydeen?" she asked.

"I don't know."

"Isn't he with you?"

"No."

Junaidah looked into the room. There were five children inside, two girls and three boys. Mydeen was nowhere to be seen. Junaidah asked her husband if he had seen Mydeen. He answered no, too. She looked into the remaining bedroom and the toilet. He wasn't under the bed, behind the curtains. The storeroom? Nothing but boxes and a vacuum cleaner. She walked to the front door. The gates had been left open—but to receive visitors, not eject strangers. She looked at the swarm of footwear at the threshold. What was Mydeen wearing on his feet? She put her fingers at her temple and tried to recall. She picked up a small pair of black sandals and shouted into the living room.

"Whose sandals are these?"

"Those are mine," one of the boys answered.

Junaidah asked Haikel again, "When was the last time you saw him?"

"He was inside the room with us just now."

"Were you playing with him?"

"No."

"So what was he doing inside?"

"He was just watching us."

"Why didn't you play together?"

"He's not our friend."

Junaidah was stunned. She grabbed Haikel by the shoulders and shook him.

"Do you know whose baju kurung you're wearing?" she asked, bitterly. "I asked you to take care of him, didn't I? What's wrong with you, Haikel? Why are you like this?"

Haikel was starting to cry. Her husband said, "What are you doing? Don't blame the boy."

"He's somebody's child. He was put in our care. What will they say now?"

"Who?"

Junaidah wanted to answer, his parents, you fool, but that answer would make her the foolish one, not him. For whatever reason, Mydeen had lost his parents. They were the void in his life. But what void in whose life does the missing orphan make? Emptiness upon emptiness, one void seeking union with another. The boy who had held Junaidah's hand would forever be beyond her reach.

"Let's go look for him," Junaidah's husband said. "I don't think he could have gone very far."

A search party was formed. The grandmother would look after the children, and the adults would comb the block. Junaidah and her husband decided to scour the void deck. The rest would sweep across the corridors, knocking from door to door, asking if they had seen a Jawi Peranakan boy in a sky blue baju kurung.

While taking the lift down, Junaidah found herself sobbing uncontrollably. All she wanted was to bring the boy into the fold of a family, a typical Malay family. But now it seemed as if her family wasn't typical at all. It was too self-absorbed in its own image to pay attention to the boy. What Junaidah did not anticipate was that it was through the boy's eyes that the real image of their family was formed. They had been judged and now, deserted.

They walked around the void deck, with Junaidah calling out Mydeen's name. She did not want to sound angry at all in case it frightened him; neither did she want to sound too pleading either, because she had to cut her voice off from the panicked hope that was its source. She understood then the double vowels in his name, of how her voice had to reach across its length; built into its spelling was the sound of a wail.

There was a group of people at a Senior Citizens' corner who stared at her. Junaidah's husband had a word with them. They shook their heads, and Junaidah took a deep breath. If Mydeen appeared, it was not because he had heard her summons. It would be because the sound of her voice had congealed in the air to become him. Now all she needed to do was to find the right tone, the right volume, the right . . .

Her husband pointed him out to Junaidah. At the car park, a family, uniformly attired in shiny grey, was walking across to the main road. In their midst, in his sky blue baju kurung, was Mydeen. Junaidah and her husband chased after them.

"Mydeen, where did you go?" Junaidah asked.

The men from both families exchanged greetings. As it turned out, the family in grey had found Mydeen taking the lift alone.

"He followed our family last year," the father said. "Such a coincidence. We asked him where he came from, but he said he couldn't remember which house you were at."

"He was with you last year?" Junaidah's husband asked.

"Yes. The children remember him. You remember *abang* Mydeen right? All of you, wearing pink colour?"

The two children nodded. They were younger than Mydeen, probably still in kindergarten. Junaidah looked at them. The boy had a little tail of hair sticking out from the back of his head.

The girl, despite her young age, had red lipstick on. The father reeked of strong, unfiltered cigarettes. You did not choose your families. But Mydeen had chosen.

The mother said, "You know boys his age, they like to play with the lift. We were just about to take him back to the orphanage." Unlike Junaidah, she wasn't wearing a tudung, her henna-dyed hair blazing under the sun.

"What do you mean send him back? We'll take him visiting again, just like last year!" said the father. "You're so lucky you found him. Don't stray again ah, Mydeen?"

Not as lucky as you, Junaidah thought to herself. "I think we'll go up now," she said. "Everyone is so worried."

Junaidah took Mydeen's hand and led him back towards her mother-in-law's block. She promised herself that she would not let him out of her sight for the rest of the day. While walking back, Mydeen had turned around and waved at the family in grey. "Bye bye!" he said to them. "Selamat Hari Raya!" The two children echoed him back.

It was already night when they finally got home. They had made two visits for the day: first, to Teban Gardens, and then later to Yishun, where Junaidah's parents lived. When Mydeen was brought back to the house at Teban Gardens, everyone had fussed over him. Junaidah wondered if Mydeen was used to being the centre of attention at these gatherings. She had thought that it was better for him to blend into the background, among the children, indistinguishable; did she not, at times, also enquire whose child belonged to whom? She did not want the boy to turn out as an exhibit. But evidently Mydeen knew his place.

They made him try all the kuih, and asked him which one was his favourite. One of Haikel's uncles taught him a hand-illusion, involving a thumb that seemed to be severed from the hand. When it was time to leave, some of the relatives gave him two paper envelopes of money, instead of one. Before leaving, everyone queued in front of the grandmother, and took turns to kneel in front of her, asking that their sins for the past year be reset to zero. When it came to Mydeen's turn, the grandmother patted his head and waved him away, saying, "You've done no wrong, child. We just met you. But you must come back next year."

At Yishun, it was a similar affair, the relatives doting on Mydeen, but never to the point of smothering him with needless curiosity. They played a cartoon on the DVD player, and the children crowded in front of the television set. Sometimes Junaidah allowed herself to observe the proceedings just like she had seen it on television, the orphan boy surrounded by his surrogate family, the Hari Raya diorama of crystal glasses filled with Coke, little girls dressed like dolls in mini kebayas, the gold and silver threads on the songket worn by the men, and in the evening, the fairy lights turned on at the window, bathing the balcony with alternating waves of jewelled colours. But she would snap out of it, suddenly reminded that the boy was on loan, and that all this would vanish for him by the next day—the money in his pocket and his baju kurung being the only mementoes smuggled out from a dream.

They decided not to return the boy to the orphanage that very evening. Junaidah made the necessary call to the orphanage, and then brought out an extra towel and toothbrush for the boy. By the end of the night, Mydeen was playing the PSP, with Haikel peering over his shoulder and coaching him. Junaidah wondered if Haikel would ask for Mydeen after the latter had gone back. They had spent so little time together. But what if they had spent more? What was his place in their lives, and their place in his? And what if he ran away from them again?

Junaidah thought about Hari Raya next year. Haikel would be one year older. And so would the boy. But she knew she would not go to the orphanage to ask for him. She thought about the other family they had met, blessed by their unexpected reunion with Mydeen. She wistfully wondered whether such a thing could happen to her family too. For a lift door to open and reveal him, as if he was the answer to some unanswerable longing. Junaidah decided that she would return Mydeen the next day, and with this decision came the knowledge that she would think of him every Hari Raya for the rest of her life. Later that night, she rose from her bed, unable to sleep, her head filled with images of a lift, black sandals, a baju kurung like a shred of blue among grey clouds. She entered Haikel's room, where Mydeen was sleeping on a spare mattress. A fan was humming drowsily. The time was 11 PM; Hari Raya was not over yet. Junaidah knelt down and rested her hand at the edge of Mydeen's foot. She was asking for his forgiveness but no words came out of her mouth.

Contributors

Ann Ang's poetry, fiction and non-fiction have appeared in *Eclectica Magazine, Quarterly Literary Review Singapore, Poskod, Kartika Review, The Common* and elsewhere. Her first collection of short stories, titled *Bang My Car* (Math Paper Press, 2012), was launched at the 2012 Singapore Writers' Festival. An avid birdwatcher, she is an educator at the Academy of Singapore Teachers. "Scared For What" was originally published in *Bang My Car* (Singapore: Math Paper Press, 2012).

Yu-Mei Balasingamchow lives in Singapore and writes about history, travel and culture in Asia. She is the co-author of the non-fiction title *Singapore: A Biography* (2009), which received a gold prize at the 2010 Asia Pacific Publishers Association Awards and was named a 2010 Choice Outstanding Academic Title. She is working on her first novel, with funding from Singapore's National Arts Council. Her website is toomanythoughts.org. "Lighthouse" was originally published in *Balik Kampung*, edited by Verena Tay (Singapore: Math Paper Press, 2012).

CONTRIBUTORS

Felix Cheong is the author of eight books, including four volumes of poetry; his latest is a collection of short stories titled *Vanishing Point*. His work has been widely anthologised and featured in a telemovie, *Love Story*, directed by Sun Koh. Conferred the Young Artist of the Year for Literature in 2000, Felix was named by *Reader's Digest* as the 29th Most Trusted Singaporean in 2010. He holds a master's degree in creative writing and is currently a lecturer in journalism at Murdoch University and University of Newcastle. "Because I Tell" was originally published in *A Monsoon Feast*, edited by Verena Tay (Singapore: Monsoon Books, 2012).

Dave Chua's first novel, *Gone Case*, received a Singapore Literature Prize Commendation Award in 1996, and was recently adapted into a two-volume graphic novel with artist Koh Hong Teng. Chua's collection, *The Beating and Other Stories*, was longlisted for the 2012 Frank O'Connor International Short Story Award. His short fiction has appeared (or will soon) in places such as *Telltale: 11 Stories*, *Fish Eats Lion*, *Innsmouth Magazine* and *Singapore Noir*, and his graphic novel, *The Girl Under the Bed* (with artist Xiao Yan), was released in 2013 by Epigram Books. "The Tiger of 142B" was originally published in *The Beating and Other Stories* (Singapore: Ethos Books, 2011).

Justin Ker is a doctor in the Department of Neurosurgery at Tan Tock Seng Hospital. "Joo Chiat and Other Lost Things" was the second prize winner (English-language short story category) in the 2011 SPH-NAC Golden Point Award, posted online by the National Arts Council: http://www.nac.gov.sg/docs/gpa2011-shortstory/2nd--justin-ker.pdf.

Koh Choon Hwee is the former editor of *Kent Ridge Common*. Her writing has appeared in *QLRS*, *The Malaysian Insider* and *TODAY Online*, and she is currently studying history as a postgraduate in Beirut, Lebanon. "The Protocol Wars of Laundry and Coexistence" was the first prize winner in the 2011 Goh Sin Tub Creative Writing Competition, posted online by the Department of English Language & Literature, Faculty of Arts & Social Sciences, National University of Singapore: http://www.fas.nus.edu.sg/ell/docs/GST_1st.pdf.

Karen Kwek read English Language and Literature at Oxford University and returned to Singapore to work in publishing after obtaining a Masters degree in Literature (Renaissance). She writes amid the intensity of life with a young family, that is to say the writing happens s-l-o-w-l-y, but she is ever thankful for this whole life. "The Dispossessed" was the first prize winner (English-language short story category) in the 2011 SPH-NAC Golden Point Award, posted online by the National Arts Council: http://www.nac.gov.sg/docs/gpa2011-shortstory/1st--karen-kwek.pdf; the story draws on some of her experiences of having grown up in old Upper Serangoon.

Wei Fen Lee is the co-editor of *Ceriph*, a literary print journal based in Singapore that promotes the work of emerging writers and artists. She is also a freelance writer and researcher of

South Asian diasporic literature in Southeast Asia. She recently co-edited *Coast* (2011), a mono-titular anthology of poetry and fiction by three generations of writers from Singapore, and her work has appeared in *QLRS, Nether Magazine,* and *Softblow.* "Welcome to the Pond" was originally published in *Fish Eats Lion,* edited by Jason Erik Lundberg (Singapore: Math Paper Press, 2012).

Amanda Lee Koe is the fiction editor of *Esquire (Singapore),* the editor of creative non-fiction online magazine *POSKOD,* the communications director at studioKALEIDO, and the co-editor of literary journal *Ceriph.* With Ng Yi-Sheng, she spearheaded and co-edited *Eastern Heathens* (Ethos Books), an anthology subverting Asian folklore. Her short fiction has seen publication in *Quarterly Literary Review Singapore, COAST, Cha: An Asian Literary Journal, Ceriph, Microcosmos: Orbital Decay, Der Greif* (Germany) and *Thought Catalog* (USA). Amanda's first collection, *Ministry of Moral Panic,* was published in 2013 by Epigram Books. "Randy's Rotisserie" was originally published in *Quarterly Literary Review Singapore* vol. 11, no. 4 (2012).

Jason Erik Lundberg (editor) is the author of several books, most recently *Strange Mammals* (2013), *The Alchemy of Happiness* (2012) and *Red Dot Irreal* (2011), as well as the founding editor of *LONTAR: The Journal of Southeast Asian Speculative Fiction,* the editor of *Fish Eats Lion* (2012), and the co-editor of *A Field Guide to Surreal Botany* (2008) and *Scattered,*

Covered, Smothered (2005). His writing has appeared in over 50 publications in five countries, and he has lived in Singapore since 2007. You can find him online at jasonlundberg.net.

Vinita Ramani Mohan's previously published works include *Parvathi Dreams About His Sex* (Math Paper Press) and non-fiction essays for various publications. A novella, *The Grand Arcade*, is forthcoming. A recipient of the National Arts Council (Singapore) Arts Creation Fund grant, she is currently writing a novel. She likes making soundscapes in her spare time. She's at: vinitaramani.com. "The Hearing Aid" was originally published (in slightly different form) in *Ceriph* no. 5 (2012).

Eleanor Neo is a Literature graduate and teacher who has written short stories and dramatic pieces for *Ceriph*, *The Ayam Curtain*, the NUS Arts Festival and the Singapore Arts Festival. She wants to continue learning, creating and recording stories wherever her place in life, with a particular curiosity for people, their histories, and their unspoken romances with the ordinary. "Copies" was originally published in *Ceriph* no. 4.3 (Sleet) (2011).

Ng Yi-Sheng is a full-time writer of poetry, fiction, journalism, non-fiction, drama and slam. His books include *Eating Air*, *SQ21* and *last boy*, the last of which earned him the Singapore Literature Prize in 2008. He has co-edited *GASPP: A Gay Anthology of Singapore Poetry and Prose* and *Eastern Heathens*, and co-organises the monthly interdisciplinary event SPORE Art Salon. He is currently pursuing an MFA at the University of East Anglia. "Agnes Joaquim, Bioterrorist" was originally published in *Fish Eats Lion*, edited by Jason Erik Lundberg (Singapore: Math Paper Press, 2012).

O Thiam Chin is the author of four fiction collections: *Free-Falling Man* (2006), *Never Been Better* (2009), *Under the Sun* (2010), and *The Rest of Your Life and Everything That Comes With It* (2011); a fifth collection, *Love, Or Something Like Love*, is forthcoming. His short stories have appeared in several literary anthologies and journals, including *World Literature Today*, *The International Literary Quarterly*, *Asia Literary Review*, *Quarterly Literary Review Singapore*, *Kyoto Journal*, *The Jakarta Post*, *Asiatic*, and *Esquire (Singapore)*. He was an honorary fellow of the Iowa International Writing Program in 2010, and a recipient of the NAC Young Artist Award in 2012. "Sleeping" was originally published in *Quarterly Literary Review Singapore* vol. 10, no. 2 (2011).

Alvin Pang is a poet, writer, editor, anthologist, and translator. Working primarily in English, his poetry has been translated into over fifteen languages, and he has appeared in major festivals and anthologies worldwide. His most recent books include *When the Barbarians Arrive* (2012), *Other Things and Other Poems* (2012) and *What Gives Us Our Names* (2011). "The Illoi of Kantimeral" was originally published as "Coast" in *Coast: A Mono-titular Anthology of Singapore Writing*, edited by Daren Shiau and Lee Wei Fen (Singapore: Math Paper Press, 2011).

Phan Ming Yen is the author of fiction collection *That Night By the Beach and Other Stories For a Film Score* (2012) and co-compiler of *Edwin Thumboo: Bibliography 1952 – 2008* (2009). A former journalist, magazine editor and arts manager, Phan is presently an Assistant Director (Academic) at the School of Technology for the Arts, Republic Polytechnic. "Anniversary" was originally published in *That Night By the Beach and Other Stories For a Film Score* (Singapore: Ethos Books, 2012).

Alfian Sa'at is known for his provocative works and is often referred to as Singapore's *enfant terrible*. A prolific playwright and poet in both English and Malay, he has won multiple awards for his writing. His most recent books include *Malay Sketches*, *Cooling-Off Day* and *The Invisible Manuscript*, all published in 2012. He is the Resident Playwright with professional theatre company W!LD RICE. "The Borrowed Boy" was originally published in *One: The Anthology*, edited by Robert Yeo (Singapore: Marshall Cavendish, 2012).

Verena Tay (verenatay.com) is a writer, storyteller, theatre practitioner, and voice and speech teacher. *Spectre: Stories from Dark to Light* (2012) was her first short story collection. She has also published three collections of plays and edited two other short story anthologies: *Balik Kampung* and *A Monsoon Feast*. An honorary fellow at the University of Iowa's 2007 International Writing Program, she is currently studying for an MFA in Creative Writing at the City University of Hong Kong. "Walls" was originally published in *Spectre* (Singapore: Math Paper

Press, 2012); the story is dedicated to Kamini Ramachandran (as well as to all oppressed and repressed souls who seek release) and was inspired by the folktale "Tell It to the Walls," collected by A.K. Ramanujan in *Folktales from India: A Selection of Oral Tales from Twenty-two Languages* (New York: Pantheon Books, 1991).

Jeremy Tiang won the Golden Point Award in 2009 for his short story "Trondheim", and has been shortlisted for the Bridport and Iowa Review Prizes. His fiction has also appeared in *Esquire (Singapore)*, *Litro*, *The Istanbul Review* and *QLRS*. In 2011, he represented Singapore at the University of Iowa's International Writing Program. Jeremy's plays have been performed in Singapore, Hong Kong, and London, and his adaptation of Hong Lou Meng's *A Dream of Red Pavilions* will be staged off-Broadway in 2015. He has translated six books from Chinese, and was recently awarded a PEN/Heim Translation Fund Grant. "Harmonious Residences" was originally published in *Quarterly Literary Review Singapore* vol. 10, no. 1 (2011).

Cyril Wong is the Singapore Literature Prize-winning author of poetry collections such as *Unmarked Treasure, Tilting Our Plates to Catch the Light* and *Satori Blues*. He also published *Let Me Tell You Something About That Night*, a collection of strange tales. A recipient of the National Arts Council's Young Artist Award for Literature, he completed his doctoral degree in English Literature at the National University of Singapore in 2012. His poems have been anthologised in journals and anthologies across the world, including the 2008 Norton anthology,

CONTRIBUTORS

Language for a New Century: Contemporary Poetry from the Middle East, Asia and Beyond. His first novel, *The Last Lesson of Mrs de Souza*, was published in 2013 by Epigram Books. "Zero Hour" was originally published in *Fish Eats Lion*, edited by Jason Erik Lundberg (Singapore: Math Paper Press, 2012).

Stephanie Ye is the author of *The Billion Shop* (2012), a chapbook of four linked short stories, and the editor of *From the Belly of the Cat* (2013), an anthology of cat-themed Singapore short stories, both published by Math Paper Press. Her work has appeared in journals in Singapore and abroad, including *Quarterly Literary Review Singapore*, *Esquire (Singapore)* and *Mascara Literary Review*, as well as in several anthologies. She is pursuing a Master's in Creative Writing (Prose) at the University of East Anglia on a National Arts Council scholarship, and is also the recipient of a UEA Creative Writing International Scholarship. She was an honorary fellow in writing of the University of Iowa via the International Writing Program in 2012. "Seascrapers" was originally published in *Quarterly Literary Review Singapore* vol. 10, no. 4 (2011).

Honourable Mentions

In addition to the stories reprinted in this anthology, the editor recommends seeking out the following works for further reading.

1. Andrea Ang, "The Dark Star," *Ceriph* no. 4.3 (Sleet) (2011): 13-18.
2. Ann Ang, "Communion," *Ceriph* no. 5 (2012): 84-89.
3. ---. "What He Want to Say, Which Is Right to Say," *Bang My Car* (Singapore: Math Paper Press, 2012), 32-40.
4. David Bobis, "Child," *Ceriph* no. 3 (2011): 40-43.
5. Felix Cheong, "In the Dark," *Vanishing Point* (Singapore: Ethos Books, 2012), 15-25.
6. ---, "The Little Drummer Boy," *Vanishing Point* (Singapore: Ethos Books, 2012), 35-47.
7. Joyce Chng, "Metal Can Lanterns," *International Speculative Fiction* no. 1 (2012): 3-5.
8. Dave Chua, "The Beating," *The Beating and Other Stories* (Singapore: Ethos Books, 2011), 19-49.
9. ---, "The Disappearance of Lisa Zhang," *Fish Eats Lion*, ed. Jason Erik Lundberg (Singapore: Math Paper Press, 2012), 365-384.
10. ---, "The Divers," *Innsmouth Free Press* no. 9 (2012), http://www.innsmouthfreepress.com/?p=16366.
11. ---, "Fireworks," *The Beating and Other Stories* (Singapore: Ethos Books, 2011), 183-201.

12. ---, "The Vanishing," *The Beating and Other Stories* (Singapore: Ethos Books, 2011), 115-119.
13. Ian Chung, "Snowflakes," *Weirdyear Flash Fiction*, May 5, 2011, http://www.weirdyear.com/2011/05/5511.html
14. Noelle de Jesus, "Mirage," *Fish Eats Lion*, ed. Jason Erik Lundberg (Singapore: Math Paper Press, 2012), 261-276.
15. Gwee Li Sui, "Grandfather's Aquaria," *Balik Kampung*, ed. Verena Tay (Singapore: Math Paper Press, November 2012), 71-78.
16. Manoj Harjani, "The Man Who Skipped Breakfast," *Ceriph* no. 2 (2011): 35-38.
17. ---, "Primordial Clam Chowder," *Ceriph* no. 4.5 (Cosmic Latte) (2011): 7-9.
18. Judith Huang, "The City," The *Ayam Curtain*, ed. J.Y. Yang and Joyce Chng (Singapore: Math Paper Press, 2012), 133-135.
19. Lucas Ho, "KY USB," The *Ayam Curtain*, ed. J.Y. Yang and Joyce Chng (Singapore: Math Paper Press, 2012), 29-30.
20. Isa Kamari, "Green Man Plus," *Fish Eats Lion*, ed. Jason Erik Lundberg (Singapore: Math Paper Press, 2012), 251-259.
21. Amanda Lee Koe, "Coast," *Coast: A Mono-titular Anthology of Singapore Writing*, ed. Daren Shiau and Lee Wei Fen (Singapore: Math Paper Press, 2011), 147-153.
22. ---, "Star City," *Microcosmos: Orbital Decay* (Singapore: Kaleido Press, 2012), 11.
23. Wei Fen Lee, "The Acoustics of Living in an Interval," *Microcosmos: Orbital Decay* (Singapore: Kaleido Press, 2012), 7.
24. ---, "Coast," *Coast: A Mono-titular Anthology of Singapore Writing*, ed. Daren Shiau and Lee Wei Fen (Singapore: Math Paper Press, 2011), 111-114.
25. ---, "Swimming Upstream," *Quarterly Literary Review Singapore* 10, no. 1 (2011), http://www.qlrs.com/story.asp?id=814.
26. Annabeth Leow Hui Min, "Ascension," *The Steampowered Globe*, ed. Rosemary Lim and Maisarah Bte Abu Samah (Singapore: AS¡FF, 2012), 5-15.
27. Desirée Lim, "Coast," *Coast: A Mono-titular Anthology of Singapore Writing*, ed. Daren Shiau and Lee Wei Fen (Singapore: Math Paper Press, 2011), 210-213.

28. Jeffrey Lim, "Last Supper," *Fish Eats Lion*, ed. Jason Erik Lundberg (Singapore: Math Paper Press, 2012), 75-97.
29. Sharanya Manivannan, "Coast," *Coast: A Mono-titular Anthology of Singapore Writing*, ed. Daren Shiau and Lee Wei Fen (Singapore: Math Paper Press, 2011), 164-168.
30. Natalie Marinho, "Savour," *Quarterly Literary Review Singapore* 10, no. 3 (2011), http://www.qlrs.com/story.asp?id=849.
31. Ng Yi-Sheng, "Coast," *Coast: A Mono-titular Anthology of Singapore Writing*, ed. Daren Shiau and Lee Wei Fen (Singapore: Math Paper Press, 2011), 140-143.
32. O Thiam Chin, "The Good Husband," *The International Literary Quarterly* no. 17 (2011), http://interlitq.wordpress.com/2012/02/03/the-good-husband-a-short-story-by-singaporean-author-o-thiam-chin-will-constitute-interlitqs-fiction-in-english-for-04-02-2012/.
33. ---, "What Are You Hiding?" *The Rest of Your Life and Everything That Comes With It* (Malaysia: ZI Publications, 2011), 102-120.
34. Alvin Pang, "A Better Place," The *Ayam Curtain*, ed. J.Y. Yang and Joyce Chng (Singapore: Math Paper Press, 2012), 141-146.
35. ---, "A Brave New World?" TODAY, August 9, 2012, 8.
36. ---, "Patience," *What Gives Us Our Names* (Singapore: Math Paper Press, 2011), 41-42.
37. Gemma Pereira, "The Tissue-Paper Man," *Quarterly Literary Review Singapore* 11, no. 4 (2012), http://www.qlrs.com/story.asp?id=955.
38. Phan Ming Yen, "Symphony No. 5," *That Night By the Beach and Other Stories For a Film Score* (Singapore: Ethos Books, 2012), 45-86.
39. Jayanthi Sankar, "Read Singapore!" *Ceriph* no. 2 (2011): 84-87.
40. Alfian Sa'at, "Child," *Malay Sketches* (Singapore: Ethos Books, 2012), 213-217.
41. ---, "The Morning Ride," *Malay Sketches* (Singapore: Ethos Books, 2012), 67-70.
42. ---, "Notes From a Sacked Relief Teacher," *Quarterly Literary Review Singapore* 10, no. 1 (2011), http://www.qlrs.com/story.asp?id=811.
43. ---, "The Sendoff," *Malay Sketches* (Singapore: Ethos Books, 2012), 105-109.
44. ---, "Three Sisters," *Malay Sketches* (Singapore: Ethos Books, 2012), 25-28.

45. Lina Salleh, "Artifact #1N-327," The *Ayam Curtain*, ed. J.Y. Yang and Joyce Chng (Singapore: Math Paper Press, 2012), 101-106.
46. Prabhu Silvam, "Trees Don't Die In September," *Ceriph* no. 2 (2011): 71-76.
47. Michelle Tan, "Garisan Kuning," The *Ayam Curtain*, ed. J.Y. Yang and Joyce Chng (Singapore: Math Paper Press, 2012), 67-70.
48. Verena Tay, "Floral Mile," *Balik Kampung*, ed. Verena Tay (Singapore: Math Paper Press, November 2012), 137-150.
49. ---, "The Land," Spectre (Singapore: Math Paper Press, November 2012), 25-46.
50. Gwyneth Teo, "Battery," The *Ayam Curtain*, ed. J.Y. Yang and Joyce Chng (Singapore: Math Paper Press, 2012), 55-59.
51. Royston Tester, "A Beijing Minute," *Quarterly Literary Review Singapore* 10, no. 3 (2011), http://www.qlrs.com/story.asp?id=851.
52. Jeremy Tiang, "HOPE," 2012 Singapore Writers Festival: Passages, last modified November 1, 2012, http://www.singaporewritersfestival.com/index.php?option= com_content&view=article&id=99&Itemid=66.
53. ---, "Sophia's Honeymoon," *The Istanbul Review* no. 2 (2012): 51-57.
54. ---, "Stray," *Philippines Free Press*, November 5, 2011, http://philippinesfreepress.com.ph/?p=4388.
55. Jen Wei Ting, "Belle and Sebastian," *Quarterly Literary Review Singapore* 11, no. 4 (2012), http://www.qlrs.com/story.asp?id=949.
56. Samantha Toh, "Swimming Pool," *Quarterly Literary Review Singapore* 11, no. 2 (2012), http://www.qlrs.com/story.asp?id=918.
57. Kristina Tom, "So Far, So Good," *Ceriph* no. 5 (2012): 52-60.
58. Catherine Rose Torres, "Coast," *Coast: A Mono-titular Anthology of Singapore Writing*, ed. Daren Shiau and Lee Wei Fen (Singapore: Math Paper Press, 2011), 219-232.
59. ---, "Her Sacred Dust," *Ceriph* no. 4.2 (Ivory) (2011): 5-7.
60. Tse Hao Guang, "Salt," The *Ayam Curtain*, ed. J.Y. Yang and Joyce Chng (Singapore: Math Paper Press, 2012), 137-139.
61. Ronald Wong, "The Taxi Ride," *Ceriph* no. 5 (2012): 66-68.
62. Daryl Yam, "Apocalypse Approaches," *Fish Eats Lion*, ed. Jason Erik Lundberg (Singapore: Math Paper Press, 2012), 153-185.
63. ---, "The Girl and Her Giant," *Ceriph* no. 4.2 (Ivory) (2011): 9-20.

64. J.Y. Yang, "Captain Bells and the Sovereign State of Discordia," *The Steampowered Globe*, ed. Rosemary Lim and Maisarah Bte Abu Samah (Singapore: AS¡FF, 2012), 114-144.
65. ---, "Where No Cars Go," *Fish Eats Lion*, ed. Jason Erik Lundberg (Singapore: Math Paper Press, 2012), 213-248.
66. Stephanie Ye, "The Billion Shop," *The Billion Shop* (Singapore: Math Paper Press, 2012), 43-65.
67. ---, "Bons at Sirius A," *Ceriph* no. 2 (2011): 12-20.
68. ---, "Coast," *Coast: A Mono-titular Anthology of Singapore Writing*, ed. Daren Shiau and Lee Wei Fen (Singapore: Math Paper Press, 2011), 58-73.
69. ---, "The Story of the Kiss," *Fish Eats Lion*, ed. Jason Erik Lundberg (Singapore: Math Paper Press, 2012), 19-29.
70. Yeow Kai Chai, "Coast," *Coast: A Mono-titular Anthology of Singapore Writing*, ed. Daren Shiau and Lee Wei Fen (Singapore: Math Paper Press, 2011), 99-100.
71. ---, "Tahar," *Balik Kampung*, ed. Verena Tay (Singapore: Math Paper Press, November 2012), 39-53.
72. Yong Shu Hoong, "The Great Dying," *Balik Kampung*, ed. Verena Tay (Singapore: Math Paper Press, November 2012), 57-67.
73. Yuen Kit Mun, "Feng Shui Train," *Fish Eats Lion*, ed. Jason Erik Lundberg (Singapore: Math Paper Press, 2012), 279-297